THE STORY OF KEILAH

by

Joann Keder

The Story of Keilah

Copyright © 2019 Joann Keder (www.joannkeder.com)

Cover Art by Rizky Nugraha

Other works by Joann Keder: *The Something that Happened in Pepperville*

ISBN: 978-1-7336639-0-8 – Paperback
ISBN: 978-1-7336639-1-5 Ebook

First Edition March 2019

Printed in the United States of America

For Doug and Barbara
Thank you for believing in me, even when I didn't.

ACKNOWLEDGMENTS

I am grateful for the help of so many good people who helped me see this project through. Debbie See and David Penpek, the three of us together would make one magnificent brain. I couldn't have done this without either of you. Your creativity, patience, attention to detail and love have helped this book become a reality. Amber Richberger, your skills gave Keilah the polish she needed. Nichelle Paz and Jenie Smith thank you for being such good resources. Michelle Rau and Cheri Lasota, you are always there when I need a writerly friend. Kathy Carrigan, I am appreciative beyond words for your encouragement of my work and your incredible friendship. My wonderful family – spread all over the world – you have given me the stability to do what I love.

"Let us be grateful to people who make us happy, they are the charming gardeners who make our souls blossom."

Marcel Proust

Prologue

HARLEN BROWNWELL

Dear Son,

You know I don't write so well, but my lawyer offered to put my words on paper. When you get your inheritance, as is happening if you are reading this letter, I want you to understand how we came to own this fine acreage. I figure you're owed the truth.

You know about the One-Armed Man who sold us the farm. Here's the rest:

The year was 1937. That man loved his animals. He trained several and the others he kept safe from the circus folk. Llamas, tigers, elephants, and I'm sure there was more.

He acquired a leopard he named Millie, after his mother. Her trainer left her chained in a small cage. She could not even stand up. Once she was settled at the farm, he planned to work with her to build up her trust. Millie jumped every time she heard a noise.

He started leaving the cage door open just a bit while he sat beside it, reading some of his favorite books. I don't know if the man was bold or dense or both. Millie sat in the back of the cage and he read Dickens. Who the heck is Dickens is what I wanted to know. But the One-Armed Man said this helped her stay calm.

One day a visitor got off the train in town. She had a voice like a dentist drill and dressed real fancy. She asked tall and short alike where her son lived, but they didn't know what to make of her so they just shrugged and kept walking.

Her name was Millie, just like the leopard. She was a rich lady, a widow, who came from New York City to see the dirt farm her son had been hiding in for ten years. He walked out on his daddy and their finance company and she wanted to know why. That's what she told me on the ride out to the farm.

I was in town to buy new seed. That was a bad summer, with all the hail and insects poking holes in just about everything in the field. A recent two-hour storm had destroyed all I planted and took the paint right off the barn. But when I saw the poor woman looking lost in her fancy clothes, I said to myself, "Harlan, there's somebody farther down than you. Help her out." So I drove her to the fanciest farm-house outside of town.

On the way, she told me how upset she was that a handicapped man was working a farm in the middle of nowhere by himself. A real embarrassment to the whole family. I tried telling her about the good things her son was doing for the community. He made dinner once a month for those without. Violin lessons at the school and a reading program he helped start. It all fell on deaf ears. Millie was dead set on being mad.

I dropped her off in front of the big iron gate,

locked like always. Millie said, "Do you really expect me to walk? In these fancy shoes?" I tipped my hat and drove off.

For some reason, I set up all night thinking about the strange woman. Not about my lost crop and how I would feed my family. About the mean, miserable woman who didn't understand her son was a fine young man. I thought I might check back the next day to make sure things were all right.

For once, the big gate was unlocked. Never seen such a grand place in my life. Windows tall as a combine and fancy rockers on the long porch. I knocked on the big wood door with the lion head-shaped knocker.

The One-Armed Man pulled me in the house and told me to sit down for tea. I told him I still had to get to town to buy seed, but he really needed a friend, he said. I couldn't say no to that.

Right away, he told me his folks loved him and he quit being their son when he refused to work on Wall Street. He made me some fancy tea that tasted like grass clippings while he told me all about growing up with nannies and beatings and no love. When his daddy died, the One-Armed Man took the money he got and moved far away.

When I got tired of his stories, I asked where his mother might be. Instead of giving me an answer, he asked if I would be interested in buying his farm. I chuckled at the thought. I was going to beg the bank for a loan to pay for the seeds I needed to replant. How would I buy another farm?

"How much is seed?" he asked. "More than $100?" I barely had a chance to think before he said, "I want to sell you my farm for $100."

I could see he was not in his right mind. "No," I said, "that ain't right. You need to get your head square, then you let someone make a fair offer."

When he told me the whole story, about how he needed to leave town right away, I had to say yes, crazy as it sounded. I was helping a poor fella when he needed it most. I told him I would go to the bank and get a loan as soon as I could. He even offered to help.

He had two conditions for the sale.

One was that we always display the portrait of Millie, his mother, above the stairs. It reminds me of a dentist drill to this day, but I had to keep my end of the bargain. She will watch over the place for as long as we own it. Twelve feet of her.

The next thing ain't so easy to talk about. That pretty garden in the back your mother tends so well? That ain't just a garden.

When Millie came up the driveway that day, she was madder than a hornet's nest about the long walk in the mud. She was yelling and screaming. The One-Armed Man was reading to his Millie as usual. He put down his book and tried explaining about his Millie, how she liked quiet and how he named his leopard after his mother so he could finally talk to her.

In the middle of his explaining and her yelling, Millie the leopard jumped over his head and right on *poor Millie. The One-Armed Man ran for his gun. By the time he got back, his leopard was back in her cage, licking her paw and content as could be. There were still bits of Millie's flowered dress on her whiskers.*

The poor man was beside himself. He spent his life rescuing animals from cages. Now he faced the fact that he might be the one behind bars.

He took what was left of his mother and put her in the ground that day, covering the big city woman with plain old country dirt. He made a promise to her and himself that he would spend the rest of his life making things better for other folks.

"Well," I said, "you're already doing that. What with your work in the school and all."

"No," he said, "I want to go somewhere nobody knows me and start over. I'll call my kin once I find a new place and tell them Millie died of fever on her visit. Nobody will know."

I nodded my head out of not knowing what else to do. I was not going to turn in the man and send him to prison after all the good he did.

"My last request," he said, "is that you make a nice garden 'round Millie. She loved gardens."

He packed up his animals and left town the next week, heading to parts unknown. Even took Millie, because it wouldn't be right to leave her when she was just trying to protect herself and her owner. Everybody was upset. He was loved.

Right away, we planted a nice tree over the top of that mound of dirt-oak. We decided to call it a

Memory Garden on account of remembering those who no longer walk among us. Your mother and grandma planted begonias, tulips, lavender plants, and lilies around the tree. I put together a nice wood bench and carved REMEMBER in the back.

The One-Armed Man had a giant portrait made of himself that we thought deserved a respectful spot outside the farm. We donated it to the Pepperville Farm and Ranch Museum. They had a nice gold plate made and mounted it underneath. It says: PEP-PERVILLE'S ONLY ONE-ARMED ANIMAL TRAINER.

Now, son, it is important that you destroy this letter. You got your truth but it serves no purpose to hurt anyone else. The One-Armed Man is long gone. This town has too much gossip. Tell your kids and grandkids about how an uneducated man came to own a fine farm and fancy house. Just tell it the way the old-timers did, round a campfire. I'm counting on you, Kenneth.

Love,
Your Pa Harlan Brownwell, year of 1972

Chapter One

SANDY SALTS
2012

"**N**AME'S DEELORIANDRA. Not after the fancy car, just a relative." She sticks out an olive-skinned, bony hand. "I'll tell you that story if you stay 'round long enough. But everybody just calls me Dee."

I shake her hand and try not to stare at the pile of hair on her head. I've never seen an elderly woman with such a complicated hairdo. It is teased up high and each layer has been sprayed to make it wider and higher. Like a reverse beehive. Maybe the fact that I didn't sleep the entire night before this day-long road trip is affecting my perception, but she seems like a dandelion ready to blow away—a tiny little stock of a body with so much on top you can barely see her face.

When I found this room for rent online, I wasn't thinking clearly. Father's funeral – actually, the reading of his will –really threw me for a loop. I had to go somewhere so I could figure out what led me to this improbable place in my life. That place turned out to be the town of Sandy Salts, Iowa. Twelve hours from everything and everyone I know. Better than sinking into yet another puddle of grief.

"Nice to meet you, Dee. I'm Keilah," I say, trying to glance behind her without being rude. "Is my room upstairs?" I point to the bright-orange staircase to the right of her hair, where a black-and-white spotted cat is crouched, eyeing me suspiciously.

"Yes, yes. That's you. Up the stairs and to the right. You can have the bathroom and the hall closet. I just cleaned out my husband's things last week. I'll tell you that story too, if you're still around. The new quilt on your bed, I just finished." She puts her hand up to her mouth and begins squeezing her chin with her thumb and third finger as if she's thinking hard about something I said. I'm resisting the urge to get back in my car and head somewhere else. But I don't know where "somewhere else" would be. I'm too tired to think about that right now.

"Ok, then." I shift my heavy purse to the other hand and stare at the shag carpeting under my feet. "I'll just head up and maybe take a breather before I unload." I walk gingerly past the old woman, who smells like Mother after a day of gardening. I make my way up the steps, ignoring the loud protests of the cat.

"Never you mind, Gentry. He's noisy but he likes everyone. Interesting story on the name. You might hear that later!" she calls after me.

I push open the lavender-painted wooden door with a loud squeak. The room is clean and barren, with shiny wood floors, a tall, comfy-looking bed, and a lone floor lamp standing in the corner. I flop my red leather bag, the one my brother Kenner had given me for good luck, onto the bed, and then myself beside it.

The multi-fabric quilt underneath me feels strange. Nothing like the fuzzy one on my bed at home that survived multiple pizza spills and make-up accidents, the one my

Rosabel and I used as a landing pad to share our deepest, darkest secrets.

I lay down just for a moment to let my eyes rest. Twelve hours is the longest stretch I've ever driven by myself and my eyes hurt from staring at the vast emptiness of the open road. I rub my hand back and forth on the foreign fabric, finally realizing that the reason it feels so strange is because the quilted squares were made from men's suits. I study the grays and blues and plaids with fascination. This must've been how Dee "went through" her husband's things.

Despite the strange feel, I pull the slick quilt around my weary body and slip into a quick, delicious sleep. There is a brief dream; my Rosabel, my brother Kenner, and I are playing in our castle world in our barn. As usual, she creates a giant moat to keep the Evil Ones away. It is my favorite dream. Something begins to beep.

I feel something wet on my chin and realize I have been drooling all over the lawn-green leisure suit square. For a moment, I forget where I am. It has been less than twenty-four hours since I pulled out of our long driveway, watching Kenner put his hands in his pockets and turn away without waving.

On the floor behind the lamp, I notice a small, digital clock with the words "Property of Deeloriandra" taped across the top—the source of the persistent squawking. It continues, despite my feeble attempt to shut it off, until I bang it hard with my palm. Six pm. Everything that matters to me has been sitting in my unlocked car for almost two hours.

I stumble to my feet and quickly make my way down the stairs and past the kitchen, where Dee is furiously stirring something that smells sweet and woody—a combination completely foreign to my senses. Her large pile of hair moves rhythmically as she stirs—in one solid, well-sprayed chunk.

"Makin' some dinner. We'll talk about divvying up the food expenses later."

"I left my things in the car. Unlocked. I have to hurry!"

"No need to worry!" she calls after me. "Small town folks leave the keys in the car all the time!"

I try not to smirk. My hometown of Pepperville is almost as tiny and I know from personal experience how "trustworthy" people are.

For the first time since I left home, the image of Kyan, my judgmental older brother, drifts into my mind. His stupid smirk, which he somehow displayed while simultaneously telling me that I wouldn't be getting my portion of the inheritance. *Not you, Keilah. You know why.*

I'm relieved to see my back seat still piled high with clothes and bedding. Even my charging devices are right where I left them. I take a big scoop of things back inside, where Dee is waiting with one frail hand on the screen door to let me through.

"See?" she says, winking vigorously. "Told you. Folks 'round here know when to leave things be."

I carry my belongings upstairs and flop them on the bed, snatching my wallet from the top of the heap: a lop-eyed driver's license picture, all my cash, and those notes, some of which have been too painful to read since her death. This wallet contains everything I was until today. I catch my reflection in the seashell-framed hallway mirror, my red hair tangled like a well-rolled tumbleweed and my eyes framed by the ever-present dark circles. At least my new landlord will be getting to know the real me.

When I rejoin Dee, the table is already set. Two steaming, colorful plates of beans, tomatoes, potatoes, and broccoli drenched in a deep, yellow sauce sit on top of a purple-and-white-checkered table cloth. A vase of yellow and pink flowers sits in the middle. It is one-quarter the size of Mother's table, but just right for the two of us.

Dee brings a bowl of rice and sits it down with a *thunk* beside me before pulling out a wooden chair for herself. "Don't eat the meat," she says, placing a checkered napkin in her lap. "Seen too much of it spinnin' on a stick at work. Makes your stomach queasy after a while."

Despite that fact, she treats her vegetables as if they are a respectable steak. She saws them into tiny pieces until her plate is covered with bits of squash, onion, and peppers.

"So, tell me about yourself... What brought you to our neck of the woods, and all?" She doesn't look up, concentrating on her sawing.

I've always struggled with explaining myself. There's too much to say and no words in my head to make it interesting. *College drop out? Official family outcast as of yesterday? Strangely missing large pockets of my life? That, until just last month, I had been employed at the same coffee shop I worked at since high school, using the locker with the name of one deceased "R. McCallister" to hang my purse every day?*

"My father just died," I start. "Unexpectedly. He had a heart attack and fell off the tractor sometime during the day. My brother, Kyan, didn't find him until late at night." I picture my brother's normally-emotionless face, twisted in agony as he made the gruesome discovery. "He runs the farm now."

"Oh, my. I'm sure sorry about that, honey." Dee pats my arm with her bony hand. "I know how it feels to lose family."

"No, I don't feel bad about that..." I put my hand over my mouth for a moment. *I really don't feel bad. I don't know why.* "It's just that we didn't expect it to happen that way. I mean, he was old and all, but..." Suddenly I realize Dee must be older than Father. "Not so much old, but he was just so active, we didn't expect it. I needed a change."

She nods.

I sigh. Talking isn't my strong suit. "He barely knew I existed. Father. My move was really more about my friend, Rosabel. I promised her that I would find someplace that looked just like the moon. She thought... well, I thought... a long time ago, that it would be a fascinating place to live. Something peaceful about the rocky dry landscape, you know?"

Only partially true.

Dee continues cutting her vegetables with the precision of a master wood carver.

"We found this place a long time ago when we were searching the internet for moon-like places on Earth. They sent us brochures. We thought we would visit together. And my younger brother, Kenner—he was a track star in high school—will be here in six months or so. Just like we talked about on the phone." I shudder, thinking about how Mother will react to this news. And Kyan – who is my parents' favorite, even though I hate him more than the smell of rotten garbage baking in the sweltering summer sun—will be shaken by the loss of a farm hand.

"Did you tell me you got a job at the coffee shop here?

Workin' for old Jack, at Jack's Beanery?"

"Ummhmm."

"Well, I work down at Salty Gas 'n' Snacks. Been there for goin' on twenty years. Didn't realize when my husband left I'd be there for life. But it's a place to meet folks. And I make all the pastries. You'll be my sampler on Wednesdays and Fridays, if you please." She smiles at me and I notice she has quite large teeth for such a small woman. Many of them are gold.

She finds a sudden interest in my face and leans forward. "You're what – thirty-two?" she asks. "I can tell a lot by the way folks take care of their skin."

"Twenty-four," I say, blushing. "I don't care a lot about the way my skin looks, I guess."

I can see the wheels in her head turning as she reaches toward my tangled hair.

"So, do you have any kids?" I blurt, jerking away.

She leans back and crossing her arms. "No, Mr. Fisher and I never had children. Always wanted 'em, but he couldn't produce, if you know what I'm sayin'." She puts her tiny hands up to her face and I think she's going to do that awkward thing with her chin again. Instead, she picks food out of her teeth.

"I'm just fine here with Gentry. He and I do just fine, don't we, boy?" she calls out. The cat meows in the distance, probably from my bed where all my clothes are getting their first dose of white cat hair.

"Now, I s'pose I should give you the do's and don'ts, more so than I did over the phone." She gets up and takes our dishes to the sink. "I don't allow strange men in here," she lets out a deep breath, "least for my boarders."

I cringe.

"And you do your own laundry. Any day but Thursday, when I do my thinkin' and breathin' in the garden. I don't go for the sound of machinery when I'm stirrin' up the earth.

"You'll probably want to go by the grocery sometime soon. It closes at six on weekdays, seven on the ends. Just watch for traffic. Don't want to end up like my last cat."

Dee turns around to face me, wiping her hands on her purple towel with her name embroidered on two lines – Dee – Loriandra. "Small towns are full of stories. You should know that already. Case you don't, I'll tell you all you need to know when the mood strikes me. They'll say, 'Oh, that Deeloriandra did this, or oh, that Deeloriandra did that...' Don't you go believin' any of it."

I know all about stories. I'm starting a journal for mine. So they will all make sense in my head.

"I won't, Deelori – Dee."

"Yes, I s'pect you're wondering about that. I'm not named after the car. Just an uncle who had all sorts of money."

I frown. I haven't heard of any car with that name.

"You know – there's a fancy car from a movie with a similar sounding name."

"Ohhh... The Delorean."

"That's the one. Well, it's not where my name came from. So, put that one to rest in your head right away."

I can't understand why she would be named after a car that was so clearly made after she was born. But it seems important to her. "No rumors. Got it." I suppress a yawn. That short nap wasn't enough to overcome all the sleepless nights.

"Yes, you'll be needing your rest. Off you go," she says, pulling vigorously at my shirt.

"Thank you," I say awkwardly, "for the food."

She smiles – a wide, toothy grin. "I'll make scones in the morning. Just this one time on a Tuesday."

Chapter Two

THE DAY ROSABEL MCCALLISTER entered my life was the first day I breathed. Not like an infant does, with no sense of the world. But a real breath, absorbing the colors and smells and sounds. She did that for me. She had a way of making everyone better, just by being in her presence. She saved many lives in one way or another. Rosabel McCallister certainly saved me.

From as far back as I could remember, I had this embarrassing problem. I had these two green streams running down my face. I got so used to them, I didn't remember they were there until I happened to look in the mirror. My parents didn't seem too concerned, so I wasn't either. When it got too uncomfortable, I just wiped it on my sleeve and went on with my day. No one explained to me why this might be happening, so I accepted it as part of my lot in life for many years.

It wasn't until I started kindergarten that I realized other little girls didn't have goo all over their faces, or at the end of the day, mushed through their hair. Most of them had carefully-styled hair anyway, not like the red nest of twigs and knots I carried around. I think most of the parents decided they wanted their kids to have nothing to do with the walking germ I had become.

I spent all of my recesses alone, pushing the teeter totter up a few inches and then falling back to the ground with a thud. I imagined what it would be like to sail high into the air as I pushed off and my teeter partner descended gently to the ground, before pushing off again. The unspoken rhythm of friendship. By the summer after second grade, I was tired of being alone and decided I was done with school. I was just as adamant about staying home as I was about changing my name.

One particularly hot day in July, a family of three came walking up our long driveway. It wasn't often we had visitors, so everybody (the hired hands, myself, and Kenner) just kind of stopped what they were doing on the side of the house to see who it was. Kenner, being shy and afraid as always, hid behind me, hoping not to be noticed.

They were an odd-looking sight, two disheveled adults and one very pretty and freshly-pressed little girl. The parents were older, just like mine. The girl approached our house while the adults hung back, staring at our glistening white porch. The girl rang our bell but I knew Mother wasn't in earshot as she was busy pulling the last of the "devil's-sense-of-humor" rhubarb.

I cleared my throat as I positioned myself behind them. The mother jumped in her skin and turned around quickly, followed by the other two. My eyes fell immediately to the girl, the most beautiful person I had ever set eyes on in all of my eight years.

She had thick, chestnut-brown hair, waving in and out around her gentle, round face and emerald eyes like none I had seen before or since. She and her hair bounced off the porch and down to where I was standing.

"Hi, there, little one. What's your name?" she asked. I could tell she was about my age, but it didn't offend me at all that she treated me like I was a young child. I noticed a small, perfectly round birthmark on her left cheek.

"I'm Keilah. Keilah Brownwell." I stuck out my hand, uncharacteristically forward for me, forgetting for a moment that most people recoiled in horror when the snotty-nosed kid offered to share her bacteria.

Without hesitation, she took my hand in hers; a warm, comforting feeling enveloped me. She held firmly and pressed her other hand on top, sealing our connection. She didn't seem afraid of my germs at all.

A big, warm smile overtook her face. "I'm Rosabel McCallister. This is my mom and dad. We just bought the place next to yours and wanted to say hello." My eyes had been transfixed by hers, but suddenly I remembered we were not alone.

I looked over at the two sullen grown-ups who didn't seem to match this girl in looks or personality. The woman stared at the sky as if she wanted to be somewhere else. The man's eyes were bloodshot and he swayed slightly. If we had met them on the road, Mother would have told me to look away and not make those down-and-outers feel uncomfortable. I wish I would have known then what they were capable of. I would have taken Rosabel and hidden her away safely until she became an adult.

I turned to Kenner and gave him the look, the one that meant "Go find Mother." I couldn't bear to let go of her gentle hands.

"What grade are you in, Keilah?" the mother finally

asked, as Kenner scampered down the porch and around to the back yard.

"Going into third. If I go to school. Not sure if I will yet," I said. Actually, I was pretty sure that I wouldn't be setting foot in that place ever again.

"I'll be in third grade too!" Rosabel squealed in a little voice that sounded like bells tinkling. "We can go together!"

If only she had arrived before I made my decision. I would have had an ally, at least until she understood how the cruel hierarchy of grade school girls worked.

"Well, if I go. I might be homeschooled," I said. Immediately I regretted uttering those words, as her perfect little face fell and her smile, as bright as the morning sun, clouded over to a late-afternoon darkness.

"Oh," she said. "I sure hope you go. I won't know anyone."

Mother came around the corner then. She was wearing her usual scowl and a grey, boxy, floral-print dress with a ring of sweat at the top. She never allowed strangers to see her perspiring, but in this case the potential to deposit all the excess rhubarb outweighed her vanity.

She chatted with the McCalisters about this and that. I heard them say they had come from Texas, anxious to get out of the heat and try some of the rich farm ground. Mother nodded, shooting a glance at the rhubarb piled up on the side of the house. The fact that she had lost interest so quickly meant that she found these new people below her in social standing.

"Do you want to see our barn?" I asked the beautiful creature. The barn was where Kenner and I spent most of our summer days. We had our own little corner for play, blocked off with hay bales. We took our Barbies and Matchbox cars out and played in our square from morning 'til night.

"Sure!" Rosabel said enthusiastically. She didn't let go of my hand as we skipped over the gentle hill. Kenner trotted behind us.

"Oh, my!" Rosabel gasped. "We can make our own little world, right here!" she bubbled. She sounded just like a character from a book; a person so enthusiastic about a little square of concrete that she couldn't be real.

We all sat down together, trying to imagine what we could create from this space in Father's barn. Rosabel stroked my hair absently as she spoke. Suddenly she turned to me and put her hand on my chin. "Your hair is so beautiful, Keilah. It reminds me of a fiery sunset."

I didn't want her to stop.

"I have some cloth we can use to make scenes, to make our own little village," she continued. She didn't seem to notice the smell of oil from Father's big tractors or the swarms of flies. "It will be awfully hard if you're not in school with me," she added.

"No, don't worry," I grabbed her hand tightly, "I could change my mind." Just a few hours earlier I had made up my mind about staying away from that place. But I just couldn't let her down. This stranger. The most extraordinary person I had ever known for all of fifteen minutes.

The next day and the next one after that, she came over first thing in the morning. "Might I spend some time with Keilah and Kenner?" she would ask, smiling brightly. As if Mother would turn away a free babysitter.

"They can play for a bit." Mother would turn to our

two eager, freckled faces, already perched at the top of the stairs. "As long as chores are done before supper," she would add sternly each time.

Our chore list had suspiciously become longer with Rosabel's entrance into our world. Maybe she was using our friend's enthusiasm to her advantage, or maybe she was just glad she finally had a carrot to dangle in front of us. We did them without complaint.

Kenner and I would follow Rosabel, like ducklings, to our barn. At first, we stood, awkwardly. We really didn't know how to play make-believe. We had never had friends over and didn't quite understand how it went.

But Rosabel seemed to understand and led us gently into her world. She wanted to take our square of concrete and turn it into a village of peasants and high society. She brought bright swatches of fabric and painted pieces of cardboard to create a kingdom and a skyline, unlike anything we had ever imagined. Kenner and I forgot our simple playpen had ever housed basic cars and dolls, because now it was filled with lords and ladies on horseback, from a magical time when dragons flew overhead. I forgot we were still sitting on a concrete floor behind the motor of an old tractor.

Rosabel positioned Kenner on her lap while she explained the most important rule of Magnolia Kingdom to both of us.

"Lords and ladies are always to be kind to the little ones, no matter what kind of violence happens outside of the castle." She combed Kenner's hair with her hand as she spoke.

"The Little Ones always have to be protected, don't

they, sweetheart?" He nodded. From the moment we met her, Kenner was just as enraptured by Rosabel as I was.

As our Kingdom grew more complex, so did its inhabitants. We had semi-wild cats in our barn for the express purpose of eating mice. Our parents and Kyan didn't pay any attention to them, other than to toss our table scraps into a big pile behind the barn for them to eat every evening.

Rosabel decided we needed to have centaurs protecting the Little Ones in our kingdom from harm. She went home and made little costumes for the tamest kittens. She tied the brown and white bibs gently around their necks and then Kenner and I plopped them right in the middle of Aegis Square. They were another level of protection, for the Little Ones.

We played like this for hours every day, only pausing long enough for Rosabel to braid my hair into two compliant plaits. Every day she repeated the same phrase, as if it had been in her since birth just waiting for a way out.

"You two are... the sun and the moon. No – you are my red Robin and her little Sparrow. I can't imagine life without either."

Mother was relieved to have us out from underfoot until it was time to pick the beans, onions, tomatoes, and peas from her massive garden. This unnecessarily large square sat directly behind the big barn, where two, tall pieces of lattice – for the beans to climb – framed the rolling green hills. It was her place of peace, an unlikely, physically-demanding retreat for such a large and uppity woman.

But even then, Rosabel was glad to help. It seemed like spending her days with our miserably dysfunctional family was more appealing than going home to hers.

Like no other summer, this one sped by and soon it was time for school. I had decided, for Rosabel's sake, that I would give school another try. It would have been difficult to convince Mother to spend her days tutoring me anyway.

I didn't tell Rosabel why I didn't want to go back to school. I wanted her to continue loving me only as the best Constable of the Kingdom she had come to know. It was hard, knowing that the moment we hit the playground she would discover I was nothing more than a pebble in her shoe, a creature, something to be discarded.

We didn't get new people in our school often. Pepperville is a small community and folks don't seem to wander in much. So, when there was new blood in the school, every kid from kindergarten to sixth grade would gather around to see if they might attach themselves to someone foreign. It was another notch on their social belt if the person turned out to be funny or clever. Everyone wanted their chance with her. I tried to take my natural position, in the back of the crowd where my two-lane highway of mucus wouldn't offend anyone.

It was only a minute before Rosabel pulled my hand until I was close enough to grab her arm and feel her pulse, a powerful beat protecting us both. "Move it, slimer," someone said, trying to yank me to the side.

She spun around, my lovely girl, and in the strongest voice I had heard her use in two months of friendship, said, "Never, ever hurt the Little Ones!"

Someone tried whispering something in her ear, but Rosabel tilted her head in the opposite direction. "Let's get on the teeter totter, Keilah," she said, pulling firmly in the direction of the formerly dread-inducing equipment.

For the first time in my entire grade school experience, I got on that thing with another person. And it was glorious. Up I went. And then down. And then up again. My hair fluttered in the breeze. I felt the sun on my cheeks. There was such light in my chest I didn't want any of it to end. Rosabel had already given me more than anyone else in all of my nine years. She made me feel normal.

The school year went by so much quicker. I looked forward to doing my homework because there was someone who would check it for me when I finished. She taught me how to smile when people spoke and look at them as though they were the only important beings in the world. She fixed my hair on the bus every morning and told me stories of her life in Texas. The only things she hadn't taught me, as I saw it, was to be the respectable baker she was.

Kenner and I wanted to make a cake for Rosabel's birthday the following spring. Instead of the masterpiece I'd imagined, a flat, goopy brown mess sat on top of Mother's brand-new stove. It looked nothing like the wonderful creations Rosabel had brought our family each week. Reluctantly, I asked Mother to help. After much hesitation, she agreed. I sulked off to my room, secretly relieved that my friend would have the cake she deserved.

Mother did not disappoint. She whipped up a three-layer, oatmeal chocolate chip cake with burnt-butter, toasted-coconut frosting. I think she even surprised herself with how good it turned out. She put it in one of those fancy hat boxes from the last time Father had gotten her a way-out-crazy hat for Easter. It certainly wasn't about impressing Rosabel. It was about making sure our family name was represented – in the form of a cake – as something respectable.

Kenner and I wanted to surprise Rosabel and deliver it to her house since our normal playdate wouldn't be until Sunday and the magnificent creation would be stale by then. We were even given the luxury of a trip in the car to preserve our surprise and Mother's hard work.

While Mother agreed to drive us, her charity ended at the car door. She had decided right away that she didn't care for Rosabel's parents, rhubarb receptacle or not, and standing on their porch would be a gesture of neighborliness she wasn't interested in making. I doubt she even put the car in park while Kenner and I unloaded ourselves and the cake.

Strangely, in all of the months we had known her, we had not set foot inside the McCallister's house. Rosabel was always eager to come play in our kingdom and we eagerly obliged. But today, standing on her paintless porch, I realized it wasn't normal for two friends not to show off their bedrooms and toys to each other. She knew of every well-oiled banister and neatly-stacked closet in my house – including the one containing my hidden cookie stash. I didn't even know what color her room was.

I balanced the cake box, first on one of my knees and then the other, as we knocked on her door several times. Finally, her mother appeared. The last time we had seen her was when they all stood on the stately Brownwell veranda and introduced themselves in a most unfriendly manner; she looked somewhat normal. She had also been wearing a clean shirt that day.

Today her hair was a greasy mess. She smelled like something I wasn't familiar with – sweat mixed with something sweet. Her eyes were bloodshot and barely open.

"Whaaaa... do you want?" She was swaying back and

forth, holding tight to the doorknob with both hands.

"We came... It's Rosabel's birthday..." I stuttered. I had never encountered someone in this particular state in all my eight-and-a-half years of living.

She nodded and released the door, throwing it wide open. Mother had pulled away by then or she most likely would have yanked us off the porch. She is big on how things look to others in the community, and it would not look right if two of her offspring entered the house of a sloppy drunk. No matter that we were in the country, miles from any prying eyes.

"We're here to see Rosabel," I said again, trying to adjust my sight to the dimly-lit room. There was trash strewn everywhere. Beer cans littered the floor and there were dirt spots on the couches and chairs. I took Kenner's sweaty hand and pushed the cake box under my other arm as we tried to hop around the empty beer cases and old newspapers, toward the light source at the other end – a bright, yellow kitchen.

I could see my friend's magic touches all over. Smiley faces cut from poster board and painted neon green were on all the kitchen cabinets. A muffin tin sat on the counter with a recipe for orange bran muffins sitting on top. A basket and blue-checkered napkins sat to the side. She would be making these for her next visit to our home; they were Kyan's favorite.

The kitchen table was full of newspapers, endless beer cans, and a plate with a smearing of syrup and bits of scrambled egg. Suddenly I felt hot breath on my shoulder. I spun around with my fists in the air, ready to throw myself between whatever evil was lurking and my baby brother. It was Rosabel's mother, who reached out to steady herself by grabbing my shoulder.

"Girl's in her rrrroom," she said, pointing with her free hand to the door off the kitchen, a door covered in more smiley faces.

We set the cake on the counter, relieved we had made it that far without an incident. Kenner knocked on her door. The sound of classical music filled our ears. I had only heard orchestral sounds once before, in the Sears bathroom. Rosabel opened the door; her usual beautiful smile greeted us.

"I will in a moment, Ma..." Her beautiful smile fell.

"I wasn't expecting you," she said in a quiet voice. Immediately I felt sorry we had come. She didn't want to share this part of her life with us, with good reason. Now that we had seen it for ourselves, there was no denying its existence.

It came to me that the gift she had given me at the beginning of the year, acting like she didn't know why I felt like I was an outcast, was the same one I could give her. "I love your smileys!" I said enthusiastically. "Aren't they wonderful, Kenner?" I squeezed his little hand, but there was no need. He knew.

"Nice smileys!" he said, limping into her room. He had a beer can stuck to the bottom of his shoe, cemented on by a piece of old gum on the side.

"Oh, thanks. Smiles, no matter what," she said. "There are so many children who have nothing. I have so much," she said. I could tell she had transported herself to some other place, where neglected children sat at her side as she stroked their tiny, thin faces.

"Keilah baked you a cake," Kenner said proudly. I

blushed. I hadn't asked him to lie for me.

Rosabel, who had been working on removing the can from Kenner's shoe, stood up quickly. "What did she do?" she asked.

I went back to the kitchen and returned with the cake box, successfully navigating around two spilled bags of trash.

She put her hands on her flushed cheeks. "What is this?" she asked. "I...um..." It was strange to see Rosabel off-balance. It was like she did so much for others that she didn't know how to handle it when something nice came her way.

"Can we sing?" Kenner asked. That was his favorite thing to do. Sing and blow out candles, no matter whose birthday it was.

"Of course, Sparrow," Rosabel said, rubbing his head. "I want to hear your handsome voice."

She went and got plates and a knife, now back in her element helping others. While she was gone, I looked around her room for the first time. Her walls were covered in flowers and pictures of starving children, both she had found in magazines. Hollow eyes next to pictures of blooming daisies. She was trying to comfort them the only way she knew how.

We spent all afternoon in her room, laughing and talking. Not once did we see or hear her parents. "This tastes wonderful. I can't believe you made it all by yourself," she commented, putting tiny bird-like bites in her mouth in between spooning bits into the mouth of Mr. You-Are-Too-Big-For-This-Treatment Kenner. She babied us and we sopped it up like pancakes in syrup.

"I… um… I tried to bake it. I really did, but…" I looked down at the floor. "I did try."

"Don't worry, Robin. Your baking skills can be fixed." Rosabel took my hand in hers. "Things can always be fixed."

Chapter Three

SANDY SALTS
2012

I WAKE UP TO SUNSHINE beaming through the frilly, lavender curtains. Gentry is insistently scratching at my door. I'm not used to cats being inside; they are mice-eating machines back at the barn. Once upon a time, they doubled as actors in Magnolia Kingdom.

After a quick shower, I go downstairs to see if Dee has something that passes for coffee until I can get to the store. I've become a coffee snob in my seven years in the industry, which always disgusted Father. "No difference 'tween the kind that costs me fifty cents at the co-op and the stuff you make, other 'n the fancy cup."

I find a fresh pot next to a plate of oatmeal and orange peel scones. There is a note, written on cat print stationery that reads: "Scones, today only. Help yourself. I'll be back at five." Smiley face.

The air is thick with hairspray, so I figure my first landlord hasn't been gone for too long. I pour myself a mug of surprisingly good dark roast, and notice the local newspaper, all four pages, sitting on the table. Father spent many mornings reading the obituaries out loud to Mother, despite her protests. She already knew they were dead.

Sometimes I grabbed the paper before he got to the table

and just started blurting them out: "Norma Wills! Age seventy-five! Died of a heart attack!"

"Stop it now, Keilah!" Mother snapped. "Why do you have to be such a foolish child?"

I danced around the table, laughing an obnoxious *ha-haha-haha* to drown her out.

"She can't help it, Mother. She's slow, and those kinds don't know how to entertain themselves," Kyan would chime in, half-trying to grab my arm. I was always too quick for his beefy fingers.

Today, I can read out loud if I want. No Kyan or Mother to interfere.

The Salty Sun, established 1902
Obituaries and Weather Forecast, Page 1
Vanessa Withers, Reporter
Jericho Phillips, age 87

Mr. Jericho Walker Phillips died Thursday, while on his morning constitutional, just as he would have wanted. He was born in Stanton, the only surviving twin to Nora and Wall Phillips. The new family moved to Sandy Salts when Wall was offered a job as a bricklayer. Nora subsequently gave birth to eleven children and all were raised in the four-room shanty which still stands on the outskirts of Sandy Salts.

At the tender age of 13, he joined his father, who by now had started his own bricklaying business. The father and son spent long days creating the foundation for many beautiful buildings around town, built to last a lifetime. Only two of their creations survived the great tornado of 84: The Fred and

Alma Louis place on 12th and the beauty shop on Main/Highway 97.

Jericho married the love of his life at age 26. Jenny and Jericho spent 42 years together before her untimely death in the combine incident of 1995. Jericho asked that her remains be placed in his casket so they could spend eternity together.

Jericho is survived by 3 children; Philbert, Phylicia, and Phelps. With those 3 children, he also has a legacy of 9 grandchildren: Philmore, Phrankie, Phlorence, Philbert II, Phawn, Phaith, Phelps II, Phelida, and Sandy.

I laugh out loud, enjoying the fact that I'm enjoying an obituary, before the sobering realization that it has been just over a month since my own Father's obituary appeared in *The Pepperville Daily Times. Why don't I care?* Kyan didn't want it known that Father died on the tractor. He thought it sounded much more dignified if he just died in his sleep. I argued that, technically, he was unconscious, and why did it matter? Well, at least in my head. None of us had really communicated since Rosabel's death five years earlier. Father hadn't looked at me since... I did things. Everyone else just drifted off. By the time he died, we were like different species occupying the same land.

"Hello? Dee?" The backdoor screeches open and a short, brunette woman with a wide face and inviting smile steps in. Her clothes make me think she's in her forties. Upon closer inspection, I realize she is close to my age.

"Dee's not here. I'm not sure I'm supposed to let strangers in..."

"Oh, that's ok, hon. Just dropping this book off for book club. You'll let 'r know?" She lays the novel on the counter, then turns around to leave.

"Wait!"

She turns around and walks toward me. She has freckles, just like Kenner and me.

"I'm Keilah. Dee's new boarder." I stick out my hand to shake. Putting on a big fake smile, just the way Rosabel taught me.

"Vanessa. Withers. Pleasure to meet you." She shakes my hand and there is a comfortable, pillowy softness to hers.

"What brings you to our little town? We don't get a lot of young folks moving in."

"I... um... I came to work at the coffee shop. It seemed like a good place for an adventure. Adulting and all..."

"There aren't many people close to our age here, but you'll find friendships in places you wouldn't have looked otherwise. Oh, and if you want to join our book club, please do. Next month we'll actually be meeting here. Ask Dee all about it. Gotta run!"

The door smacks shut before I have a chance to reply. The wound of insignificance is still too fresh.

"And for my daughter, Keilah, this stipulation: She must move off the property and live for five years before receiving her full inheritance." Kyan smirked. I think he even winked. *"At this time, the sale of her portion may be negotiated if she doesn't wish to return."*

"All you've ever done with life is pour coffee," Kyan reminded me, again. *"Father helped build this farm up from a few weeds to the largest wheat producer in the county. He knew what he was doing."*

A small part of me hoped Mother might protest. Her only daughter and all. Instead, she seemed almost excited. "It'll give you time to write that journal. Like the psychiatrist said."

They wanted to push me off my farm? Fine. I wasn't good at grief anyway. Room for rent. $200 per month, got your own bathroom and closet. Keep it clean and no funny business. Contact Dee Fisher – 555-292-0728. We'll talk about the rest later.

The newly acquired book hits the floor with a thud. Gentry is now perched on the counter, blinking at me innocently. I bend down to pick it up and, to my horror, the cover of *Midnight Tapestry* is a naked man splayed across a couch, covered only by a discreetly placed doily. I toss it back towards the counter, the suddenness of the sound causing the cat to jump to the shelf above it.

"Sorry about that, Mr. Gentry."

I notice that beside his furry body are old-timey pictures in antique frames with swirly edges. The people in the pictures almost look like caricatures. They're posed in funny ways and the expressions on their faces go from unhappy to downright suicidal. In this cartoonish house, they could be pictures she found at a garage sale. My family would have at least pretended to be happy, for the sake of the picture. I make a mental note to ask Dee about these later.

Chapter Four

JOURNAL – PEPPERVILLE
1988

I CAN'T REMEMBER how many times I heard, "We thought there'd be just the one..." That was in reference to the birth of my sainted older brother, Kyan. One strong, serious boy is all they needed to run the farm when Father was gone.

Mother, for all of my life, has been completely focused on her firstborn. The child with no sense of humor or personality to speak of, Kyan is much like her. She gets him.

A broad, pale face with dark hair and dark eyes gave him the menacing look of a serial killer, even at the age of ten. He didn't resemble either of my parents, other than the menacing half grin they all seemed to have no matter what their moods.

Kyan has always done everything he was told and that made the threesome – Mother, Kyan, and Father – a perfect fit. My father had him out on the tractor when he was barely five and that suited Kyan just fine. In the winter, Kyan played basketball, just as they told him he would. I'm sure Mother and Father were there cheering him on – in their non-excited way—all through school. Everything went about as planned, day after day. Nothing to change their perfect world.

And then I came along.

Six pounds and nine ounces of screaming, red-haired chaos entered their world on July 9th, 1988. Right smack in the middle of the mighty Iowa harvest. Usually, Mother cooked for the entire crew, sometimes as many as thirty people, three meals a day. What a hindrance I was straight out of the shoot. The way she tells it, she was boiling up chickens from our yard and baking apple pies just a day after giving birth.

My father, a no-nonsense, straight forward kind of man, didn't trust the harvesters who came in from a neighboring state to harvest his crops, so he watched them, from sun up until sundown, until the job was done and they were safely off his property. He wasn't there for my birth and told me several times that if he had been in attendance, no wife of his would have gone home with a red head. I think that was his attempt at humor. At least I hope.

Katherine Eugenia Brownwell, born to the Brownwell Farm family in the middle of a bountiful harvest. That's what my birth announcement said. I disrupted harvest the way I did the routine of the perfect little threesome.

That awful name sounded like it should be announcing an entirely different girl's entrance into the room. It didn't suit me at all. When I looked in the mirror, I saw someone else. For years, I thought I had been such an inconvenience during harvest that Mother just hastily picked a name from the phone book.

Eventually, the story came out. Katherine, my Mother told me, was the choice of her mother-in-law, the woman who so graciously allowed a homeless, pregnant teen into her home weeks before Kyan's birth. The only time Kyan inconvenienced anyone, it seems, is when he made his entrance into the world.

Mother was a popular girl from a strict home. When she became pregnant in high school, through a "one-time" experience with the terribly-unpopular-but-quite-wealthy boy who became my father, she was immediately removed from her home. Father promised she would have a home with his family.

Though she never explained in detail, she said there were certain conditions to her living in the fanciest house in the county. The first one is obvious: my parents drove to the next county and married just days before Kyan's birth. As for my name, Mother didn't seem to regret giving away the naming rights of her only daughter.

It wasn't until I met my namesake, Katherine Brownwell, Father's great aunt, that I realized the extent of the burden placed upon me. She came to stay with us for a week every summer, starting the year my freckles and bucked teeth came into full glow. Only once did I hear Father call her Katherine. The rest of the time it was "ma'am". I hoped he didn't use her name out of respect for me, but the more I've thought about it, I've realized he was just as afraid of her as we were. Her personality was stern like Mother's, but she had a real mean streak. She referred to my brother and me as "field vermin".

I asked why I was given the middle name of Eugenia, instead of Elizabeth like my great-great aunt. It just seemed cruel. It was an unnecessary albatross to hang around the neck of a snotty-faced girl who was trying hard to fit in. Every time I brought it up, Mother would turn even more serious than usual. "None of your concern," she would mutter.

Two years after my unexpected birth, another surprise Brownwell joined the team. It was yet again a warm July day when Kenner Harlen Brownwell entered the world with the same shock of red hair, round face, and tiny nose.

Without detailed information on the back of each photo, no one would know whether they were looking at me or my baby brother. Three weeks early, my beloved little Sparrow once again interrupted harvest. From the day he came home, I was his protector.

Mother was over forty and tired of little babies. She had only planned on the one, as she constantly reminded me. The truth of the matter is that Mother never even planned on Kyan. When I reminded her of that story, she drew her hand back and slapped me hard across the face and brow. It wasn't the only time, but it's certainly etched in my head.

She left a lot of the care for this new bundle of Brownwell goodness to his only slightly older sister. Some of my earliest memories are of playing with my dolls in my bedroom with Kenner parked right beside me, in his bouncy seat. I didn't mind.

Mother's indifference toward us paled in comparison to Kyan's outright hatred. He didn't want me so much as breathing in his space and felt only slightly more charitable towards Kenner. We were dumb and silly and disrupted the perfect circle of three he and Mother and Father had created years earlier.

As Kenner got older, we would finish each other's sentences. He was painfully shy and, often to make it easier for him, I would just continue his thought out loud. We would ride our bikes into town for ice cream and as the man leaned over the counter to ask for our flavor preference, Kenner would tug on my sleeve. "He wants the special today," I would say.

"How do you know that?" the man would ask.

"I just do," I replied.

Even though as we grew I was able to look in Kenner's face and see my own, I couldn't find myself in my name. It felt like a shoe that was on the wrong foot. I began to loathe it to the point that I refused to come when called. I was a girl without a title. "I don't understand you, girl," Mother would huff as she yanked me by the arm.

Every time I looked in the mirror, I was trying to find her – the person who was staring back at me. Several trial runs failed along the way. Salome was exotic enough and sounded pretty well in my head. The next one I settled on was Zasma. It is a star in the constellation Leo and sounded space-like and very new age.

"How 'bout I just call you 'idiot'?" Kyan said. "Stop tryin' to ruin our family's reputation by soundin' like you need to be covered in tin foil." Just once he could have been supportive.

The next time we went to the library, I checked out a book of baby names. I opened it up to the Ks, thinking I wouldn't sound as rebellious if I kept that first letter. *Katie.* Too perky. *Katalinka.* Too easy to misspell. *Kaylie.* A babysitter from down the road who smoked pot with her boyfriend and let kids run in the fields.

Keilah. A strong name meaning lively and aggressive. It felt right. I looked in the mirror and gave it the test. "Keilah!" I shouted in my parents' you're-in-trouble voice. "*Keilah, darling!*" I said again, this time in my dreamy, *someone-important-loves-me* voice. Keilah. Keilah Middle-

Name-To-Be-Determined-At-A-Later-Date   Brownwell.   I
decided to close the book and think about it overnight.

That night I had a dream about a giant Viking ship. I
was riding to battle, in the middle of a foggy night with
several fur-clad shipmates, horned hats adorning their heads.
"Keilah! Prepare your weapon!" a voice cried out. "Keilah!
To the bow!" I took my fur-covered body to the front of the
ship and peered into the dense air. A beautiful princess
motioned to me. "Now, Keilah! Shoot your arrow now!"
And then I woke with a start. I knew. It was a sign. From
the Vikings. If they could call me to battle with that name,
my own family should be able to learn it, for heaven's sake.

The next morning, I announced at breakfast that I was
no longer to be referred to as Katherine. Kyan snickered.
Kenner clapped his hands together. Mother shook her head
and opened her mouth, in anticipation of what was sure to
be a lengthy lecture.

"That's my name. I've been searching for a long while,
and this is the one that chose me," I answered matter-of-
factly. "It won't change again. Call me anything else and I
won't answer," I added. My family ate in silence. I could tell
they weren't taking me seriously. "When school starts, they
have to call me Keilah or I won't answer," I added, feeling
slightly more confident than I should have. I pushed my
oatmeal away forcefully to make sure my point registered.
No one on the other side of the big, shiny Macassar Ebony
table was paying any attention. My bowl slid right off the
side and down to the floor, splattering all over the olive shag
carpet Mother had cleaned the day before.

"Smooth move," Kyan snickered.

"Clean it up, Katherine. You'll get no more," Mother

snapped, as she always did.

"It's Keilah. Keilah Brownwell. That's it." I crossed my arms, ready to dig in for the long haul.

"You'll do as you're told, Katherine," Mother said, taking my bowl to the kitchen and eyeing my father, who would normally come in for the kill at this point.

My father looked at me for a good long time, which normally would make me squeamish enough to rethink my point entirely. That day, I sat stoically.

"You're serious about this, are you?" he finally asked.

"Yes. Dead serious," I replied.

"Don't believe her, Dad. She's just bein' a dramatic little brat like she always is," Kyan said.

Father leaned back in his chair like he was ready to negotiate the price of grain he had been holding in his bins, knowing it had hit the sweet spot. He crossed his arms and put one knee over the other. "Now, there's no going back. Once we all settle into this new name, you can't up and change it again."

"I know that, Father. I'm keeping this forever."

He raised one eyebrow, as he always did when he wasn't sure he was going to believe what you were saying. "A name's a serious thing. People have to know who you are to size you up. If they can't remember your name, likely they won't think too long about the person behind it."

I paused for a second. Was it wrong to give Katherine away for good? I saw the image of Kenner and I running in the summer sun while Great-Great-Aunt Katherine called us orange-headed yard vermin from her chair on the porch. "No. I won't change my mind. This is my forever name." I smiled at him.

"Well then, I 'spect we should honor that," he replied. Kyan huffed and got up from the table.

It was the one and only time I can remember my father looking me in the eye and telling me that he respected my choice. I sat taller in my seat. In Keilah Middle-Name-To-Be-Determined Brownwell's chair.

Chapter Five

SANDY SALTS
2012

Salty Sun, Established 1902
Vanessa Withers, Reporter
Dannerly Breadwith, age 59

The Breadwith family is sorry to announce the passing of their beloved Dannerly. Locally known for her inappropriate language around children, she died as she lived—with gusto. Dannerly was out shooting at the crows on the power lines, as she liked to do every Monday, when she was attacked from behind by a wild dog.

She was widely known for her tall tales and her ability to consume more alcohol than all of her coworkers combined. Her service will be held on Friday at 6 pm, behind the Salty Bar and Grill, where everyone will be asked to share a good story and a pint of her favorite whiskey. In honor of her life, mourners are asked to bring clay targets for shooting practice immediately following. No children in attendance, please.

I get my keys for my usual two-mile drive into Pepperville, to the Cup of Dreams where I've worked on autopilot, barely awake for the last five years. Then I remember I'm already in Sandy Salts, just a block from the main street that doubles as a highway through town. There's a sort of freedom in realizing my exploration is only limited by the tread on my sneakers. Not like living in the country, miles from anything and anyone. Sandy Salts isn't remote when you think about it that way.

Today I'm meeting my new boss, Jack. At Jack's Beanery. My old boss, Mary Anne, offered to call as soon as she heard. He offered to hire me, starting as soon as I got my bearings.

As I walk, I notice the rocky, barren surroundings are just as they had appeared on the internet. Just a few shocks of green here and there, but they are weeds. There isn't a tree for miles. Nothing like home. My old home. Rosabel would have loved this place. Kenner's going to thank me.

"You won't chicken out on me, right?"

"Six months – I promise."

"Why did he hate me so much, Sparrow?"

"I dunno, sis."

"I'll keep a journal, so you don't miss out on anything."

I'm standing in front of the Sandy Salts Library, the current incarnation of a former saloon. I can almost picture ladies dressed in silk, fitted bustiers with one leg draped over the balcony railing. I step up the squeaky steps and in the front door, relieved at the first bit of air conditioning since stepping out of my car yesterday.

I walk up to the desk, a long bar area that reminds me of the dark, polished woodwork from our farm. A woman dressed in tan pants and a tan shirt opens the swinging doors and steps up to the counter. She doesn't recognize me.

"Sorry," she says. "I just finished unloading the packages. Can I help you?"

I stand, silent. She points to the sign above the counter/bar: Sandy Salts Court House, Library and Shipping Center.

"You were just at my... Dee's... house. You dropped off a book...." I stammer.

She bends over, shifting things under the counter, not paying attention to my face. "Oh, court date? One of those out-of-town speeders? Up the back staircase to the rooms marked 'court'. And slow it down your next time through. Or don't. Those fines keep the lights on here." She stands and fluffs her red hair before crossing her arms.

"No, that's not it. I just moved here. I'm living with Deelor... Dee. From the next block. Just..."

"Ohhh... Sorry. I have so many things on my mind. Three jobs and all. It's a library card you're after? You should've said so." She doesn't seem embarrassed at all by the book she left. There's shuffling from underneath the counter and suddenly a large bundle of papers is being pushed toward me.

"All of this? For a library book?"

"Just in case you do end up needing the services of the court upstairs. That way we've already got your information on file and I don't have to do that extra paperwork."

I try not to laugh. "Well... I'm planning to walk around town a bit and meet my new boss. Can I take it all with me?"

"You're working at the Beanery, right? No secrets in this town. You'll have your hands full with Nova."

"Like a star?"

Vanessa rolls her eyes. "So not like a star. I shouldn't gossip though." She surveys me for a moment and then hands me yet another paper from under the counter. "You can do the expedited form for now," she whispers. "I'll get your pre-court forms from you later."

I grab the paper and turn to leave. "Thanks," I say. "I'll bring this back soon. Nice to meet you..."

"Vanessa!" she yells. "Remember, you can join our book club next month if you want!"

I stop. "Wait – are you the lady who writes the obituaries?"

"Yeah. I have a passion for the obits. For showing people's lives had meaning. Ya know?"

I nod. There's a weird lump in my throat. Rosabel's life meant so much more than the paltry few words in the paper. I can't think about it. I have to get out of here.

Turns out there isn't much to see on Main Street/Highway 97. An insurance agency, an ice cream shop, and a gym are all the business life that exists. I continue on, past empty lots and five fancy-looking three-story homes. There is a huge green sign up ahead, dwarfing everything around it. Lighted tendrils extend from the top, and in between each one are the letters J-A-C-K'-S B-E-A-N, and then jammed into the space after the last tendril are the letters E-R-Y.

Looks like every car in town has filled the parking lot. As I get closer, I realize this was the coffee shop where I would soon be filling my days. The facade didn't fit the old west style of the other homes and businesses.

Jack's Coffee Beanery is a large, dark, log-cabin style building. It has a porch full of wooden tables and rocking chairs and is covered in green vines. Looks like something that should have been sitting in the middle of the woods instead of the desolate landscape of Sandy Salts.

As I approach, several people stop what they're doing and look up at me. That was also the way it went in Pepperville when new blood appeared; everyone stopped in their tracks to scrutinize a new face. This is my first experience being on this end of the process and I don't like how self-conscious it makes me.

I push my windblown hair behind my ears as I walk up the steps and pull the oversized screen door open, trying not to think about the eyes following each move. Two older men who are sitting by the door playing chess smile. "How-t-do, miss," one says.

I nod my head, unsure of how this dance goes from the outsider's perspective. Inside the musty-smelling room with dim lighting, people are similarly staring. They sit at long log tables and put their drinks down as I walk by. I try tiptoeing but it makes no difference to the creaky floor. My every step seems to create new sound and interest.

Someone is playing a simple beginner piano piece (*Heart and Soul?* Rosabel taught me that one on the dusty piano that sat in her living room). In the dim lighting, I can make out a tall, white piano stuck in the recess of the large room. I walk up to the counter where two women are shaking and mixing drinks.

"Looking for Jack!" I say, too loud for the space.

"What?"

A short, heavy-set girl with brown-rimmed glasses and straight black hair wipes her hands on her pink apron and moves dutifully behind the cash register.

She doesn't say anything more, doesn't greet her customer as I've always been taught.

"Do you have espresso?" I ask.

The girl nods.

"I'll have a coffee. With a shot of espresso. Needing something to get me moving." I hope she'll ask me why.

She looks over at the blonde girl whose chest is bulging out of her two-sizes-too-small shirt, who seems engrossed in deep conversation with some overly-muscular guy at the end of the counter. I guess she's hoping her co-worker has heard my order so she doesn't have to speak. It suddenly occurs to me that I've come all of this way and there's no one to talk to at the end of the trip, except for Dee and maybe the girl from the post office/courthouse, and the jury is still out on her. I miss conversation.

I scooch down the counter to the girl making my order. "I love this Maplewood counter," I say, suddenly grateful for Kyan's constant admonitions as he polished his many wooden creations. *"Don't get too close to that Maplewood totem with your greasy hands!"*

"Yeah. My dad did that. He gets into that kind of stuff." Her voice barely registers over the rumbling of the blender. I wait until she's done and then stick my hand over the bottles of flavored syrup. "I'm Keilah. I'll be starting tomorrow." I'm smiling, the biggest fake smile I can muster.

She wipes her hands on her apron and offers one in my direction. "Nova. My dad is Jack, your new boss. He's out fishing, like always." She is stunning – cascading blonde hair, high cheekbones, and perfect movie star teeth. I notice her pink apron lowers into a V, matching the shape of her shirt. I'm a little ashamed to make that observation.

"New in town, right? From somewhere out of state?" She looks down at the drink she's mixing without waiting for my response.

"Same state – Pepperville. It's a twelve-hour drive," I say with a sigh, hoping she'll appreciate that I've done that all by myself.

Nova has already re-directed her attention to Mr. Muscles, who seems to be whispering something hilarious. The other girl shoves my coffee forward on the counter without looking in my direction. She sticks two fingers in the air and stares at the ceiling.

"That's Lorraine. My cousin," Nova says, giving me a look that means *she's only employed because she's related.*

I nod and take my coffee, leaving only what is owed. After spending the last seven years of my life working in a coffee shop, I know the value of a good tip for an underpaid employee, but I don't want Lorraine to think she had done something tip-worthy.

I turn around to see that, thankfully, everyone else in the room has returned to their conversations and I no longer seem to be the center of attention. Someone is playing "Close to You" by the Carpenters. The piano twangs like it is in pain. Just like Rosabel's. Suddenly I have a surge of homesickness. There is no familiar rhythm to this place. The funny smell, the strange people; it doesn't quite feel like someone died in this building, but they sure wanted to.

I sit down at one of the long tables and take out the ringed notebook I've been carrying in my purse since I left home. My story. *Who are you, Keilah? Just write your story. It will fill in all the blank spaces.* I don't know, Third Counselor I've Seen In A Year. I'm too much. Too little. *It's all explained right here.*

Mother has always been fascinated with my life in the service industry. She and Father thought it was beneath someone in our family to work that kind of a job. When Rosabel and I initially took jobs to buy our prom dresses, she was sure I would quit before school finished for the year. Then when we didn't, she insisted we quit before the end of summer. I convinced Mother that Rosabel needed me by her side and my friend wouldn't have any money for school lunches and craft projects unless she worked. There was no arguing with that logic.

Strange landlord. Good scones. Smelly coffee shop. Fill in more later.

The quality of this cup of coffee surpasses my expectations. I put my cup in the dirty dish bucket and think about saying goodbye to Lorraine, but she refuses to meet my gaze. Nova is still deep in conversation, at least from the chest down, with Mr. Muscles.

As I step out on the porch, I notice that traffic is really buzzing through town on the highway. I paused to contemplate my next move. The two older gentlemen are still sitting there, engrossed in conversation.

"Careful on that street now," one says, pulling a chess piece into his lap as his friend looks my direction. "Lots of them young ones 've gotten hit. Traffic don't stop like it's supposed to."

I suck in my breath, trying to keep unwanted memories at bay. An older woman, older and feebler than Mother, stands at the corner by the crosswalk. The cars zoom by so quickly her hair lifts as each one passes. As soon as she sees a break in the cars, she runs like I've never seen Mother do. Two bananas flop out of the bag she's carrying but she doesn't dare stop. When she gets to the other side, she puts her hand on her chest and stands there, glancing briefly at me and then at her lost produce. It is only a matter of seconds before a truck comes barreling through, flattening her fruit.

There isn't any option other than to follow the path of this elderly woman and hope that I don't meet the same fate as her bananas. Two cars, then three. Finally, I see my spot and I run. I keep my eyes closed, thinking I don't want to see it happen. *How horrible she must've felt in those last few seconds.* I trip when I hit the curb, but I've made it safely.

On this side of the street, there's more to see: two hair salons, a restaurant, and a body shop. I still haven't found the grocery store or Dee's place of employment. How hard could it be to find in a town of this size?

I walk into the beauty shop and, just as they had done in the coffee shop, everyone stops what they're doing to stare at me. It is an older, repurposed home with four hair dryers and two sinks; it smells of permanent solution and the same mustiness I noticed in the coffee shop.

One of the hairdressers, who looks about Dee's age and has the exact same hairstyle, comes over to the counter and thumbs through her appointment book.

"Don't see as I have anyone new on the books. Do you want to make an appointment?" she asks, without looking up. It seems to be a common trait in this community.

"No, I'm just looking for the grocery store. I'm... living with Dee..."

She looks up quickly. "Oh! You're the new boarder! Keema, isn't it?"

"Keilah." I stick my hand out for a minute until I realize she isn't interested.

"Dee mentioned you was coming. From out of state? Things'll sure feel different here, I'd imagine." She turns her head to the other beautician, who is wearing thick, brown gloves while intensely scrubbing someone's head. "Frances, come see Dee's new girl."

The other lady comes to the counter and looks over her clear half-glasses at me – up and down a couple of times. "You got a boyfriend, honey?" she asks. I blush as I shake my head no.

"Dee'll make sure she has one. Constant stream of men in and out…" someone in curlers yells from the back of the salon.

"Well, there ain't much to choose from here," Frances says. "But we'll get you fixed up. Nice hair you got. Don't see that burnt red color much 'round here. Must be a new kind of Clairol they have in the big cities. I'd put some frost in there, lighten it up for ya and make it less of a mess, for real reasonable." She turns around and walks back to her client, without acknowledging me further.

I grab the back of my hair and smooth it down. "I'm looking for the grocery store? And that gas station where Dee works? Where is that?"

She put her hands on her hips and her back hunches into a C as she points out the door. "Grocery's two blocks that way. To the left across Main."

Please let it be on this side of the highway.

"And Dee works at the Salty Gas 'n' Snacks, over at the

other end of town, off the new exit they put in. Sad case, that woman."

"Is it... on THIS side of the street?" I gulp.

"Yep. Sure is. Just down a ways. Come back when you wanna do somethin' with that hair o' yours."

Chapter Six

R OSABEL DECIDED IT was her obligation to make me a real baker. She discussed, very seriously, the options for my baking education with Mother. Mother nodded, only looking at her watch once. In front of Rosabel, Mother appeared interested in helping me.

When my friend left, Mother questioned why I would go asking for things from other people. Especially people of less social standing. "You can figure things out in your own house," she said tersely. "Start easy."

"But she knows how to do everything. And she's got a big kitchen, almost bigger than ours." And my own mother wouldn't be there to criticize everything I did. She finally gave in and allowed me to join a junior baking group.

Everyone pretended to like my creations except for Kyan, who by now was engaged to the structurally-perfect-but-personality-devoid Melanie, his high school sweetheart. He didn't spend much time eating with us, in part because Melanie didn't believe in food, at least not the kind that came from our refrigerator.

In junior baking, like everything else in the world of a child, it was all about competition. Our leader told us we would soon be competing in a cooking demonstration contest in front of judges. I wasn't dumb enough to think that I could do it on my own, so I begged Rosabel to be my partner. The winners would receive a giant trophy while everyone else got ribbons of different colors signifying their status in the contest. Even if you didn't win the contest, you were still competing against everyone else for the top ribbon color.

We practiced our Snickerdoodles (Rosabel thought chocolate would be overdone) endlessly, reading from our cheat cards until we didn't need them anymore. Rosabel thought it would really set us apart if we used fancy words to describe what we were doing. "Now, *incorporate* the flour *conglomeration*. Mix until the dough is uniform and buttery in color," I announced proudly.

We even practiced once at Rosabel's home, where her parents cheered suspiciously loudly, given the fact they had sworn they were both sober and eager to listen. Mother insisted on braiding our hair into fancy swirls on our heads and adding matching ribbons and ruffled aprons to make people think we were kitchen help from the mid-1800s.

We sat through chocolate pudding, chocolate-dipped fruit, quick chocolate fudge, and chocolate brownies. Rosabel was right, as usual. We would stand out from the crowd of chocolate bandwagon demonstrations. It was finally our turn.

Rosabel began by giving the history of the Snickerdoodle as I put everything in order and mixed the cinnamon and sugar. She continued on with the importance of handwashing before getting into the contents of our recipe. We seemed like a well-oiled machine, her confident voice and my steady hands. We didn't look at our cards once. It was my turn to talk and all I could think about was how Kyan's track trophies would have to sit in the barn when my cooking trophy took over the mantel. "Now incorporate the fl... fl..." My nose had the familiar tickle that it got every time a sneezing fit began. I continued mixing as I tried mentally squeezing my nostrils together.

I had to get these words out and continue on, get past it. I took the bowl and turned to the side, hoping to throw the sneeze over my shoulder unnoticed. It seemed like it had passed. "Mix until the dough is *uniform* and buttery in color." Then out it came with such force the green slime jumped out of my nose and into the bowl, where I inexplicably continued to stir while the green strings incorporated into my once-perfectly-pale-yellow masterpiece.

The only sound in the room was that of the judges' pencils, demolishing our judging form. Rosabel looked helplessly at Mother, who in turn looked sternly at me. Mother made a twirling "wrap it up" motion with her finger. Rosabel grabbed the tray of finished cookies from behind me and presented them to the judges for tasting, explaining our mixing, rolling the balls in cinnamon sugar, and baking process while she smiled graciously at each one. Only one judge took a cookie, but I never saw him eat it.

I set the bowl down and ran into the bathroom, sobbing as I went. The only good thing I could think of was that most of the kids had already gone home and wouldn't be able to report back to school that I ruined our chances of a trophy with my green toxicity.

I took tissues and rubbed my nose until it was raw, trying to remove any lasting traces of the awful muck that flowed from me like sweetness and light flowed from Rosabel.

There was a knock on the door. "They're going to announce the winners. Come on out, Robin. It'll be fine."

How could I face her after I humiliated her like that? The one person who mattered in my life? I ruined her chance to shine in front of everyone.

"No, I'm not going to embarrass you anymore, ever. Just forget about me, Rosabel. I'm worthless."

I didn't hear anything for several minutes. I thought she had taken my advice. *Good. I'll just go back to being alone, the way I deserve. The popular kids have been dying to hang around her. I could go back to the homeschool plan and never leave Brownwell Farm again. They could bury me in the back, beside the mother of the One-Armed Man. That hateful woman and I belonged together for eternity.* I started to sob and the green river roared down my face once again. Suddenly there was another knock.

"Robin?"

"Just go away, Rosabel," I responded, in the meanest voice I could muster to respond to such undeserved kindness.

"I was just wondering... are you planning on living the rest of your life in that bathroom?"

"Yes... maybe. I don't know."

"Well, I really have to pee."

We both burst out laughing. It turned out that after I opened the door and hugged the best person in the world, we got a blue ribbon. In the ribbon world, it was like 2nd place. The judges thought our presentation was excellent but commented that when one "has to perform an indelicate act, it's best to leave the room".

Somehow, the absolutely humiliating experience made

me more agreeable to Rosabel's parents. A high-and-mighty Brownwell with a major flaw. They told her to invite me not just once, but every Thursday for dinner. More often than not, Kenner came as well. As much as Mother found them all distasteful, she valued a peaceful dinner with Father and Kyan much more and readily agreed to the plan.

They were completely sober and pleasant, different beings entirely – even telling stories at dinner about funny things they had seen and done in Texas. "Call me Uncle Ted," her father insisted. They even cleaned up their messy living room and wore clothes Rosabel had washed for them.

While Rosabel's mother was furiously beating the flank steak, Uncle Ted told us stories about growing up on a large cattle ranch. "You wouldn't believe the horns on them things. Longer than you are tall, boy," he would say.

Kenner would perch himself on Rosabel's lap, with his arm draped over her shoulder. "Why do they need long horns, Uncle Ted?"

"Well, them cattle really stick together. More'n any other breed. They round up in a circle and put their heads down to keep the intruders out." Uncle Ted would squint at Kenner as he told the story for the umpteenth time, rolling a toothpick in his teeth.

"They're probably protecting the Little Ones in the middle, right Rosabel?" Kenner asked.

Rosabel would look down nervously. "Ummhmmm," she would say.

A few months later, I was even invited to spend the night. Uncle Ted had been out of town all week for work and now that he was returning, he and Aunt Penny wanted to go out to celebrate with friends. They bought frozen pizza and popcorn for Rosabel and me. Having our own food and the run of the place made us feel like grown-ups.

Rosabel surprised me when she pulled a key ring out of her pocket with the words, DAWG TRACK dangling down the side. "Do you know what these are?" she asked with a devilish look in her eye. I shook my head.

"The keys to the liquor cabinet and the beer refrigerator in the garage," she replied. Even at our young age, it was what you did on a Friday night. Just not Rosabel. She seemed too mature to sink to this level of pre-teen mischief.

"Are you serious?" I asked, not sure I really wanted to become another Monday morning story about the girl who got drunk and threw up after she did something really embarrassing.

"We won't have to act like we know what they're all talking about because we tried it ourselves."

Rosabel was always right about everything.

We went straight to the liquor cabinet because beer just didn't seem as glamorous. My eyes caught the Cinnamon Schnapps label right away.

"Do you remember when Allie talked about Cinnamon Schnapps and Coke?" I asked. "And then she puked all over her brother's science project?"

Rosabel took the bottle and found her parents' fancy wine glasses. If we were going to do this, we were going to be classy about it. She poured half of each into our glasses and we clinked them together. I shuddered as the spicy harshness coated my throat. It was the best thing my twelve-year-old taste buds had ever tasted. We made another batch and ate our frozen pizza.

After the first glass, the room started to spin and Rosabel's silvery laugh became a hideous cackle in my head. She insisted I lay in her bed and she tucked me in, drooling on my face as she pulled the covers up tight.

The next thing I remember, a hand was roughly shaking my shoulder. I didn't want to move because surely it couldn't be morning yet. I rolled over to see Aunt Penny swaying over the top of me.

"You girrrrrls... c'mon now..." she slurred.

"Huh?" I asked. The more I got my senses about me, the more I realized we must've been caught. Rosabel must've put me to bed and then left the remains of our Cinnamon Schnapps experiment out in plain view and now her parents were home and wanted to confront us.

I rolled over to see Rosabel sitting up beside me. "C'mon, Keilah," she said.

"Where are we going? I'm not feeling the best," I asked, half-hoping she would take pity on me and face the consequences on her own.

"Breakfast," she replied. I looked at the clock. It was three am.

We stumbled to the kitchen, both still wearing our clothes from the day before. As it turned out, that was a good thing. There were at least ten adults smoking and laughing and telling stories. Rosabel got all of her pots and pans out and handed me a skillet and the egg carton from the fridge. She didn't seem the least bit concerned by this strange turn of events.

"You're making the eggs," she said. I broke them all and put them in the pan, not sure what came next. We hadn't covered what to do with a simple egg in my baking adventures. I wanted to ask Rosabel, but she was hurriedly putting bacon in a pan and trying to stir biscuit mix at the same time. I tried to study her face to see if we were dreaming, or if this was some kind of strange joke they played in Texas. She showed no emotion at all. I had never seen her quite so closed off from the world before. The usual joy she found in everything wasn't there.

"Keilah! Stir! You'll ruin them!" I looked down and the pan was bubbling furiously. Apparently, eggs were something that needed lots of attention.

Aunt Penny sauntered over to inspect my work. "Where's the pepper?"

I shrugged. She took the container and shook it in wide motions, the way the high school band director had directed last week's John Phillip Sousa tribute.

"Stir!" she commanded, echoing her daughter.

When I finished, the adults pushed me out of the way as they fought for their share. I stood in the messy living room, trying to make sense of the nightmare. They all ate like they hadn't had food in days, shoveling it in with fingers and spoons. One man put his hand on Rosabel's behind and she twisted her body away from him quickly. I diverted my gaze to the coffee table, where our two half-empty wine glasses still sat. I picked them up and moved them behind some empty beer cans. The smell reminded me of our earlier adventure. The scents of breakfast and Schnapps and leftover frozen pizza didn't mix well and I ran to the bathroom. It was all too ugly. All of it.

I went back into her bedroom and pulled the covers over my head, hoping I would wake up in my own bed. The next morning, Rosabel tapped me on the shoulder. I squinted at the clock. It was nine am.

"We shouldn't lay in bed forever," she whispered in my ear. I rolled over and studied her face. She looked absolutely perfect. Like nothing had happened.

"Did you get sick?" I asked, not certain my stomach wouldn't be anxious for a repeat performance soon. I was thinking, hoping the whole breakfast episode was some strange dream, what must happen to everyone when they had Cinnamon Schnapps for the first time.

"Just a little. But I'm fine now. Or I will be." She smiled, rubbing my arm.

"You know what we need, Robin?"

I wasn't yet ready for a new adventure, no matter how spectacular it was sure to be.

"We need to walk into town for tacos!" she said excitedly.

Tacos were the last thing on my mind. "Are you sure?" I asked. I knew she wouldn't lead me astray, but that didn't seem like something smart, given what we put our stomachs through the night before.

She convinced me it was a home remedy for hangovers she had heard at school. I put on some clean clothes and we tip-toed out her front door, something that seemed completely unnecessary given her parents' thunderous snoring coming from the bedroom.

I had never walked to town before. Taking the shortcuts, across several neighbors' fields, it was about two miles. The sun felt warm and soothing on my head and, by the time we made it to Torta's Taco Corner, I was ready for food.

As we sat on her patio munching on our hangover cure, I struggled to find the words to ask her.

"Rosabel?" I asked. "Do you remember what happened

last night? I mean, when your parents came home?"

She sat quietly for a minute. I felt silly bringing it up. Of course, she knew.

"It doesn't happen that often," Rosabel said. "My dad just got home and all." She lowered her head. "It really doesn't…"

Somehow, I didn't believe her.

I crunched the end of my delicious taco. "You know what?" I said.

"What?" Her eyes were still fixed on the cement in front of her.

"I am quite amazed to say this, but tacos are the best hangover cure."

She smiled.

We began drinking every time her parents left. We even got in the old, beaten-up car in the garage and drove it through the pasture. Because we could. We were unsupervised and wanted to see just how far we could push our luck.

Then, as suddenly as it began, it ended. Rosabel invited me to spend the night and I arrived, as usual, with my brown, leftover-from-Kyan's-camping-days sleeping bag. I had researched mixed drinks and had plans to do something really upscale, depending on what Uncle Ted had in the cupboard that week.

As soon as they left and our pizza was in the oven, I took the key and began the familiar ritual of opening the liquor cabinet. Rosabel put her hand on mine. "Not today, Robin," she said.

"But why? I have some great ideas. We can even use toothpicks and olives," I protested.

"I don't want to be like them. You shouldn't either."

We had never before discussed the way her parents were different from mine.

"I don't understand…" I said, even though I did.

"Sometimes, it's just awful, Robin." She looked away for a moment. "We have things to accomplish in our lives." She looked at me and smiled. "You want to find someplace that looks like the moon, right?"

"Yeah," I said. "But every once in a while, just for fun…"

"No!" Rosabel said sharply. "You don't understand…"

I looked up at my friend, surprised. She very rarely spoke in that tone. "Did something happen? To you?"

She shrugged her shoulders. "Things happen to everyone." She turned to the coffee table, covered in crunched beer cans, and pulled the *TV Guide* from underneath them. "Some silly 1940s romance movie?"

At that very point, a good friend, a smart friend, would have insisted on a full explanation. Someone who cared enough to demand to know who or what had hurt her and find a way to make it better. She would have done that for me. But I wasn't her.

I was nothing like Rosabel. I was only worried about how I could stay up late and eat pizza and brag to Kenner about going to bed at three am. I didn't care that something in her world was terribly, horribly wrong.

And the great irony? My sweet, sweet Rosabel tried keeping me safe from the very thing that took her life.

Chapter Seven

Salty Sun, Established 1902
Vanessa Withers, Reporter
New Today:
Grampy Winston, age 69

Genuine (Grampy) Winston died of complications from a catnip allergy. Somehow, the doctor said, he just developed an allergy to all 42 of them almost overnight. Not much is known about his early life, but Grampy could be seen about town, covered in cat hair of all different types, always ready with a story to tell about his farm or something funny one of his cats had done. Services will be held on Wednesday at 2 pm on the Methodist Church lawn. All attending are asked to bring a box or animal carrier.

It's my first day of work after an awkward dinner conversation with Dee about her lack of friendships and the big event she would "tell me about later". I'm uneasy about everything here.

I didn't sleep at all last night. I went to bed early, hoping that the sheer act of pulling the sheet over my head would induce slumber. I tossed and turned for hours, wondering how a girl who lived in a constant fog could manage learning a new job in a new place. Sleep and beautiful dreams finally consume me: the days of running through the wheat fields with Rosabel and Kenner, our skin brown from the unrelenting summer sun. I felt free and, most importantly, whole. With my best friend and my brother by my side, there was nothing I couldn't accomplish. When Dee's alarm clock goes off at five-thirty, I don't want to open my eyes and leave that safe place.

I decide to get gas first because I need to see a familiar face before I begin this part of my journey. The same turquoise Chevy Beretta I've seen in front of Dee's house is now parked by the "Please See Me for the KEY, Folks" door. It's a busy place, most likely the only place for miles to get gas. I walk inside, surprised by the smooth voice of Frank Sinatra playing on the sound system.

I find Dee in the back, unpacking boxes of candy. *"It's quarter to three, there's no one in the place except you and me, so, set 'em up, Joe, I got a little story you oughta know... Da de da... Make it one for my baby and one more for the road..."* Dee has a surprisingly rich, throaty alto voice.

"Hi, Dee, just thought I'd drop by..."

She jumps, sending several candy bars over her shoulder toward me. Somehow, she ends up sitting on the ground. "Good gravy, miss. You scared the dickens out of me!"

I offer my hand to help her up. "Sorry, I just wanted to..."

She shakes her head back and forth. "Small town, but this is a highway and there're some real unknowns comin' in every now and again. Gotta learn not to sneak up on a lady."

I step back to let her push her way through the boxes. Instead, she leans back and hops up quickly, in one motion. Like an elderly ninja.

You findin' your way around then?" Dee asks as she steps over the candy mess and moves to the potato chips on the other side of the aisle, dusting off the shelf with her green smock.

"Well, sort of. I haven't found the grocery store yet. But your coffee and scones are amazing."

"Humph," she says gruffly, pushing me aside to continue a task that seems to gain importance because I'm in her way.

"Coffee came from your coffee shop. Jack grinds them beans for me every week. Don't want to drink the lukewarm motor oil I'm servin' here. Did you meet him? I dated his dad a few years back. I'll tell you that story sometime."

"Just Nova and Lorraine."

Dee rolls her eyes and then looks at me straight on for the first time today.

"That Nova. A runabout. Everybody knows. Never met a back seat she didn't like. And that cousin of hers has some wires crossed. The engine doesn't fire on all cylinders, if you get my drift."

She pauses for a moment and put her hands on her hips, jutting them forward as if she were thinking really hard about what to say next. Then, as quickly as it came, it's gone. She goes back to her dusting task.

Ding dong. Someone has come inside to pay for gas and Dee grabs my arm and pulls me closer. "That's one of Nova's right there. He's a looker, can't have a lick of sense if he's sowin' his oats with her," she says with her hand over her mouth, though not in a whisper.

There is something familiar about the guy standing in front of the pork rinds and gum. He has blond, wavy hair and the upper body of a bodybuilder. He would have been perfect for Rosabel.

"I s'pose you'll be wantin' to get to work," Dee says, motioning for me to walk with her to the front of the store. "You'll do fine, Keilah. Girl like you, all the boys will be leavin' the big tips."

I resist the urge to argue.

She pats the rear of the blond man, who is now standing at the cash register with a bag of popcorn. "How's it all today, Phillip?" she asks. "No gas this time?"

I gulp.

He turns around and I see it is the same person who couldn't take his eyes off Nova's chest yesterday. I know his type. No use feeling sorry that Dee had her hands on him.

"Hey, new girl. I saw you yesterday!" He flashes a grin that matches Nova's in symmetry and perfection.

"Keilah, this here's Phillip," Dee says as she rings up his popcorn. "That'll be $2.53."

I smile, just a little, and nod. Not wasting a fake smile on him. Not on his type. I head for the door. "Thanks for the scones!" I call over my shoulder. *Oatmeal. Just for today.*

"'LO THERE. You must be Keilah. I'm Jack Merlin." He sticks out a beefy hand and shakes mine vigorously. He isn't a tall man, but he has a commanding presence. His wide nose is partially framed by a bushy brown, mustache flecked with grey. The green-plaid shirt he is wearing is covered in flour and doesn't properly meet his pants. The last time I saw a man with a belly this big was at the Pepperville Holiday Pageant, and Doody Martin always wore a layer of padding to create his. Jack's appears to be natural. "We've been lookin' forward to your arrival. Big city girl, come to show us the ropes."

I blush. "Yes, sir. Pepperville's got a whopping 4,000 people. Just 2,000 more than Sandy Salts, but…"

"Well, I come in for prep time, which will be your job from now on. Then I show up here and there throughout the day, just to make sure everybody's got their act together. I come back to do the clean up when everybody's gone. I like it done just so." He smiles again.

I'm relieved that he takes care of the "just so" part of the day.

"There's a place to fish here? I haven't seen water for miles," I say, thinking back to the last four hours of my very dry journey.

"Oh, there's a fishin' hole that's not too bad, 'bout twenty miles north a here. Problem is, ever'body and their dog are out there lookin' for a place to swim and splash later in the day. That's where you come in. I'll let you be in charge of all the early morning stuff so I can get out there while the sun's still layin' on the ground and those noisy heads are all on their pillows."

He locks his fingers behind his head and looks toward the kitchen. "It's not hard work once you figure out how to get on with everybody. I s'pose you kinda figured so."

I nod. It's a relief he realizes what I'll be up against with his daughter and niece. Not like Mother, who ignores

Kyan's awful treatment of me and Kenner.

"Well, then, I'll take you back and get you set up with Tucker. He comes in to help with the bakin' and such. You'll be his boss too."

My heart starts to beat quickly. Suddenly I feel naked. I haven't ever been the boss of anyone. I could always hide behind Rosabel and she would take care of things that made me uncomfortable. Even in the years since her death, I remained the employee who kept her head down. I've learned my lessons the hard way.

Tucker turns out to be the quiet sort, not saying anything unless he's asked. Jack calls him "slow but just fine". I decide Tucker would be the least of my worries.

To my relief, a large box of commercial muffin mix sits in the middle of the counter. I don't want to disclose my lack of baking skills just yet. *Just add water and stir.* Thankfully.

"So, your boss there told me you were lookin' to start fresh? Kinda knock the cobwebs out?" Jack asks as he sets the first muffins on the counter to cool.

"Yes. I'm trying to figure it all out. Find myself, I guess you would say."

"Mmmhmm... Well, there's lots of space for that in Sandy Salts. Not much else for the young folks to do. You got family?"

"I... uhh... We needed some time apart. They don't seem to want me around. They think I'm an embarrassment to the family and they don't think I'm capable of helping run the farm because..." Immediately I regret sharing something so personal with someone I've just met. "I'm not really the farm-girl type, which doesn't work well on a family farm."

"Good thing you put some miles between you then."

Tucker, Jack, and I work for about an hour until Nova and Lorraine saunter in.

They both put their purses in the lockers and primp for a good twenty minutes. Nova fluffs her hair and then turns her head upside down to shake it out. Lorraine stares at her reflection, pulling the sides of her mouth into a smile and then letting them fall again to their natural, sad-jowl state. Eventually, they each take an apron and close the locker doors.

Jack puts his large, hairy arm containing a Timex Fisherman's Special watch with fishing pole arms up in the air. "It's after eight, young lady. The doors shoulda been open ten minutes ago."

Nova continues to touch her hair, pulling this strand up and that strand out. A can of hairspray has materialized and she has turned away from her father, facing the mirror. It strikes me that her hairstyle, though an entirely different color, is another version of Dee's.

Lorraine coughs, loudly, and fiddles with her bangs.

"Did you formally meet our new employee yesterday? Didn't think so. Now's the time to be polite, Lorraine. This here's Keilah. Shake her hand like a good business person does," Jack commands as he adjusts the brim of his blue and white Salty Fishin' cap.

Lorraine sticks her hand out but looks away. Her hand is sweaty and it barely stays in mine while we shake. Father taught me that a firm, lengthy handshake is the mark of a true professional, a "good egg". Lorraine tries to head to the front of the store, but Jack blocks her. "You have to show this one the ropes – ya 'hearin' me, Lorraine?"

Lorraine looks to the side, where the Cornflower Blue purse Rosabel had sewn for me senior year is draped across the back of the break room couch.

She pushes her glasses up her nose and sighs. "Ummhmm," she mumbles.

Jack moves to allow her to walk to the front of the store, shaking his head. He turns around to me and folds his arms. "Don't know what's wrong with that one. She's my brother's girl, so I gotta keep her employed, least for now."

"So nice to meet you, Keilah." I turn around to see a hand stretched out and a large smile, with all those perfect teeth visible. Either she has been paying attention to her cousin's mistakes or Nova has some business sense. Sticky from the hairspray but very firm.

"When you're done with Dad, come on out and I'll show you the design of the pastry case and we'll make practice coffee." She turns and heads to the front of the store, where I can hear customers already.

Jack says he'll let Nova take over for a bit and motions for me to follow her.

"I'll work on the coffee with you. It's a complicated machine and you might not be quick enough to catch on." Nova is using the same sweet tone she used when Jack was watching, but her words are completely different.

She carefully measures the beans she has just ground and presses them into the head. The milk is steamed and a beautiful, frothy latte is placed in front of me. "Now it's your turn." She pulls the corners of her mouth up slightly. I put the exact same amount of coffee in and she grabs the head from me before I can go any further. "That's not right, sweetie."

I load it up again and try a second time. And a third. It seems each time she wants a different amount. Something I have been doing since high school is now completely foreign. The fourth time, as Nova opens her mouth to criticize me, I feel someone behind me and turn to see Jack looking over my shoulder.

"Quit makin' an issue where there isn't one, Nova. She's doin' fine. We've got customers to worry about," he snorts. To my great relief, she is mostly silent for the rest of the morning.

By around two o'clock, things begin to change dramatically. I notice that Nova's sweet demeanor has melted; she has started snapping at customers and, for no apparent reason, at Lorraine.

"Did you not see that syrup on the floor? How many times are you going to step in it before you get the mop? Moron!"

"I told you we ran out of blueberry muffins like ten times! I swear you were dropped on your head at birth."

No matter what she says, Lorraine does not respond. As horrifying as it is to watch Nova's nice-girl façade wear into something this nasty, I'm relieved she hasn't decided to turn her angry comments toward me. Rosabel was always the peacemaker, keeping everyone calm and polite. She would have handled Nova with ease. I wish that somehow I could turn back the clock and observe her in action, so I would know what to do right now. Instead, I assume my familiar position, in the corner, feeling helpless. She is a "shell", what Rosabel and I called the people we knew in high school who invested more of their energy on their outer selves than they did on their inner beings.

At two-thirty, a mysterious honking begins. After a few minutes of agitated grunts, Nova pulls off her apron and throws it in Lorraine's general direction. "I'm outta here," she announces, to no one in particular. The air in the room immediately feels lighter.

The rest of the day has the familiar rhythm of my job in Pepperville. I mastered the coffee maker, at least for today. Just before closing, Jack comes back to show me how to finish up and pats me on the back. "Good job, Miss Keilah. It ain't always easy dealin' with my baby girl, I know. You'll figure her out, though. Got a good head on you, I can tell."

I'm not so sure.

DURING A DINNER of roasted sweet potatoes, fresh spinach salad, and homemade whole wheat bread (which Dee insists is a one-time deal since it was my first day at work), I tell her all about my experiences with Nova and Jack and Lorraine. She picks her teeth with her finger and taps her toe until I finish.

"That Lorraine's an odd bird. Least that's what I've heard. Course they say those things about me too. You didn't hear any stories about me today, did you?" she asks, suddenly sitting forward in her chair.

Not since my trip to the beauty shop has anyone mentioned her name. "No, nothing at all," I say. "Just to say they knew you from your job."

"Oh, well that's fine, I imagine." She gets up and takes my plate to the sink. "They've all had their time, you know. Gossipin' about me."

"What do they... I mean, what kind of gossip? Because

you're alone? Lots of people are – I lost my Rosabel and she was all I'll ever have."

She throws the dishes to the side and puts her hands on her hips.

"Never mind. It's none of my business," I say quickly. "I should head up to my room. Thanks for dinner, it was so much better than anything I could have made." I stand, wanting to make a quick exit before I do any more damage.

"No, it's better you have an idea, least some of it," she sighs. "Otherwise, you'll be like Gentry starin' down my headlights on a rainy night every time it comes up at the coffee shop." She wipes her hands on her apron and smiles.

"I 'spect this'll be a new one for you."

Chapter Eight

SANDY SALTS
2012

"**S**IT YOURSELF DOWN, Keilah," Dee says. "Some things need told 'round a table."

I sit back down and cross my legs uncomfortably.

Dee puts the turquoise tea kettle on the stove. "Want some?"

I nod.

"My family treated me like a princess, see." Her hands are on her hips again, in that weird posture. "Well, a commodity, while they thought I would bring them some return. Named me after my great uncle, Delorean Fisher. Mom and Dad always had some sort of somethin' they were concoctin' to get rich. Uncle Delorean was old money bags. Loaded with it from his days owning a brick manufacturing company." The tea kettle chirps and she takes it off the stove, filling two strawberry-painted mugs. She drops homemade tea bags in each one before bringing them to the table. "Basil and chamomile. To soothe the stomach."

She sits down beside me with a thud and scooches her chair until our knees are touching before continuing her story.

"So, when I was born, they had this idea to name me after my good ole uncle and make me the favored child. He was sickly by then and they didn't think they would have to work too hard at it. Dressed me up and took me to his fancy home every Sunday. All week long they coached me in what to say and do, so by the time we made it to his house I was as nervous as a cat in a house full of toddlers. 'Go sit on Uncle's lap, Deeloriandra. Remember your poems and give Uncle a kiss on his wrinkly, old cheek.'"

She shakes her head and takes a sip. "I was a puppet and never did I say or do the right things. On the way home, they would smack me and tell me I was a stupid girl for forgettin' to tell him I was hungry or that I was too poor for somethin' they wanted. My brother didn't know any better and joined in for fun."

"Oh, Dee. That's awful. I'm so sorry." Her strange behavior is starting to make sense. I take a sip of my tea and try to slide my chair slightly in the opposite direction.

She shakes her head. "Not the worst of it. When the old coot finally died, all he left us was his deaf cat and a box of baseball cards. $250 was all those cards was worth. All my fault, they said. There I was, trying to live with what I done to the family." She starts picking at her teeth and looks over at Gentry, who is lying on the kitchen windowsill, lazily blinking as if he has heard this story a thousand times before.

"Then my brother was gone, and they lost all that mattered. It wasn't fun to be told you were the cause of your family's ruin every day." She raises her chin and glances at Gentry once more. "You understand me, don't you, boy?"

"What happened to your brother?"

Dee waves her hand in front of her face like she is swatting a fly. "Just gone. Removed. No more to say."

As curious as I am, there's no point in asking more on that topic. At least for today. "How did you finally get away from them?"

Dee presses her lips together. "I found Mr. Fisher. Thought that was my reward."

"Wait – his last name was Fisher too?"

"Yes. Strange as it sounds. I thought that was a sign we were meant to be. Anyhow, he was flashy all right. Barth Fisher, or Red, as he went by. Handsome devil, with straight white teeth and blue eyes a person could fall in and drown. And a red mane, thick and wavy. Not as pretty as yours, of course. Everybody stopped what they was doin' when he walked by. He smelled good, he looked good. He was THE man about town. Told me I'd be rich and fancy if I married him."

I remember the type. I'd even slept with a few. "You did your best," I offer, bringing the tea to my lips uncomfortably.

Instead of understanding my attempt to be comforting, she squints hard. "You think you wouldn't have fallen for him?" She leans in uncomfortably close. "Well, Miss Fancy Pants, I had never been anywhere in the world but class skip day when we all drove to Farmertown to meet Lucille Ball's stand-in. So, to me, he was the best I had ever seen."

"I'm not judging you, Dee... I..." I don't know what to make of this woman. I stand up and, for the second time, hope to make a quick exit. "I promised I'd call my brother tonight."

"Oh, sit for a few more minutes." She tugs on my arm until things become weird. "Let me finish while you drink up that tea."

If I wait much longer to call, Kenner will be in bed, as he has to rise with the sun each morning to do his chores. But I sit, reluctantly.

"When he asked me out, I couldn't believe it," she continues. "We were a sight to see. He was Mr. Tall How-De-Doo, and I was this pretty little thing with no more 'n a whisper to my name. Guess that's why it all worked so well. Mr. Slick did all the talkin'."

I'm trying to imagine Dee with someone so popular and handsome. It doesn't seem to fit.

"When he married me, I couldn't believe it. I thought maybe things was about to head down the golden path I should have been on all along. Then he started ignorin' me and comin' home late, or not comin' home at all. That sounded more like the way things worked for old Deelori-andra.

"Well, off he ran with his bookkeeper. Mavis was her name. Bleached wig and a chest big enough she sat her lunch on it every day. They left for parts unknown. Left me with next to nothing. Two ratty old cars and this house to show for my life. And enough gossip to keep this town a-movin' for years to come."

We sit in silence for a while and I try to process everything she said. I wonder where Red Fisher is now. I hope he's completely miserable.

"I started workin' at the Salty Snack 'n' Gas after the business went belly up. I needed the money, what with Mr. Fisher nowhere to be found. I thought it would be for a few months, 'til I figured it all out. Still there today." She leans back and taps her fingers on the table.

"Had to start takin' in boarders to pay for the retirement. Since I'm an old single gal and all…" Her eyes start to fill with tears, which she wipes on the front of her shirt. "That's enough of that now. You know the basics of old Deeloriandra." She stands and lets out a deep breath with an *ooooh* sound. "You'll have to wait for the rest."

Chapter Nine

JOURNAL – PEPPERVILLE
1998

"YOU CAN BUY YOURSELF *a trampoline and jump, Robin,*" she said. "*Close your eyes and you'll feel weightless. Open them and you will see the barren landscape of your dreams.*"

At one point, I fantasized about living in a spacesuit on the moon. How it would feel so freeing to be without gravity. I didn't want to go through astronaut training or learn about science. I just wanted to feel it. Weightless and removed from the worries of life.

It was sixth grade, the best year of grade school and also the last. We were no longer little kids to be pushed around. We were finally grown-ups, at least in the eyes of Pepperville Elementary School.

Miss Seagull was new to our school system and everyone knew that the fresher the teacher, the more you learned. She was tall – taller than both our fathers and very muscular. Her face was broad and tight and reminded me of Kyan's.

In reality, she was nothing like my brother. When she spoke to each student, she bent down, like a gentle giant reaching down to the bunnies in the forest. As her head came down, her hair caught the breeze from the drop and spread on either side of her face like wings gracefully lowering her giant body to the forest floor.

If you had a question, she dropped down each and every time to hear what it was. She let us all choose a friend to sit beside at the beginning of the year and promised we could stay, provided chattiness didn't become an issue.

Rosabel and I had become quite adept at passing notes. One of us would tilt our paper to the side and place the note underneath. The other person leaned to the side, and with her elbow, slid the note from underneath the page. We were never caught in all our years of school.

Sometimes she helped me study for a test, as I had test anxiety like no other. I'm sure it had something to do with Kyan, who was my reluctant tutor. He reminded me daily that he was the best math and science student ever to grace the halls of Pepperville High School. *You can't be that dense, Katherine.*

During one particular tutoring session, Rosabel was waiting for me to finish so we could go out to the barn and work on the cottages we recently created. Our little kingdom had become quite the extended village of workers and farms, much like a real community. Even though we had grown well beyond the kingdom in the eyes of others, we felt safe in a world where we created all the rules.

Rosabel sat very quietly at the other end of the table, looking through Father's coffee table book of natural disasters. She didn't make a sound and didn't look up, but she was adept at taking in everything around her.

It was a lesson on decimals, which to me just looked like a poor use of a period. "Round up! Round up! How many times do I have to tell you?" Kyan said, slamming his hand on the table. Melanie giggled from the other room. "I don't know what else to do for you, Katherine. Figure it out or have them transfer you to the remedial class."

"I have a writing project due tomorrow," I said. I had recently discovered the quick and easy way to get rid of him. My brother had no interest in anything creative, especially something that might have to utilize my bizarre way of thinking. Kyan darted out of the dining room before I could close my book.

Rosabel and I got up simultaneously and held hands as we headed out to the barn. We never spoke of my tutoring sessions. That would have been humiliating for me, to acknowledge that my brother thought of me as a loser. Not that she didn't already have that figured out.

The next day, I closed my eyes and tried to picture an A on the top of the paper. The Rosabel method of thinking would turn out well if I imagined them. As I started down the page in utter frustration, Rosabel's paper turned to the side and a folded note slid to my side of the desk. I looked at her face, panicked that she wanted to start a conversation when she knew I would struggle through the entire test, without keeping up my end of a conversation. I slid the note over and opened it. The first ten answers were placed on the line: After Cats Barf Beets, None of the above Can Binge on Alcohol A. Bravo!

There were only twenty questions on the test. That meant I would get at least a 50 percent, plus the bonus ten points of writing your entire name (Keilah Middle-Name-To-Be-Determined Brownwell) and end up with a D, not even taking into account the questions I accidentally guessed correctly.

After class, we walked to Rosabel's locker. "Why did you do it?" I asked. She had come to my rescue so many times, but never before had she risked her own grade in the class to help me in such a brave way. It was too embarrassing to ask for her help when we seemed like equals creating our world together in the barn.

She took a tissue from her locker and gently wiped my nose. "Everybody has smarts in their own way, Robin. Yours don't come from a grade on a math test."

Miss Seagull called me in after class the next day. I couldn't let Rosabel take the blame. I had to come up with a reason for cheating, other than the fact that I didn't understand what she was teaching. Maybe Kyan was right about my needing to be in a lower grade.

She bent down beside me, her hair wings taking flight. I tried to stay calm.

"Keilah, you really stepped things up with this last test," she said, patting my back as she would someone who hadn't cheated.

"Thank you," I responded, staring at the ground and waiting for what would come next. I had already decided I would blame it on Kyan's poor tutoring skills.

"I can see that this is very hard for you. I might have a solution for that." She took out a piece of paper and handed it to me, along with a Kleenex for my ever-runny nose.

"Give this to your parents. This is a doctor who may be able to help." She raised herself back to giant level. "He gave me my life back," she said. "You deserve good things, Keilah."

No adult had ever said that to me before. I got up and ran out of the room, crying hard even though I didn't know why.

I got on the bus, but instead of my usual spot beside Rosabel, I sat right in the front. I could feel her sadness burning into the back of my head, but it was just too hard to talk about. I didn't want her to know I was crying for no reason and I didn't want to explain something that defied explanation.

The paper I was handed was the number for an allergy doctor. Mother didn't think it was necessary, that my problems all stemmed from laziness and a strong desire to be dirty. Father thought we should at least hear what they had to say, especially if it was going to turn me into a student like Kyan.

They did lots of tests and decided I was allergic to dust, grass, and most importantly corn. It was the biggest crop we had on our farm that year and Mother and Father looked at it as one enormous slap I was giving them in their hard-working faces. How dare I be allergic to the one thing I couldn't avoid.

When we told Kyan that night at dinner, he made his usual snorting sound of disgust. "Found another way to get yourself out of harvest, did you?"

They did give me the medicine, though, a thick, brown goop that tasted like bitter pop without the carbonation. And shots, one in each arm every week. Eventually, my yellow rivers started to go away.

Suddenly, I looked like everyone else at school. My grades improved, though not to the miraculous level my family had been hoping for. I started smiling at people and forgetting to put my hand over my face. For the first time, I looked forward to getting to my desk every day.

Miss Seagull was big on making plans for the rest of your life. At the beginning of the year, she informed us that we would be creating a list of things we wanted to accomplish in our lives. Certainly, nothing I would have completed at that stage of misery.

"You are your truest selves now," she said mid-year. "Before the world corrupts you, we need to document and preserve who you are."

She suggested we frame it and put it on our walls to remind us what we wanted to do. That's how Miss Seagull had become the successful teacher she was. "I want to eat bugs, that's gonna be number three," I joked to Rosabel on the bus ride home.

To my surprise, she had a serious look on her face. She already had a piece of paper out and was jotting some things down.

"Well..." she began slowly, "I'm still working this over. It's very serious, don't you think?"

I nodded. If she said it was serious, then it was.

"You've always wanted to go to the moon..." she offered.

I wanted to live someplace that looked like the moon. Maybe pee in a space suit. Not really travel there. She didn't understand my curiosity for living removed from life.

"And be a princess," a voice said from over my shoulder. It was Kenner, who usually sat in the back with the other boys his age.

I turned and patted his hand. "Thanks, buddy," I said. "Come sit down and help us."

Kenner plopped down beside Rosabel, squishing our two-seater into three. He was now too big to fit in her lap.

She tore a new sheet out of her notebook and wrote *Seven Things Keilah will Accomplish in Her Life* on the top. "Ok. Number one, go to the moon," she said.

I put my hand out. "Wait – make it number six."

"Why? You've always wanted to go. Might as well make it your priority," Rosabel said.

"The moon will be a lovely place," I began, "but it's a long trip. I want to get other things done first." I looked out the window, trying to avoid her gaze.

"Like eating something with mango or chickpeas," he said.

"That's a great goal, Sparrow," Rosabel smiled at him. "But we need something to really set your sights on, a big plan for life."

I had no plans. Rosabel took care of me. I didn't want that to change. "Number one will be helping you set up the orphanage."

Her eyes shot up from the page. "Really? You'd do that for me, Robin? I don't want you to miss one minute of your life working on my list."

"We'll all do it. Keilah can help you with kids and I'll be the handyman. I'm gettin' real good with a hammer and nails," Kenner offered.

She put head first on my shoulder and then on Kenner's. I'd never actually seen tears on her face before. "Oh, I love you two," she said softly.

As we reached our stop, she sat up straight and looked at me. "You need a serious list. Maybe you can open a business, something."

I collected my backpack and started walking out. "Maybe," I said. "After your orphanage is up and running."

1. Help Rosabel create the best orphanage in the world.
2. Live somewhere exotic.
3. Eat candy all day.
4. Eat something with mango or chickpeas.
5. Have a savings account with at least ~~two~~ three zeros.
6. Be someone special.

I couldn't think of anything important to put on it. I knew that beyond my graduating from high school, my parents didn't have high hopes for me. I would help around the farm, in some capacity. I hadn't ever thought about being something. Being someone. An important someone.

That night at dinner I was going to read my list at the table. I thought it might be my chance to really impress Mother and Father.

"You're sharing your homework? That's quite a thing, Kath... Keilah. See, dear? We should have taken her to that doctor years ago."

I wrinkled my brow and looked at Mother. "You knew about this doctor before Miss Seagull gave me his name?"

Mother shrugged. "Didn't think it would make any difference. You should thank your father for convincing me it was a good idea this time."

Father could see I was beginning to boil. "Doesn't matter now. We've got things fixed, like we always do. After dessert, you can read your homework. Maybe play that trombone of yours too. Need to hear what my investment sounds like."

Mother clucked her tongue. "Girls shouldn't be playing those gangly things. When will you be done embarrassing your family?"

I didn't want to have this argument again. Playing the trombone was something I did because they didn't think Rosabel and I should be in every class together.

As Father finished up his last spoonful, I pulled my list from my pocket and stood up. At the same time, Kyan rose from the other side of the table. "No! It's my..."

"I was gonna wait on this 'til Melanie came over tomorrow, but I got to make this announcement now." Kyan didn't even glance in my direction, almost as if he had timed it to the second to let the air out of my one-and-only-dinner-announcement balloon.

"Oh?" Mother said, not even looking up from her second bowl of the green-and-orange swirl. "Pass me the sugar cookies, Keilah, will you please?"

Kyan cleared his throat. "You know Melanie graduates in May. We've been talking... I'm gonna ask her father tomorrow for her hand."

"What?" Mother stood up. I wasn't sure if it was a shocked or sad stand or if she had just spilled sherbet on her dress.

"Why do you need her hand?" Kenner asked. I looked at him and giggled. Then we both started to laugh, thinking about Melanie's long fingers, topped with bright pink-frosted fingernail polish attached to Kyan's muscular and hairy arms.

"Quiet, you two!" Mother snapped.

"Well, it's to be expected," Father said, acting not the least bit excited. "Not a summer wedding though?"

"No. We were thinkin' end of September. When planting's done."

Mother actually hugged Kyan. She wasn't one for any

kind of affection, at least around me, so it took Kenner and me by surprise.

"That's just plain ol' good news," she said, slapping his back. Before he had a chance to respond, she picked up his sherbet dish and took it into the kitchen.

"Will they live here?" Kenner asked as we pulled my covers up around our necks. "They'll live in their own house." As I said that, it occurred to me that Kyan's room would now be empty. We might be able to create a whole new kingdom inside, away from the allergens and the barn cats.

"Will I get married?" Kenner asked.

"Oh, sure," I said. I looked at his beautiful long eyelashes and wavy red hair. "There will be some perfect girl for you."

"Do you think she'll look like Rosabel?"

"Just as beautiful. And kind. You deserve the best," I said.

"What about you?"

"I have Rosabel. I don't need anyone else."

"Oh," he replied. "Maybe we can just be together forever. All three of us."

"Maybe." I doubted he would end up like me. "If we don't die from tickle wars first!" I reached over and tickled his armpits until we both dissolved into laughter. I sat up, suddenly remembering that my one moment of pride in front of my family had been ruined.

"Can I read you something, Sparrow?"

He shrugged.

I pulled out the list and read to him what I had written. Afterward, he jumped off the bed and clapped. "That's real good, Keilah. I could never come up with that. I wish I was as smart as you."

I pulled him in close and hugged him hard.

The next day I told Rosabel all about Kyan's upcoming wedding.

"Do you think you'll be in the wedding?" she asked as she braided my hair.

I cocked my head to the side. "Are you kidding? She hates me." I couldn't imagine one of her eighteen bridesmaids would be Kyan's little sister. One of the things they bonded over was their mutual hatred of me.

"But that's tradition," Rosabel insisted, gently pushing my head upright. "The groom's family is always part of the wedding party. I bet our little Sparrow will be the ring bearer."

"The reception's going to be in the barn. Melanie thinks she can turn oil stains and rusty walls into a Disney movie."

Rosabel made a faint sound of disapproval. I could tell she was excited but didn't want to tell me.

"Did you make your list?" I asked, changing the subject. "For class?"

Rosabel patted her notebook. "I have one. And a back-up."

I turned to face her. "Why a back-up?" Now I was worried that I really hadn't understood the importance of the assignment.

"Well, in case this one isn't enough. For Miss Seagull." She looked at me, completely serious.

I still didn't understand how this assignment could be so much more important than anything else we had done all year.

"If she doesn't think my list is a good use of my life, then I'll give her the other one, even though I'd rather not. Go ahead and read this one, Robin. See what you think," she said. I could tell she was nervous. "Oh, but before you start, I just want you to know that I understand."

"What?"

"I know you don't want to go to the ACTUAL moon. You want to find your own moon. Someplace foreign and exciting right here on our planet. We'll make it happen."

A lump formed in my throat, but I said nothing. I carefully unfolded the sheet, entitled MY LIST OF THINGS I WANT TO ACCOMPLISH, *smiley, smiley, heart face.*

1. Give someone inspiration.
2. Buy a home for my parents.
3. Create an orphanage for unwanted children.
4. Blank space – everyone must have some for great, unexpected things to come!
5. Feed those starving – with food and love.
6. Bring many animals to the orphanage for all of the children to love and care for.
7. Help my Robin get to the moon.

I gulped. "These are spectacular, Rosabel. Why would you make another one?"

She shook her head. "I just wasn't sure. There are other things of importance, but we must do what's best for others first. I want to make sure I make every minute count."

"And what about number four?" I asked.

"You should always save room for one unexpected thing. That gives life a little breathing room." I smiled. My chest squeezed, just thinking of my own list.

Chapter Ten

SANDY SALTS
2012

"YOU WAITED A LONG TIME to call. Startin' to think you forgot about me."

I sigh. "I'm sorry, Sparrow. It's been busy. You know – getting acquainted and starting the new job."

"Well, don't make me guess. How's the new place?"

I look across the room, where my blue notebook containing all my observations is resting inside my purse. I haven't even gotten to Nova and Jack and the strangeness that is Dee yet. I roll over and switch the phone to my other hand. "Yeah, it's great. Really dry and barren, just like I thought."

I mentally scan the businesses on the main street. "There's a body shop right on the highway that would be perfect for you to work. You know all about machinery."

"Mmmm... maybe. How's your job?"

I take a deep breath. "There's Nova, the boss's daughter. She's gorgeous and horrible. Horribly gorgeous. Her cousin Lorraine works there too. And then Dee, the lady I live with... I just don't know how to describe her... but she makes the best scones. I can't wait for you to meet them all."

"Yeah, me too."

"Kenner, I've been wanting to ask you about the day Kyan read the will..." I hear a female voice in the background and my heart drops. "Is someone there with you?" I already know the answer.

"You should talk to Mother, she'll be wanting to know you're safe. Hang on." Then he is gone.

"But I don't want..." I ache for his friendship. The way we used to be. A comfortable place for my mind to rest at the end of the day. "Love you, Sparrow!" No one replies.

I hear another muffled voice, this one I recognize as Mother's. "You made it alright then? Everything's workin' out?"

My insides tighten. It's not that she doesn't care, I keep reminding myself. At least that's what the stupid psychiatrist she forced me to see for two years always told me.

"Yes. I have a job, if that's what you're asking."

Why didn't you stand up for me? Why didn't you tell Kyan he was wrong? That I deserved to inherit my share at the same time as everyone else?

"Kyan thought you might be stuck in a ditch somewhere." She chuckles to herself. Apparently, in her world, that's pretty funny.

"No, I found it just fine. My new boss is great and I'm sort of in charge." I'm hoping she'll remember I worked all those years in Pepperville without a promotion.

"Oh? Melanie's goin' to take me out shoppin' next week for my birthday. You remembered it was my birthday, didn't you?"

"Of course I remembered your birthday." I reach for a pen off my nightstand. "I thought I would send you some coffee from our shop. Jack roasts all the beans himself."

Send coffee and a b-day card, I write. "Are you doing okay? Getting out in the garden at all?"

She sighs, with Kyan-level irritation. "The garden's done for the year. You know that, Keilah... You should be told that Kyan and Melanie want me to move in with them so that I'm not alone all the time. It wouldn't be forever, just until they've got things fancied up in here."

I feel my stomach lurch. Melanie had been whispering about redecorating the big house for years. This is just the first step. Get Mother out, then she can erase any trace of Brownwell that exists within those walls and make it some kind of showpiece where she can entertain fancy rich people from towns out of state. We all knew her plan was to claim our childhood home as her own right from the start. Eventually, she would move in and probably have Mother living in a glorified shed in the back yard. "Oh, Mother. That's my house too. And Kenner's. You've lived there your whole adult life! Why would you abandon it?" Then I remember nothing is currently mine. I have no piece of this life I lived.

"I'm not abandoning anything, Keilah. I'll still be up the road," Mother says, defensively. "'Sides, I haven't decided for sure. It's too big for one person. Kenner's hardly here anymore. Just an idea for now. It wouldn't be forever. She's got plans to change the rugs, some kind of fancy Persian..."

I distract myself by watching Gentry, who has pushed his way through my door, sniffing at my open and still-unpacked suitcase in the closet. When he decides to claim it as his own, I reach the limit of my tolerance. "No, kitty! Shoo!"

"So, that Salty place is where you plan to spend your

whole time? Until you can come back? You think it will fix that fuzzy head o' yours? Probably not even eatin' right."

"It's Sandy Salts, Mother. And yes, no problems eating." I think about Mother's farm cooking and how simple it seems now that I'm experiencing Dee's complex, vegetarian dishes.

"You know I had to leave. Father didn't want me there."

"The headstone came in. It's that brown marble, like he would've wanted. I took some flowers to other graves while I was there."

I swallow hard.

"Thought I might have to dust hers off, but it's just covered in stuffed animals and little plastic flowers. Someone's been keepin' it nice, though I doubt it's her people."

"Oh... I guess that's good. She loved her stuffed animals." I feel more guilt about abandoning my Rosabel in the cold, hard ground than I do leaving my family. Her "people" wouldn't involve family, that's for sure.

"I'm worried about the boy," Mother says suddenly. She never confides in me about anything.

"Kenner, you mean? Why?"

Gentry jumps up on the bed beside me and, despite my best efforts, plops his shedding, purring body on top of my arm. Immediately I worry that Kenner had somehow spilled the beans about our plan. If Mother got wind that we both were leaving, she would find a way to make him stay.

"It's that girlfriend of his. She's got her hooks in him so deep he can't take a breath by himself. He won't even eat dinner with the family unless she gives the okay. He has to call and ask her first."

I feel queasy. I knew she had taken over simple things for

him when Father died, like paying his cell phone bill and doing his laundry. He had become desperately sad, despite the fact he and Father were never close.

"I'll talk to him. Probably nothing to worry about." If only she had paid attention. Kenner has been trapped for years. If only she were the type of mother I could tell.

"Well then, I need to get to bed. Write your things, like you're supposed to. Keep in touch now."

I resist the urge to ask why she thinks I wouldn't. "Ok, Mother. Sleep well."

I hang up, feeling more exhaustion than an entire day's worth of Nova and Lorraine. Flowers left on Rosabel's grave by someone who wasn't me. Mother, abandoning our home and our secrets, the ones we had worked hard to protect our entire lives. For the first time, I'm not there to oversee that life and I begin to feel like I'm being choked. I put my head on my pillow and let out a hearty scream.

"Gracious, girl! Did something bite you?"

Dee is standing in the doorway, the silhouette of her head looking very different. The beehive is now cocked slightly to the side.

I sit up and take a deep breath. "I'm just having a hard day. I called home and things are a mess."

Dee comes over and sits on my bed, where now I see clearly that her hair has two dark strands of blue swirling around the beehive core of gray. It could be a twirling mass of tornadic activity just as easily as a new hairstyle.

"Just got back from the beauty shop and heard you from the minute I opened the door. Thought for a second there was an intruder the way you were bellerin', but ol' Gentry wouldn't go for that."

"I know. I'm sorry, Dee. There's so much going on at home and I can't seem to get a handle on it. I moved here to start over, but that life won't let me."

She pats my leg. "Well, the world keeps spinnin' no matter where we are. You can always spill it to me, you know."

I think for a moment about telling her everything, but by then she's stood up and turned away from me. "The girls at the beauty shop sure liked you. Hopin' you'll come in and get yourself all purtied up sometime."

They were so judgmental of Dee I was surprised they spoke to her like a friend. "We'll see." I can only imagine how they would talk about me, if they knew everything.

"Let's go get us some supper and work it all out."

I tell Dee the story of my Rosabel, as best as I can muster, over black beans and rice with homemade mango salsa and pita bread. She nods her head and clicks her tongue. When she finishes eating, she sits, picking her teeth with a toothpick in the chair while the joy of Rosabel continues to pour out of me.

"Never did have friends like that. You are a lucky one, Keilah."

I never thought I was lucky. All I had was Rosabel, and once she was gone, I wasn't anything. "I'm not lucky. I had someone wonderful, who made me important. When she was gone, I became... nothing."

She stands up and throws her toothpick on the plate. "Luck ain't your problem. Ya got that brother of yours coming soon, don't you? You have all those memories with your friend, fuel enough to keep things runnin' after all these years? It's the way you look at life that's got you stuck."

She takes her plate to the sink and tosses it in carelessly, causing beans to jump over the sink and out onto the floor where Gentry immediately runs to make sure it wasn't something meant to land in his mouth.

Her strange outbursts are starting to seem normal.

Dee spins around and stares at me. "Somethin's missin' in your head. A big chunk. Don't know what, but I know it's gone. Never wrong about these things. I have a gift, some say." She turns back to the sink and wipes off a dish. "Someday I'll tell you that story," she mutters.

Chapter Eleven

JOURNAL – PEPPERVILLE
1999

I T WAS IN THOSE DARK DAYS before the funeral that I felt I had ceased to exist.

I wanted to speak at the service, even though I was terrified to stand up in front of an entire gymnasium full of people. It seemed like the right thing to do as her best friend. I owed her something. I dug through my closet looking for inspiration.

There were remnants of our time playing in the barn, the little costumes she made and all sorts of weaponry we used to protect the Little Ones. Nothing inspired me as I thought it would. I closed the door, pretending that my world was completely unchanged.

I put it off as long as possible, hoping the words would come to me. Perhaps Rosabel herself would appear in a dream and give me the perfect speech, the way it always happened in the movies. Something profound would come from me, for the first time ever, leaving the entire town of Pepperville on the verge of tears. But there were no dreams or inspirations.

Finally, the day before her memorial, I knocked on her mother's door. It took a long time for anyone to answer. I had to resist the urge to just walk in as I had done for so many years when Rosabel was busy baking something or sewing in her bedroom. A relative from Texas, sharing the same weather-beaten face as Rosabel's father, opened the door and let me in. The lights weren't on, as usual, and I had to make my way carefully through the dirty dishes on the floor and ashtrays full of cigarette butts to Rosabel's room.

Her kitchen was covered with dirty dishes, half-eaten casseroles, and empty liquor bottles. I gulped as I walked through, trying not to think about all of the days I sat at the counter and watched as Rosabel created something magnificent for us to devour later. I tripped over a full trash can and almost fell on the dirty floor, but someone caught my arm.

I looked up to see Rosabel's mother, Penny, her eyes redder than normal, holding on to the countertop to keep herself upright. "Nice you came," she said flatly, maybe even sarcastically, studying me as she had the very first day we met.

I wanted to run as far away from these people as I could, but I had made a promise, probably the last thing I could do for my friend. There was an eerie silence in the house that felt like someone other than my Rosabel had died. She would have wanted laughter and happy thoughts of her life permeating the thick, smoky air.

"I need to get into her bedroom," I said. I gazed over to her door, where cards and flowers sat in a makeshift memorial.

She shoved me a little, causing me to lose my balance. "Go on then. Just don't take things. Her things stay put."

I was shocked she would treat me this way. No matter what I really thought of them, they were Rosabel's parents. I stepped over the flowers and very carefully opened her door. For a moment, it took my breath away.

Her room was exactly as she had left it just a few mornings prior. The smell of her perfume, *Enchanteur*, still lingered. It was like she had gone away for the night and would return soon. Pictures of hollow-cheeked, teary-eyed children plastered on her walls now seemed as if they were crying for their lost savior.

I opened her dresser drawer, where her socks and underwear were arranged by color. I felt around until I found it: The Sacred Folder of Life. We each kept all our important things, life guidance, in one with strict instructions that, should something happen to either one of us, the other was to retrieve it. It contained the lists we made in sixth grade, things we wanted to accomplish in our lives, along with the blue notebook where Kenner wrote down all the plots to our stories we acted out. Things I would have thrown away.

Somehow Rosabel knew it was important. She knew I would need it to carry on without her. I opened up her folder and immediately had to sit – not on her bed which was still pristine from her last time pulling up the covers and repositioning the daisy-patterned pillows. That was hallowed space. I sat on the floor. There, on top was our list from 6th grade. *Seven Things I Will Accomplish in My Life*. I felt an immediate rush of emotion. For others in our sixth-grade class that year, it was just another mindless assignment. For Rosabel, it was a directive for the rest of her life. I set it aside.

Next were pictures of Kenner and me from a party. That Halloween, Rosabel had dressed as the Queen of Hearts and Kenner and I were in matching outfits as scepters in her court. She had carefully sewn the outfits and put matching hearts on each one. She insisted we have our pictures taken without her because everyone in the queen's court was important.

Underneath that picture were several flowers she had picked from our farm. She had pressed them into a book and left them lying flat until they were dried, promising one day she would use them in a memory book she was creating for me. Hesitantly, I opened the paper.

"You must be Keilah," a voice said from behind me. I turned abruptly to see someone identical to Penny in features, but at least ten years younger. "I've heard so much about you."

I shook her hand. It was puzzling that she had heard so much about me, yet I knew nothing of her. "And you are?"

"I'm Rosabel's Aunt Patty. Penny's twin." She smiled and handed me the tissue that was in her hand. I hadn't even realized I was crying.

"Thanks," I said. "I was just getting some ideas for my speech." I felt like I needed to explain why I was lost in a room where I usually felt so at home. "You know, for the memorial. But don't worry, I won't take anything."

Patty shook her head. "I heard my sister talking to you. You have to know this is extremely difficult for her. And losing them both... that's too much for one person." She put her hand on my shoulder. "I can't even imagine how this is for you," she whispered.

I nodded. I didn't want to think about it.

"I wish it all could have gone differently..." she said.

I didn't know how to answer. How did this woman know how anything had gone? Why wasn't she here, helping her sister before now?

"You take whatever is meaningful to you. I'm sure Ros-abel would have wanted that. She'll always be in here," she patted her chest, "but you'll need something to touch. Spend as much time as you need. I'll close the door and give you some privacy." She patted my shoulder once more and slipped out.

I set her *Things I Will Accomplish* list aside and took everything out of the Folder of Life, laying it in front of me. In one of the notebooks she retrieved from Kenner, listing all the characters in our kingdom, I found a folded paper stuck in the middle like a bookmark. As I unfolded and read it, my hands shook. It was something I couldn't fathom. I hadn't expected such a turn of events. And yet I had.

Chapter Twelve

SANDY SALTS
2012

The Salty Sun, Established 1925
Vanessa Withers, Reporter
Jenny Jacobson, age 82

Our dear Jenny went to be with the High and Mighty yesterday at 4 p.m. She wasn't upset about dying. As she told this reporter during a chance encounter at a coffee shop, "This lady has gotten her work done and you can only lounge in the sun so long before the sand in your crack becomes unbearable."

Jenny was born in Wallyville. Her folks were out shopping for a new car that day and lost track of time. She barely outlived her mother, who died at the age of 103 a week ago last Thursday, after finding a big spider's nest in her bathtub.

Most of Jenny's life was spent giving to others. After graduating with a teaching degree, she moved to Canada where she taught English and P.E. for twenty-five years. Upon retirement, she decided to move back to Sandy Salts to open a secondhand goods and firsthand ice cream store, called D' Ya Want Seconds? Folks who couldn't afford the ice cream could trade clothing or good, used appliances for a scoop. Nobody went away hungry.

She closed the place two years ago in order to fulfill her lifelong dream of traveling the world with a younger man. After finding her companion via an online ad, Jenny and Javier spent time in Spain, Greece, New Zealand, and Cancun. She died last week in the garden of her Sandy Salts home with a smile on her face.

Services will be on Sunday at 2 p.m. at the Sandy Salts Community Park. Please wear bright colors and bring something chocolate to eat in her honor.

I'm getting used to the rhythm of this coffee shop, so different from the ebb and flow of my days at the coffee shop in Pepperville. We always knew there would be a crowd at seven-thirty and then again at ten, and then some quiet for cleaning. Jack's Beanery is always buzzing. It's the only social gathering spot in town for everyone, young and old.

I enjoy coming in early and working with Tucker, getting all the baked goods ready to go and going over the list of specialty drinks. My new favorite is a Drippicino: chocolate-flavored powdered milk and ice with espresso and cream. *Dee's sour cream muffins would be the perfect accompaniment*, I thought each time I drank a "mistake".

The least enjoyable part of my day is dealing with Nova and Lorraine. Lorraine keeps her head down, doesn't say much, even when I try to make conversation. She doesn't do anything she isn't specifically told to do.

"What do you do for fun, Lorraine?" I ask, more than once.

She shrugs her shoulders. "Dunno."

By the time I come up with something else to ask, she's off to another section of the coffee shop, dragging her rag slowly up and down a table or staring at the highway outside like it's a complicated puzzle.

I would gladly work with ten Lorraines if I didn't have to deal with Nova. She is awful. Whenever she speaks, she has a smile on her face, but her words don't match.

"Oh, you're going to use a SHORT shot in that?" Wink. "You know that's half a shot, right?"

"That's what he asked for."

"Is that so? Hmmm." She smiles, then purses her lips. "You might want to re-check your orders each time, just to make sure, until you really learn everything just right, sweetie."

Just like during the millions of conversations with Kyan or Mother, I clamp my jaw and say nothing. If Rosabel were here, she would remind me that even though I couldn't confront the boss's daughter, I have twice her experience.

I start to enjoy seeing regular customers each day. At first, it feels strange for people to look at me without a sense of pity. Everyone in Pepperville would, even five years later, expressing their sympathy for the loss of Rosabel.

"Sure sorry 'bout the way things turned out for you," they would say. "Just awful."

"I know," I would reply, glad that the customers understood our unique bond and wishing I had something more profound to offer. I should have been able to quote one of her wonderful bits of wisdom, but there was nothing in my head beyond the next order to make. Something in me had died next to Rosabel that day on the road.

"Keilah!" Nova snaps through her toothy grin. "Customer!"

"Oh, sorry." My face is flushed. "What was your order?"

"Double shot latte."

"She's new." Nova winks. "Sometimes she can be a little ditzy." She leans over the counter, making sure this customer, who is at least her father's age, sees her new, black-lace bra.

The men who come in to whisk her away are a constant parade of beauty in all shades, each one more appealing than the last. Strangely, they all seem attracted to Nova, despite her personality. She's a shell, as Rosabel used to say. Just bits of outside beauty with no real filling.

Many days I watch the clock, begging the hands to move to the magic two-thirty mark. It's always the same game. One of her endless boyfriends shows up "unexpectedly". She leans across the counter, whispering in his ear while she looks in my direction, as if she needs to figure out how to negotiate her departure. She walks over with that sick-sweet smile on her face. "I've got to do some business for the shop. You'll be alright on your own? Won't burn the place down, right?" Wink, wink.

I look over at Lorraine, who is twirling a straw between her fingers. "Yes. Fine on my own."

About ten minutes after she leaves, one of the more handsome boyfriends shows up. The guy Dee pinched on the butt my first full day.

"Hey there, new girl." He flashes me that irritatingly perfect smile.

"Can I help you? Your girlfriend is gone for the day." *As usual.*

"Nope. Just came in for a coffee. Black."

"Seems kind of boring." *But perfect for an idiot like you.*

"I'm a pretty boring guy." He puts his arms across his chest. "Hey, Lorraine, what're you readin' these days? Anything I can borrow?"

I'm ready to jump across the counter and attack him like a cheetah snatching its prey. *There's no reason to tease Lorraine. Jerk.*

Lorraine walks over to the dirty dish tub and pulls a paperback from behind it. *How have I never seen that?*

She shoves it across the counter. *Did the corners of her mouth just raise slightly?*

"*The Book Thief?* I heard that was super intense. You'll have to let me know how it ends."

She nods, pats the cover, and then places the book back where she found it. Her interaction with humans has ended and she goes back to dusting the window.

I realize I have been staring at this unlikely interaction and haven't made his coffee at all.

Flustered, I fill the cup quickly and place it in front of him. "Sorry."

"No worries. Tell Nova I was here, would ya? And say hi to Jack for me."

He does that annoying clicking thing with his mouth that the fakest of men use on the dumbest of women.

"Good day to be in coffee?" Jack asks a few minutes later. He lays his fishing hat on the counter alongside a greasy wallet.

I take a deep breath, prepared to give him my usual, "Everything went fine." Instead, I drop the broom into a pile of scone crumbs and begin shaking violently.

"Hell fire, Keilah! You gonna be alright?" Jack asks as he pulls me in and hugs me tightly to his musty jacket.

"I...I..." I can't express to him how good it feels to be held so tightly. We stand, he in a protective stance and me enveloped in his strong arms, for several minutes until it passes. When it does, I look up at him and smile weakly. These things always zap all my energy.

"What's that, some kinda seizure?" he asks. "Maybe we should get you to a doctor."

I blush. "No, it's something that's happened to me for five years now. Since my friend died. The doctor said it's just how my body reacts to stress." I feel guilty for bringing Jack into this intimate act that previously only happened when I was alone.

He shakes his head. "I'm not sure 'bout that. Seems like you shoulda been better by now."

Chapter Thirteen

JOURNAL – PEPPERVILLE
2001

IT WAS THE BIGGEST SHOCK I experienced thus far in my young life: Melanie told Mother she wanted me to be in her wedding. It turns out that in her very elaborate wedding planning, she found no relative the right age to act as a junior bridesmaid. When she realized I was her last resort, she also discovered she had no boys in her extended family to stand on the other side to act as junior groomsmen. Kenner was already cast in the role as ring bearer, a title he found terribly insulting.

As far as my partner on the other side of the aisle, Melanie consulted a wedding planner who suggested adding another junior bridesmaid to the groom's side, so that when we all stood for pictures there was an even number of people.

She asked, or rather *told,* Mother that both Rosabel and I would be her junior bridesmaids. I think she was secretly hoping I would come down with something awful and it would just be Rosabel, who would look stunning in whatever dress she picked out. If it were up to me, that would have been the week I came down with the measles.

The burnt-orange, floor-length dresses were like something out of a cartoon. The sleeves puffed up to twice the size of our arms, making us both look oddly muscular. The skirt fanned out (thanks to a ridiculous hoop skirt underneath) so large that when we walked down the aisle, the material touched each side. The front of the dress made a V dangerously low for girls of our age. I had nothing but a straight road from my chin to my belly button, which left a big gap of material that would warrant constant reminders to hold the thing flat to my front every time I bent over. Since Rosabel had started to develop lovely curves, hers looked better.

On top of those cruelly-designed dresses, I had just gotten braces. It was a grand total of six months between the time my nose dried up and the braces appeared. I looked normal for less than a year. Braces; red, frizzy hair; freckles; and gangly, long legs that never went in the direction I commanded. And yet, my Rosabel was still just as beautiful and perfect as the day I met her. She had no awkward phase.

When Melanie realized it was going to take too long to have everyone's hair professionally done, she insisted her second cousin-in-law and her junior bridesmaids do their own. So, we set out to find beautiful things to place on the top of our heads, distracting from the hideous mess covering the rest of our bodies. We found white and purple wildflowers that we took turns winding through each other's hair. I thought we looked quite beautiful, all things considered. We took pity on the last bridesmaid/cousin and brought her some flowers as well.

The wedding was at two, so after we got dressed we had to sit and wait for what seemed like days in the fancy sitting room at the church. "Want to hear a good story?" Rosabel asked. *Like I had ever said no.*

"Ummhmmm," I responded.

"I've only been to one other wedding ever. It was my cousin. Second, I believe."

"Girl cousin or boy?"

"Girl. She had lots of bridesmaids too. Not eighteen like this one, but six or seven."

I tried to imagine what she would look like. Probably with the same perfect smile and heart-shaped face, but with one obvious flaw.

"My parents had a bottle of whiskey under the front seat, so when they dropped me off at the front door and told me they were going to park, I knew they weren't coming back," she said matter-of-factly.

"But not to worry, I found another cousin, I think – a grown-up cousin – and sat right beside her. She passed me funny notes all through the ceremony. A couple of times I started laughing out loud, and everyone turned and stared. When it finally ended, she snuck me out the back door. I stayed at her house for two days, in my fancy wedding clothes – a flowery summer dress and shiny shoes, if I remember correctly."

I was horrified. "How did they... your parents... know where you were? Did they think you'd been kidnapped by some sick wedding stalker?"

Rosabel smiled. "I don't know for sure. I wasn't worried. I knew they would come and find me when they were ready." She looked at my wrinkled brow and patted my arm. "This is a GOOD memory, Robin. No need for that face," she said assuredly. "We ate sugar and watched cartoons. It was heaven for a child."

Right about the time she finished that story, Melanie

came racing into her dressing room, screaming and yelling. Her maid of honor, her best friend, and co-captain of the cheerleading squad had not shown up. She and Melanie had gotten in a fight during the rehearsal dinner the night before about how many members of the squad would be invited to get up and dance during the special guests dance. Melanie wanted to make sure that the people bringing the most expensive gifts were able to dance without interference from low-dollar spenders, like her teammates.

Rosabel and I had been sitting on the brick patio of the Beef and Bean, the most expensive restaurant in town, when the argument broke out. We had been eating blue popsicles, daring the syrupy liquid to stain our matching sky-blue peasant tops. The two friends stormed out the door and began an all-out brawl right in front of us. We sat, completely entranced, with blue syrup dripping from our lips.

It was the most violent fight I had ever witnessed. Hair pulling, cheek twisting, even trying to break off each other's expensive nails. They spat at each other and then said some nasty words; some I wasn't really sure were real but I nonetheless made a mental note to ask Rosabel about later.

When they finished, both stormed back in the building without even acknowledging we were there. Rosabel and I looked at each other, stunned. Finally, she giggled. I started to giggle. That was our language.

The next day we all just assumed things would go back to normal as they always did with emotionally-charged Melanie and her equally high-strung friend Marlie.

"You!" she screamed, pointing a broken nail in my direction. I ran through any possible transgressions in my head.

"Keilah! Look at me!" she demanded. I reluctantly met her gaze, a bit afraid of meeting Marlie's fate.

"I want you to take the dress that's still hanging in the closet over there." She pointed across the room at the lone bridesmaid dress still on the hanger. "I want you to take that and find someone in the church who fits!"

I didn't understand at first. Did she want me to give away this dress? That seemed so kind and out of character for her. But then again, it was a hideous dress.

"Ummm... ok, but I...."

She tugged on her silk slip and smoothed the sides. She let out a deep breath and collected herself. "You're going to find me a maid of honor. That bitch didn't show. Go out and find someone as fat as she is to put this on. Then bring them back to have their makeup done while I get my nails fixed."

Rosabel and I hopped up and headed down the hall with the dress. We soon realized that beyond Marlie's obvious poor choice in friends, she had a body with more curves than Highway 59 (known for its unexpected twists and bumps). Finding someone for this fitted dress would be a nightmare to inflict upon them, even for an hour. We held it up to several people before Rosabel looked at the clock and pulled me aside.

"We're running out of options. I have pins in my purse and I can make this fit you. I've made dresses for you so often I can do this with my eyes closed. And that girl," she pointed to Mother's bridge partner's daughter, "is almost exactly your size."

I must have had a look of abject horror on my face. "Why can't you wear it, Rosabel? Melanie will think I'm trying to ruin her day!"

"I can pin easier on someone else than myself and we don't' have time. Don't think, Robin. Just do it."

Quickly we guided the other girl, who didn't mind being photographed in something that hideous, to the dressing room. Rosabel was careful to keep me out of Melanie's view until it was too late for her to change her mind. She pushed me to the front of the church and away from Melanie and her father. "Try not to move much, Robin. Anything wild and these pins may not survive."

I nodded, half-hoping they wouldn't. Suddenly, I felt the familiar tickle in my nose. I touched my upper lip with a sense of dread. The yellow highway had returned. I caught a glimpse of myself in the glass partition and found to my horror that my eyes were swollen like two golf balls.

I realized I must be having a reaction to the wildflowers in my hair. There was nothing I could do now but walk down the aisle as Melanie's maid of honor and hope the pins didn't pop when the inevitable sneezing began. The music swelled and I took my place in front of Melanie, who thankfully wasn't paying attention to anything but the people she had hired to fluff and primp her.

As I walked down the aisle, I tried to avert my gaze from Kyan. I saw Mother mouth, *Oh Keilah,* but there was nothing she could do either. Father shook his head in disgust. As I reached the front of the church, Kyan shot me a disapproving glance. For once, he was powerless to insult me.

Rosabel clucked her tongue as I arrived to take my place in the long line of bridesmaids. The rest of them tried to look away uncomfortably. My only hope was to face a slightly different direction from Melanie and hope she didn't notice. Each time I exhaled, things ran further down my face.

I decided if I looked down at the worn-out gold carpeting throughout the service, people would forget I was making such a scene. I heard the swish of Melanie's dress as she arrived beside me, but she said nothing. I continued for what seemed like hours – breathing in short breaths through a rattly-sounding nose to avoid popping those pins through the readings... and the music... and more readings. Finally, Kyan and Melanie went up to light their unity candle together and someone sang a song.

I felt a finger tapping on the back of my aching neck and brought my head up slowly. I looked up to see the minister's freshly-pressed, monogrammed hankie in my face.

"Blow!" Rosabel commanded. And I did. When I finished, Rosabel put the hankie in her dress and returned to her spot.

Melanie and Kyan turned around, and for the first time, she saw me as her maid of honor. "What the hell, Keilah..." she whispered. The hairs on the back of my neck rose. I gave a panicked glance in Rosabel's direction.

Rosabel winked, smiled at me, and then did something brilliant. She started clapping. Everyone else followed suit, and before they were even pronounced man and wife, Kyan and Melanie had a standing ovation, all to keep Melanie from making a scene at her own wedding. They smiled and I moved as far away from Melanie as I could for the remainder of the service.

I looked over at Mother and Father. Mother had a stern look on her face, but because she was at a very important public event, she couldn't appear upset. Father looked at me and squinted. It was the same look he gave the hired hands when they forgot to set the water on a cornfield on a hot day. I felt like dirt.

"Let's clean you up, poor thing," my friend said. She took me into the bathroom and gently wiped my face clean and removed the flowers from my head. "I'm so sorry, Robin. I should have known." She removed the pins gingerly.

With each pin, more emotion was released until I was in a full-on sob. "You saved me, Rosabel. You always save me."

Chapter Fourteen

JOURNAL – PEPPERVILLE
2012

A

T THE END OF THE DAY, I went home and told my stories to Dee over some unbelievable meal she had concocted, just "one more time" before I would be asked to cook for myself.

She would tap her hair and *tsk tsk* when she wasn't picking her teeth or itching an inappropriate place. "Keep lookin' forward, Keilah. That's all I've got to say. If you look sideways or backward, things can fall apart quick. Someday I'll tell you that story..."

I have yet to hear one of her stories about one of these interesting things that happened in her past. "Um hmm..." I say as I gather up our dishes. I should probably call Kenner again and see how things are going with the training of the new employee, the hired man he found to take over his spot.

Suddenly, Dee jumps out of her chair, knocking over the mason jar of lavender lemonade she intended to drink with her supper. "Say, you know what? I think I should take you dancin' with me. That'd change up your thoughts for a bit."

I bring a rag over from the sink and start mopping up the floor, grateful she can't see my look of disgust. "I'm not much of a dancer. I haven't actually done any since my high school prom."

Dee pats my head like I'm Gentry under her feet. "No, I didn't mean YOU would dance. I meant you could watch me. I like to do the polka. It's how I meet men for a little bit of fun."

I sit up quickly, bumping my head on the edge of the table. "'Scuse me?"

"Oh, you young kids do the same thing – meet a gentleman for a... what's it called? A shook up?"

I examine Dee's face to see if she is actually serious. She is picking her teeth and looking out the window. Her normal demeanor. "I think you mean a 'hook-up'. And no, we don't all do that." Well, the Keilah who was raised right doesn't do that. But the Keilah since Rosabel's death is another person entirely. She finds any stray who wanders in at the end of her shift and doesn't care too much what happens after. At least that's how it worked in Pepperville.

"Who knows what kind of creep you're bringing into your home. I'd hate to think someone could hurt you." I look at her one more time, just to be certain she isn't making a joke. Then I realize I have yet to hear Dee make a joke about anything. "Really, Dee? You can't be serious."

"You're bein' way too long-faced now, Keilah. It's the only reason new men come to Sandy Salts. From miles away. They want a little excitement and then they're off to the next whoop-de-do. I can have a little fun myself, and then go about my business."

I try to imagine Dee out on the prowl for men. Who am I to judge, after all? But I have to get up by five-thirty for work.

"You might learn a thing or two about pickin' up a man."

I suppress a giggle. I probably owe her this. To watch her in action, if that's what she wants. "Ok. I'll go with you. Just don't try and set me up with anyone." I don't do relationships. Or whatever type of man Dee would find.

I finish cleaning up the dishes while Dee goes upstairs to change and "put on her face". I shudder to think what that might look like. I hear the familiar *shhhh* of the hairspray, diffusing without pause for a good five minutes.

It occurs to me that I haven't looked in the mirror all day. I wipe my hands on my jeans and walk over to Dee's orange stucco-framed mirror. I'm shocked by the image that greets me. Big circles under my eyes and my hair looks like I forgot to comb it after getting out of bed this morning. Reluctantly, I go to my room and half-heartedly apply the last remnants of my makeup and tame my hair. I just don't care how I look.

"Ya ready up there?"

As I come down the steps, I realize I'm actually looking forward to this. Dee is standing in the kitchen, dressed in a shiny fuchsia top and a long, flowing, magenta skirt. Her hair is piled high on her head – high enough to make her appear at least five inches taller. She's wearing a thick coating of frosted pink lipstick on her lips and a full set of fake eyelashes. The change in her is so dramatic, I don't know whether to laugh or run back to my bedroom and hide until this night is over.

"Oh, Dee! You look..."

"Trampy? You was goin' to say trampy? Well, I don't care. I..."

"No! I just meant you look so different than what I'm used to, that's all. You look very... nice."

She adjusts her blouse. "Well, thank you. Now let's hurry along before all the good-looking ones are taken."

"Shouldn't I take my own car? In case, you know, there's a hook-up? That would be real awkward to have me in the back seat."

"Oh, for heaven's sake. We don't jump each other in the car like teenagers. We're more civilized than that."

We get into Dee's second car – a Crown Victoria – and let it warm up to a mild chug-chug before we head out. "This used to be the police car in town, you know. Didn't get much use so Mr. Fisher bought it for me. The last thing he gave me before runnin' off."

"I'm glad it still works."

"Well, that's the only thing Mr. Fisher had that ran properly, if you get my drift."

I do.

We sit in awkward silence while I try to come up with a different direction for the conversation. "How far is this place?"

"It's about ten miles out in the country. It's an old barn. The Canby family fixed it up all nice for graduations and dances and the like. Now they can charge admission to get into their barn. Can you imagine? Fancy people and their fancy things."

I can imagine. Many people approached Kyan about using our beautiful property for things like weddings and other special events. No way was he going to cheapen our family estate by letting it be a circus attraction, he said. It always killed me that he never got the irony of that state-ment—the property we gained from a circus attraction.

We drive for what seems like forever until we turn off on

a dirt road and into a pasture where cattle most likely grazed the day before. A man with an orange vest and a flashlight guides us into a bumpy, dusty parking lot, where we find ourselves several rows from the barn and an actual pathway.

Dee parks and then reaches abruptly between my legs. "Push 'em to the side while I get my flashlight out."

Before I can protest, she produces a small flashlight and a flask from under my seat, both of which she drops in her shopping-cart-sized purse. "We'll need both of these later," she says solemnly.

I offer her my arm as we navigate the uneven dirt. It seems so strange that people would dress up to walk through farm ground and into a barn. But there are several people around us doing just that. As we reach the doorway where they're taking money, a man about Dee's age with a dark, brown toupee and wisps of gray hair peeking over his ears steps up and takes her arm.

"Haven't seen you here in months, Dee," he says in a deep voice. "You'll be saving a few for me?"

"Oh, I don't know, Floyd. Depends on what my options are." She winks.

I'm shocked, even though I shouldn't be at this stage of our relationship.

"That's Floyd Howard. Took him home once a while back," she says matter-of-factly. Then she leans in close to whisper, "He farted all night, though – the bedroom smelled like a day-old taco for almost a week. I can do better."

Dee pushes me forward and points a bony finger inches from my face.

"See clear to the back? Where the musicians are? There's

a bar there for young folks like you to sit and watch. Make yourself comfy and I'll check on you when things get slow."

"But, I..." There is no point. She is already gone. I make my way through the big skirts and bigger hair to the stools underneath the tacky, fake-grass roof set up to look like a tiki hut.

I plop down on a stool and stare at all the people, mostly over sixty, doing some kind of weird hop and twirl, moving in the arms of their partners across the barn floor. Some couples just bounce in place for a few minutes before waltzing to another spot and starting over. Some of the men do little more than a sway, feet planted firmly in one spot as their partners dance in a circle around them.

The band, consisting of an accordion player, a tuba player, and a drummer, pulsates in sync as they play bouncy polka numbers. They seem just as happy and enthusiastic as the people on the dance floor.

I'm horrified. My parents would never, ever allow themselves to be caught in such silly, vulnerable poses. "Look at them, flailing in public..." Mother would say.

"You look like you'd rather be eating dirt."

I turn around to find Phillip, Nova's (ex?) boyfriend standing behind the bar. "Phillip? What are you doing here? Is Nova here too?" He is irritating me and he has barely even spoken.

"I tend bar here two nights a week. The tips are good after everybody gets liquored up. Keisha, isn't it?"

He has probably heard Nova refer to me as "the help" so often he can be forgiven for getting it wrong. "Keilah!" I say, too loud as the music suddenly stops. "It's Keilah," I say again, awkwardly.

"Are you here by yourself?" he asks while shaking a drink. "Doesn't seem like your crowd."

I notice a dimple in his cheek, and this intoxicating smell coming from his hair. Probably something expensive Nova bought him for being one of her harem.

"I'm here with my roommate." I see Dee on the dance floor, pinching some elderly man on the rear. I turn away quickly. "She seems to be quite the player."

"Let me make you something," Phillip offers. "To help you cope."

I shake my head. "No thanks. I didn't bring any cash with me. I'm really just here for the entertainment."

In the days and months after Rosabel's death, I drank the same kind of rot-gut whiskey her parents did. In a sick way, it made me feel closer to her. Kenner had convinced me to quit, eventually, promising me store-bought tubs of cookie dough to ease the pain instead.

"It's on the house. I insist. You'll be helping me get more practice with the fancy drinks."

I shrug. "Well, ok. But just one. I can't see how she can last too long out there."

Whatever this drink is, full of infused fruit and four different types of alcohol, it's all-too pleasing to my palate. Phillip leans across the counter, just as he did with Nova. He smells even better close up. He asks about my family. I agree to another. And then just one more.

I remember at some point Dee telling me she's going home with Ron or Don, that a woman of her stress level needs a good release and I shouldn't judge her.

"You'll see her home then?" she asks Phillip. I feel like I'm watching a play. She makes sure I have my flashlight and remember my address.

"That's ok with you, Keilah?"

I nod, my cheeks hot and my mind swirling with images of Dee as a dominatrix. Phillip assures me that everything will be fine. I've consumed three magical drinks. Of course, it will be fine.

I lost my virginity the night of the prom. I never told Rosabel directly because she wouldn't have understood how I could lose control of myself like that. I didn't have my needs and desires in check the way she did.

After she died, I lost control a whole lot. It was usually meaningless and quick. I didn't care. I needed the sensation of someone else's skin against mine. I just didn't have the headspace to invest in a real relationship, with feelings and rules. For most of the men I encountered, that worked perfectly. For the ones who wanted more, I closed the door as quickly as it had opened. I wasn't interested.

Phillip pulls up in front of Dee's place and opens the passenger door. I try to object; I'm completely capable of getting out by myself. I can hold my liquor at this point in my life. When I stand up, I realize differently.

"Let me help you, new girl." Phillip grabs my elbow and tries to steer me inside.

"KEEEEE-LAAAH!" I say as soberly as I can.

"I'm sorry. It's been a long night. Actually, a long day. I found out Nova's been sleeping with my best friend."

I snort. "Who is your friend? Kevin? Sebastien? There is a long list."

Phillip has a sick look on his face.

"You... didn't know? About ANY of them? Oh, this is too sweet." I want to laugh in his face but things are spinning a bit.

Things become quiet. He looks sad and vulnerable. I take his face in my hands and kiss him hard.

He pulls back, surprised. For some reason, this makes me desire him all the more. I grab his tight buttocks and pull him close to me. He doesn't resist.

By the time we're inside, on Dee's grape-and-tan couch, our shirts are laying by the front door. The rest of our clothing is soon to follow. It's just like my many other encounters, quick and furious. Somehow, we make it to my bedroom. I don't remember much more from the night. That is the way those things have always worked for me. As long as I don't feel, I can go on and on.

The next morning, I wake up with the sun streaking in between the flaps of my blinds. Gentry is kneading the bottom of the bed, where my feet are uncovered. Phillip's muscular arm is draped over the top of me.

I look over at his face, this perfect combination of manliness and beauty. His full lips are positioned in a slight smile. His silky blond hair laps around his face. He is stunning. Someone who would have been perfect for Rosabel. I can picture them together, laughing and holding hands. Making beautiful babies.

Some strange feeling is creeping up inside me. It might be those fruity drinks. I'm not used to fancy things accompanying my alcohol. I try to push it away.

The enormity of what I've done becomes apparent. I slept with the boyfriend of the vilest person in Sandy Salts. That's not the Keilah Who Was Good. That's not even the current version of myself. I jump up, pulling some of the covers with me and knocking poor Gentry to the floor.

Phillip rolls over and opens his eyes. "Keilah? Something wrong?" he asks sleepily.

It's such a relief that he remembers my name. "I... um... You should go before Dee gets back. And about Nova..."

He rubs his eyes and sits up. "We pretty much decided Nova's got other things going on. I'm not giving her any more of my time."

I want to hug him. It feels like I'm in high school again, brushing up against the popular boys, but instead of feeling their intense desire for Rosabel, I'm feeling some of my own. For a one-night stand. "I'm sorry. I shouldn't have gotten so drunk and forced you to..."

He shakes his head and smiles, his perfectly straight teeth and one dimple visible. "You didn't force me. That's more fun than I've had in a while."

A tingle zips down my spine.

"You sure you don't have time for more?" He pulls the sheet back to reveal more of himself than I had seen in the darkness. I gulp.

I glance over at the clock to see that I'm already an hour late for work.

"Dammit!" I grab my clothes, losing all vanity as my sheet falls to the floor. "I'm late. If I don't get there before Nova shows up, I'm going to be fired."

Phillip shakes his head. "Don't worry about it. I know her tricks. I'll call Jack while you get ready and just tell him you lost your phone while you were helping me fix a flat. He thinks women who understand cars are mythical creatures. He might just give you a raise. Just leave your phone here today."

"Thank you!" I run into the bathroom and take the

quickest shower of my life. Beyond my strange and unex-
plained feelings for Phillip, I feel sudden gratitude that
Kenner had made the effort, many times, to try and teach
me how to change a tire.

Nova would be furious that not only was I late, but that
she could do nothing about it. Anything that goes over her
head to her father is completely out of her hands. I smile to
myself as the warm water runs down my body. Phillip is
gone when I come back to my room. There is a note beside
the bed. "Again? (smiley face)"

It is a dead run to work. I walk in the back door and, to
my surprise, Nova hadn't made her entrance. Tucker looks
up but says nothing.

Lorraine is milling about in the front of the store, but I
don't need to make any excuses to her either. I put on my
apron and get to work, and by the time Nova arrives thirty
minutes later, I am busily arranging scones as though
nothing completely, utterly, earth-shattering has happened.

Chapter Fifteen

ONCE THE BRACES CAME OFF, a new Keilah Brownwell emerged. My acne had come and gone and, little by little, my chest filled out enough that I was no longer mistaken for a boy when Rosabel fixed my hair. I could have passed for pretty in any other school. But our school had the most beautiful human creature roaming the hallways. There was no way any girl could measure up to her beauty.

That didn't go unnoticed, as every boy (and probably a few teachers) desired her to the point of never leaving her alone. She refused to have anything to do with them, which made their craving for her even stronger.

They were relentless in their pursuit and eventually realized the only possibility of gaining her favor was via a gangly redhead. I was like a new car salesman but my product wasn't actually on the market, and I wasn't about to let them in on the secret. Every day it was some variation of the same thing.

"Can you hook me up with/give me the number of/make me sound cool to Rosabel?" Each thought, legitimately, that they had a shot at being the first to capture her interest.

It became a real game, like Monopoly, and I was the iron

playing piece. Some of these boys were masterful at their trade. They would touch my arm and lean in close as they whispered in my ear. Our bodies sloped against my locker, my foot propped against the wall pushing my hips forward suggestively.

I became just as adept at using them. When I wanted to reel them in, I would open my locker door and rest my shoulder against pictures of a smiling Rosabel, hair tousled from laying on our lawn. I touched an arm lightly, enjoying the sizzle of contact with the opposite sex. I didn't feel guilty at all for using my best friend for my own means. She couldn't care less about any of those people. Besides, it wasn't really using her if she didn't have any idea it was going on.

I knew they wouldn't succumb to my manipulation forever. I had to give them just enough to keep them on the hook until I was done toying with them. Just like an unsuspecting fish in the pond on the south end of our property, I lured them in with something appetizing and then tossed them back into the water when I was done.

There were dates: pizza of my choosing (just to make sure it was the kind Rosabel would enjoy) and movies (just to make sure they weren't inappropriate). Once in a while, a little fooling around too. But in the end, the conversation always turned to Rosabel. What did she like to do for fun? Would she invite them over if they bribed her with stolen cigarettes (no) or alcohol (a definite no) or if they brought their older brother with them? Could I put in a good word?

I hesitated to ask her why she didn't want anything to do with them. I had a good thing going. I knew she didn't hate boys; she loved Kenner and even flirted a little with Kyan. I assumed that, much like everything else in our world, she was beyond their simple minds. She craved higher forms of humanity, like Mother Teresa, or whoever the male version of that would have been. High-schoolers weren't even on her radar.

So, I continued "practicing" with popular boys in preparation for the real thing. It would take them a time or two before they figured out that I wasn't going to be a conduit for their advances. The strange social world of Keilah Middle-Name-to-be-Determined Brownwell.

One day after a non-date of burgers and over-the-shirt fondling that ended just as they all did, I decided it was time to ask my friend why she didn't want to participate in any of it.

"They aren't like you and me, Robin," she said.

"But what does that mean, exactly?"

She shrugged her shoulders and changed the conversation.

Soon after, I unleashed my most devious plan to date: find the luckiest boy in the Pepperville general area. Someone fortunate enough to spend an evening with Rosabel who had a friend willing to take ~~me~~ her to the prom. Mother always made it seem like the most important date in a girl's life, next to her wedding and the first time she canned every single zucchini in her garden.

"Rosabel, I was wondering if you would help me with an experiment."

"Of course, Robin! Is it another cake? I'll watch the ingredients as you measure this time. Anyone can confuse cinnamon and cumin."

"No, I was thinking we should go to prom. As an experiment, of course. Just to see why everyone thinks it's such a big deal."

She squinted her eyes and studied my face. "Is that what you want? To complete a social experiment?"

I nodded. She knew me better than anyone.

"Then we should go. As an experiment. If you decide you like it, next year I'll stay home. We'll have to choose just the right dates, though."

We got our yearbook out and went through the pictures, trying to find a boy or two we could tolerate for an evening. "Carl Ashenbrenner?" I asked. I had always admired how clean his shirts smelled, even on those muggy days when the teacher wouldn't open the window.

"He's dating Shandra Lewis," Rosabel replied. She flipped a few pages further. "What about Davon Morris? He's usually polite."

I remembered how he had tutored me through Algebra II in exchange for a picture of Rosabel's bra. "Nope, he's dating someone from out of town."

Rosabel started making a list of those she felt we would be safe with and then insisted that after we got through all of them, I should call and make "appointments". It all seemed kind of silly. But I never disagreed.

We were just barely into the sophomores, some of Kenner's friends, when Rosabel came up with an idea. "We should call Elena! She has a cousin somewhere close by."

Elena was a quiet girl who sat by herself unless Rosabel was nearby. Rosabel was a magnet for anyone who seemed outside of the social loop of acceptability. Elena told Rosabel stories of her many cousins who lived in neighboring towns.

As soon as Rosabel called, Elena agreed to set up an "interview" with one of her cousins and one of his friends. Even though I was still in high school, I felt like we were on our way to an important business deal.

In the meantime, we discussed what to bring. The theme of our prom that year was "Fairytaled: The End". Someone in the senior class planning committee had come up with the idea to make our prom sound like it belonged next door so that maybe the fairytale-themed coffee shop would want to contribute to our decoration fund. Instead of just making it about one story, the theme was about making an alternate ending to a story we loved. It could be incorporated into whatever clothing we were wearing, or it could be a prop.

Rosabel was a big fan of fairytales. It kept her from having to deal with what was happening in her home every day. I knew that things in her home weren't good. In fact, her parents had taken to drinking and gambling almost every night. I heard Mother say under her breath several times, "Don't know how those two keep a home. They don't do a lick of work."

We had stopped asking if she needed extra food and just packed her a bag every time she came to visit, hoping it would get her through most of the week. It sat on the small, mahogany table by our front door and she would take it on her way out. No words were ever exchanged. More than once, as we left, we had to swerve to avoid her father, drunk as he attempted to maneuver his old pickup into their driveway.

I decided I would be Snow White, the poor maiden who slept until she got the kiss from her prince charming. Rosabel would make me a purse in the shape of an alarm clock, with tiny cymbals hanging as fringe. Snow White wouldn't have to wait for her prince if she had something to wake her up. She would use some fabric the same color as my dress along with black and white for the face of the clock. I thought it was genius.

Rosabel knew immediately that she wanted to take her inspiration from the story of *The Nightingale*. This was the story of a bird cast out in the forest when an emperor found a mechanical bird much more to his liking. When the mechanical bird breaks, the nightingale takes pity on the emperor on his deathbed and comes back to sing for him, saving his life.

This sounded like an awful story to me. In fact, I had nightmares of being cast off into the woods after Rosabel told me the story as a child. But she was insistent. She wanted to represent the bird.

"Why not be Cinderella? Or Sleeping Beauty?" I asked. In my mind, she already was the living version of these fairytale characters.

"Because the nightingale is always true to himself," she said simply.

She changed her mind about wearing a matching dress and took it back in order to buy fabric. She, of course, designed a beautiful dress for herself. Brown and then gray layers of scalloped fabric to represent feathers. She had a black belt around her tiny waist that had tiny wing imprints, something we spent hours searching for in the thrift store.

Elena's cousin Charles and his best friend Gage showed up for their pre-prom interviews. They had just showered and reeked of body spray, the kind I sprayed on Kenner's pillow for a month until he agreed to quit using it.

They looked like twins, as many best friends do. Both had short, dark hair pushed to the side and piercing blue eyes. Gage was the taller of the two, with the lean body of a dancer. Charles was stocky, very physically fit, and had a rounder face. He reminded me a bit of Kyan, if my brother were a friendly guy trying his best to impress the prettiest girl in school and her best friend.

They wore matching t-shirts with the symbol of a frog in sunglasses emblazoned on the front with the words "Dare to Dream" scribbled across the top.

They squirmed nervously on my porch steps like two fifth-graders waiting for their teacher assignments for junior high. Rosabel noticed immediately as she walked up the steps and patted Charles gently on the shoulder. "It's alright. Really. I've never bitten," she said softly.

They both stood up, wiped their hands on their shorts, and offered them to us. I took Gage's hand and felt his strong grip, a grip I wasn't expecting from a boy looking for a last-minute date.

"Gage," he said in a deep voice. "You're Keilah, right?" He smiled at me in a way I hadn't experienced. Like someone who wasn't about to use me as a pawn to get to someone prettier. He didn't look over my shoulder for whatever came next.

I looked away and pulled my hand back, unsure at first of how to handle this new situation. I remembered my promise to Mother and turned towards him.

"Yep, Keilah. Good to meet you." I smiled a new smile back at him, like a person who, for once, wasn't about to manipulate a boy into tutoring a girl in Chemistry.

"I haven't seen you in school before," I said, motioning

for him to sit on our porch furniture. "Are you new?"

"Well, technically I live in Stratusville, down the road. My folks just optioned me into this school so I could play football for a better team," he said.

My heart sank. Another Someone Without a Brain who would inevitably want to get in Rosabel's pants and have nothing to do with me. I could feel my invisible shield rising around me. I wasn't about to let him hurt me over what amounted to little more than a business transaction.

"That's nice," I said sarcastically. "We should talk about the color of your tie and what you want to do for your theme," I continued. I wanted him to know I wasn't taking him seriously. I could tell he was hurt that I wasn't interested in his football experiences. But quite frankly, I didn't care.

"I was thinking..."

"I'm wearing a navy-blue dress and I'm taking this alarm clock purse," I began. "You'll have to find something similar, you know, so we match."

"Maybe I could be Prince Charming who..."

"I don't need a prince," I interrupted again. "The whole point of this is to show I can wake up on my own."

"I was going to say I could be the Prince Charming who didn't wake up in time. You know, with bed head and maybe a stuffed animal I sleep with," he said.

I looked at him for a moment and realized he was sincerely trying to be nice to me. "That's actually funny," I said. "I think it will work. As long as your tie matches my dress."

Meanwhile, Rosabel and Charles were deeply engaged in a conversation about pets caught in traps that were set for wild animals. Rosabel's hands thrashed about as they always did when she was passionate about something. Charles was nodding furiously in agreement.

"Are you two ok about prom? Are we good?" I was feeling irritated. This was my game, not theirs. They both stopped and looked up at me.

"Actually, we haven't even discussed it," Rosabel said, her cheeks flushing. "You're right, Keilah," Rosabel said. "We need to figure out what we're wearing and when we're leaving and all of that."

The rules were simple – no drinking or doing drugs. Most importantly, we had to be home by 11:30 so that Kyan wouldn't be out knocking on car doors looking for us. I wanted to make sure we had very clear boundaries, as Rosabel had seemingly lost her head and one of us needed to make sure the night didn't get out of hand.

When the topic of purchasing the prom tickets came up, things became awkward. They were expensive – $75 per couple. I knew Rosabel didn't have that kind of money and I certainly didn't want this stranger buying mine. I decided I would ask Mother to purchase those tickets, if she really wanted to make sure I went to prom. How could I know her purchase would mean the end of Rosabel's innocence?

Chapter Sixteen

SANDY SALTS
2012

I'M LOOKING FORWARD to enjoying my bran and chocolate chip muffin with some Sumatra roast coffee. The paper is lying neatly folded on the table, as usual, and I can't wait to see who has died. I'm starting to wonder if Dee ever reads the paper, or if it's more a decoration to accompany her morning baked goods. She goes to work a full hour before me. I never see her read it when she gets home from work in the evenings either. There is a new book club book, *Handy Man Dan*, on the table.

Reading the obituaries every morning is strangely soothing to me. Because it is someone else's loss and misery, I can focus on the life being memorialized. And they are fascinating. Picturing their loving family members gives me a feeling of belonging, even if it's just in my head.

Salty Sun, Established 1902
Vanessa Withers, Reporter
Melba Modelty, age 97

Melba was born in her parents' bed with the help of her grandma and two neighbor ladies. She was proud of that four-poster bed and told folks she planned to die in the same place she was born. Fortunately, she did.

Melba never married but lived a long life of devotion to her neighbor friends, heading the Neighbors Not Nasties group formed to cut down robberies and the annual neighborhood potluck and poker night. She ran the church ladies' bible study, VFW friends, Library Helping Hands, and Plants for Paupers, (giving produce to those in need) 'til she couldn't do them anymore. She was a friend and neighbor to all.

Melba was preceded in death by her parents, Allen and Meredyth, brother Campbell, and second-cousin-once-removed, Gentry. You may recall Gentry was the boy who disappeared on the camping trip to Friendly State Park and was presumed dead after a number of years. She is survived by Gentry's sister, Deeloriandra Fisher.

I put the paper down and try to process what I've read. Dee's brother actually *did* disappear? All this time I've been thinking he died in a car accident, or as the result of some bizarre family ritual. Somehow, I'll get her to tell me this story now instead of "someday".

Gentry comes sauntering in the room and jumps up on my lap, rubbing his head on my chin. "Not now, boy," I say absently.

I look down at his whiskered face in shock. *Dee named her cat after her missing brother?* It couldn't be. *Gentry... presumed dead.*

Standing up, I force Gentry off my lap and on the ground, causing him to scowl at me briefly before sauntering off. I fold up the paper, the way it always looks when I come down for breakfast. This will take some thought. I still have a full day of Nova to get through.

The walk to the Beanery goes quicker than usual, as I mull over Dee's loss. She is always ready to retreat to her room. Maybe she's stuck, as I am, in a place of grief.

I slip my key into the door, panicking when I find it unlocked. Did I leave it unlocked when I left? Sandy Salts is a very small town, but there are so many people who come through on the highway you just never knew when an unsavory type might find their way in to look for cash. I can't afford to make those kinds of mistakes.

I open the door slowly. If only Rosabel would have spent as much time teaching me self-defense as she wasted on three-layer cakes. "Tucker? Jack?"

"Do you always get here so late? I can't believe my father puts up with that." Nova's newly-manicured hands snap to her hips, as if she has been there waiting for hours.

I look up at the clock. Two minutes past six. I decide it's too early to point out that she never arrives before eight, and more often than not she comes in thirty minutes after that.

"What are you doing here already?" I ask, hanging my purse on the hook and slipping the butcher apron over my head. I blush as my mind drifts to Phillip, my new connection to Nova. I've slept with her man of convenience, or past boyfriend, or whatever he is to her. To me, he's magnificent.

"You don't remember?" Nova smiles, making her hastily applied makeup appear cracked on her face. "Wow, I reminded you like five times yesterday."

Yesterday she had been especially hard on Lorraine, questioning whether she was the right size to be out in the front area of the store.

"Oh, you're having your picture taken for that article, right?"

The local reporter for the *Salty Sun* is doing stories on entrepreneurs around town. In Sandy Salts and the surrounding communities, that translates to kids who inherited their folks' businesses and think that makes them successful. Nova shows up at her daddy's coffee shop most days when she's scheduled. She's sort of qualified.

"I'm not just having my picture taken, Keilah. It's an entire article. I'm hoping you'll really try to look busy while she's here." Nova puts a dark-red nail in the air, dangerously close to my face. "You're not wearing that manly thing today, are you?"

I have also forgotten, or tried to block out, her tirade about the plain white aprons her father purchased for everyone. She took her father's credit card to the beauty shop last week, where they also sold knick-knacks and kitchen items. She purchased four black ruffled aprons printed with red spoons and mixing bowls. Only Lorraine dutifully placed one over her head every morning. Strangely, Nova continues wearing her tight pink apron.

Jack isn't here to back me up and Tucker is just trying to get through the morning without having a heart attack. "Ok. I'll wear your stupid apron." As I turned around to go back to the locker, I can hear the clacking of Nova's nails on the counter.

"Aren't those muffins done yet? Get with the program, idiot. I hate it when we have to serve them burnt."

Tucker shakes his head. "We just put 'em in. It takes twenty minutes. On the timer. I can show you."

Nova crosses her arms. "I know what a freakin' timer looks like, fool. Just keep your eye on those, ok? Don't mess this up for me today, or I'll make sure it comes out of your paycheck!"

I pat Tucker's shoulder and start my usual morning routine: taking his mixing bowls and washing them by hand before they go into the sanitizer. Tucker and I have become very good at our well-choreographed dance. One of us bakes and the other washes, or vice versa. Today, however, Nova's presence is like a wooden barrier on the dance floor.

"Do you really need that much butter? That'll make them so greasy."

"Can you move a little quicker? My interview will be here at eight-fifteen and I want everything to look perfect."

"Don't you two have a way to make this a little cleaner while you cook?"

Tucker's face is red and blotchy. Nova normally ignores him, and all this unwanted attention is throwing him off his game. He wipes his face on his sleeve and mouths his routine to stay on track. *Two cups of sugar, stir well...*

It doesn't matter, however, because Nova's voice is drowning him out. Soon he puts the scone mix in the muffin tins and drops a plate of croissants on the floor. Finally, he walks stiffly out the back door, his mouth set in a grim line of anger.

"Where are you going? You don't get a break until nine-thirty!"

I turn and point to the front of the store. "Out!" I match Nova's pitch, surprising both of us. "Get out of our kitchen now!"

Nova jumps back, startled. Maybe she's never been confronted before. At least not if they expected to drink a coffee from Jack's Beanery ever again, without the additional ingredients of Nova's spit or a few pieces of her hair.

"You are so... FIRED!"

I take a deep breath, pushing away the queasy feeling inside. "First of all, you aren't my boss, so there's no way you could fire me." I let a smile creep over my face. "And more importantly, to you, if I leave now, it will be up to Lorraine to run the place while you're doing your interview. If that's what you want..." I cross my arms and lean against the counter, proud that I've handled things with Rosabel-level confidence.

Nova whirls around and storms out of the kitchen, stomping so hard the coffee cups I set on the service counter rattle. One of them falls to the floor, shattering.

"Clean that crap up before my interview gets here!"

I hear her continue to stomp, all the way to the front door where the screen door creaks, and then slams shut. I smile to myself as I head to the back door to find Tucker. The rest of our morning setup goes smoothly. Tucker calms down and falls back into his routine with a little coaxing. Nova doesn't come back until eight, just before the reporter for the *Salty Sun* walks in. I imagine her angry texting several of her boyfriends in the parking lot, long nails clacking furiously as she scowls at the door every now and then.

A familiar face walks up to the counter. "Hello, there. I'm Vanessa Withers. I'm looking for Nova?"

"I'm Keilah. We met a couple of times... Your obituaries are just...magic. I mean... that sounds weird. But I do love them!"

She shakes her head and laughs, a glorious sound that reminds me of the school lunch bell. "No one has ever been enthusiastic about those before. I remember you from the library. Had to check your references before I sent you that library card. We don't hand them out to just anybody." She winks.

"And Dee's house. The book... for your... book club."

"The Salty Sinners. I know what you're thinking." Vanessa blushes. "I really wanted to have a book club with real discussion. Everybody agreed to come and bring baked goods, but no one would finish the books. I just needed some mental stimulation, you know? So, it hit me that I needed to find a genre that caught everyone's interest." She winks again. "Now they read every single page." She leans over the counter and whispers, "I didn't even know some of those things really went on in the bedroom."

I nod in fraudulent agreement.

"And your Dee, she always brings the best desserts. She should have opened her own bakery long ago."

The swinging doors to the kitchen swoosh and Nova, as if walking a runway, enters right on cue. I notice she has a small, perfectly round smudge of flour on her face, even with her temple. She is wearing her new apron, wrapped tightly at her waist.

"I'm so sorry my help is bothering you." She extends a hand to Vanessa as she brushes by me so close she steps on my foot.

"Oh, not at all." A look of confusion overtakes her face as she surveys the production that is Nova. She turns and pulls a bright-red business card out of her large purse and hands it to me. "Call me sometime and we'll go for drinks, or whatever."

I look at the print-filled card and smile.

Vanessa Withers

Librarian/Postal Employee/Reporter/Avon Represen-tative/Non-sleeper

Nova purses her lips, obviously upset that I have made favorable contact during her moment in the spotlight. Nova guides Vanessa to a nearby table, where in a matter of minutes, her hands begin flying around her head while she describes her busy and stressful life. One of the regulars comes in and sits down at the piano, playing a lively rendition of "What About Me".

"Keilah! You're needed!" She screeches loud enough that someone on the front porch puts their face up to the screen.

I avoid her gaze and smile directly at Vanessa. "More coffee?"

"That piano. Ugh. Shut the lid on their hands if you have to, dear. They're ruining my interview." Nova turns back to Vanessa, smiling.

Vanessa smirks, ever-so-subtly.

As soon as Vanessa is gone, Nova decides her day has begun too early and she suddenly has a headache.

"Keilah!" she yells as I'm trying to scrape gum from under the kids' play table.

"What?" I snap.

"You... you'll be here tomorrow at the usual time?" she asks, looking away.

"Why wouldn't..." I begin, momentarily forgetting about our earlier confrontation. "I'll be here. Like always, Nova."

We stand for a moment, each stuck in our own struggle. A horn honks incessantly. "I think your ride is here."

"See you tomorrow."

I look at the floor, waiting for the horn to stop. I don't have to look up to know why the room feels lighter. I'm trying to finish cleaning up the tables, covered in sticky goo from the young mother's group that always comes in for hot chocolate with their multiplying broods each week, finally able to breathe when Lorraine appears at my side. She is nothing if not a persistent stander.

"Yes?" I ask, rather irritated that conversation with her is so hard. At least with Nova, I always know where I stand.

"Locker." She turns and goes back to her corner, where she often goes to escape Nova and stare at her phone screen.

I shake my head, thinking she is just talking nonsense until I remember that after our conversation about changing aprons, I never locked up my locker again. My purse and all my personal things have been sitting unprotected, exposed to Nova's imagination all day long. I drop the rag and run to the back, where my locker door is wide open. All of my things – my wallet, makeup, phone – all laying on the floor, some of it covered with a melted glop of Nova's dark red lipstick. Inside the locker is a note scribbled in her lipstick: Never challenge me in public again. Bitch."

All of the times I saw people bullied in high school, I felt sad. But I knew I was safe because no one dared bother me as long as Rosabel was there, acting as my protector. She was too good and kind for even the harshest of personalities to tangle with. All the girls who were jealous, all the boys who clamored to be by her side, none dared to play their games with me.

I feel sick inside. I'm re-living high school without my other half. I spend the next hour cleaning everything and putting it back as it had been. I could call Kenner, but he would be out with his girlfriend. Kyan would say I had it coming, for whatever reason.

Lorraine giggles in the front of the store and I panic for a moment, thinking she has lost her mind. Lorraine doesn't have a sense of humor. I peek my head through the swinging doors to see Phillip smiling broadly at Lorraine, just as he had with me the week before.

He looks up and waves when he sees me. "Keilah! How's it going?"

I storm through the doors. "Looking for Nova? She left already. With... who was it again, Lorraine? I can't keep track." I hope he feels the sting of my sarcasm.

Lorraine shrugs and walks off.

"I was just dropping off a bunch of things she left in my truck – lipstick, nail polish, and her old phone," he says. "Thought I'd say hi to you while I was here."

"How does she have any lipstick left?" I snap, not sure why Phillip is making me so angry. He has no way of understanding the great irony involved in his handing me a sack of items similar to those just used to destroy any small bit of self-confidence I had built.

Phillip frowns. "So how are things at home? Did Dee make it back in one piece?" He leans over the counter far enough that I smell whatever intoxicating scent he is wearing, mixed with sweat.

"I... well... Dee is fine. We're fine. Everybody is frickin' fine. I've got work to do." I grab the sack from his hand, unsure if I have the character to keep from dumping it in the toilet. If he has the audacity to come in here after we'd been together while I was in a drunken state, he is here to see Nova, not me. No one in their right mind would poke that sleeping bear.

"I... kinda... Well, I really came to see you," Phillip says. "I really enjoyed getting to know you the other night."

"I did too," I say before I have a chance to censor myself. I turn my back to him and start wiping things with a rag. "But we can't..." I want to spin around and pull him across the counter.

"I... we... can't have this conversation. Not here, in Nova's place. You know how she is."

Phillip shrugs. "Can I call you?"

"Maybe..." There is an uncomfortable silence as the rag *swish swishes* across the counter. I write my number down and slide it quickly towards him, even though I know there is no chance that Nova will return.

"Well, you know where to find me." He sounds hurt.

I gulp. What I want and what is real are in two entirely different universes. I wait until I hear his footsteps and the door bang shut before I turn around.

I suppress the need to cry. Actually, there is more of a need to scream. For some reason, this wonderful person has been dangled in front of my face, just slightly out of reach. I can't have him because I don't deserve anything that truly makes me happy. That has been evident since Rosabel died.

When I get home, Dee is already in the kitchen, whipping up something delicious-smelling that includes bread baking in the oven. I remember we have important things to discuss at dinner and my heart sinks. I don't need more stress today.

"How was your day, Keilah? Did that runabout give you grief again? I think I should talk to Jack about that."

I want her to hug me. To understand what's going on inside without my having to explain. "It was the same as always." I head up to my room to unpack, not only my newly-reorganized purse but also Nova's things I've inexplicably carried home with me.

There is a series of pictures from a photo booth that says: *County Fair 2011* at the top. Phillip's arm is draped around Nova's neck, and he's in various stages of trying to kiss her in each one. She is looking at the camera or looking away.

Dinner is a quiet affair, with lentil sloppy joes, home-made buns, and a small salad. I push the nuts in my salad around my plate until Dee finally notices.

"What's up, honey? I may be slow but I'm not dense," she says.

I let out a loud sigh. "Oh, just Nova..." I start. "She's awful. She and her boyfriend are playing some kind of game with me and..." I stop mid-sentence as I remember how the day had begun.

"Actually, there is something I need to ask you about. I read in the paper this morning about your Cousin Melba's death. I'm so sorry to hear about that."

Dee shakes her head. "That old coot's finally gone? She was missin' a few screws. Hadn't talked to her in ten years, at least. She always thought I did something to drive away Mr. Fisher. She thought he was the prized fish in the pond and wicked ol' Deeloriandra set him out like yesterday's trash."

"Oh, I'm sorry. The paper made it sound like she was

this wonderful, giving person."

"Course it did. Everybody thought she could do no wrong. Friendly as could be to the neighbors. But her own kin? Treated us like filth. Mr. Fisher went begging her for money to leave town, even had his girlfriend in the passenger seat. Melba wrote him out a big check and gave him a hug and said she would give me the what-for next time she saw me. Haven't talked to her much since then, the old bat."

I'm disappointed that Vanessa's obituary about this supposedly wonderful woman isn't accurate at all. "It also mentioned in the paper that... your brother Gentry had disappeared." I look down at the ground, bracing myself for whatever type of dish-throwing may come next.

Dee drops her fork and stands up. She puts her hands on her hips and paces around the kitchen. I don't know if she's going to be angry with me or just so emotional she can't speak.

"Oh, you heard about that, did you? I told ya he was gone. I was goin' to tell you the whole story." She picks at her teeth voraciously with her index finger. "I would've told you. Someday... He was my brother, you know. Kidnapped. When we was campin'."

Chapter Seventeen

JOURNAL – PEPPERVILLE
SONNET

S ONNET CRANDALL WAS THE DAUGHTER of the Pepperville
Daily Bank president and, as such, should have dressed
like she was one of the important people in our little town.
Instead, she wore long, flowing tops and jeans with patches
of different colors. Often, her shoes were mismatched and
her hair was styled completely different on each side.

Her style was to have no style. When she wore makeup,
sometimes this walking Van Gogh painting did each side of
her face differently. She could have been a famous model
walking the catwalk of a fashion show for an avant-garde
designer. High cheekbones, full, red lips, and skin that was
almost translucent, like she had never enjoyed a summer day
under the warm sun. If she were anyone else, we all might
have appreciated her free spirit. But the free-flowing outer
shell of Sonnet didn't match the inner, frighteningly evil and
manipulative being.

Our little Sparrow had gotten tall – a good six inches
over the low-to-the-ground-but-equally-muscular Kyan.
Summers of picking up heavy farm equipment and loading
the massive bales of hay on the trailers behind the tractor
left him with a real-life set of poster boy biceps. He wore
tight jeans like all the high school boys did and sprayed

himself with a nasal-assaulting body spray, something he picked up from the boys who visited my locker. Somehow, it was so appealing when it came attached to a popular boy. On my Kenner, it was nauseating.

Since anyone within Rosabel's circle became part of a walking spectacle, it didn't take long for someone of the opposite sex to notice our only male member. Cue Sonnet, technically too young for him as an eighth grader.

Somehow, she and another girl had wormed their way into ninth-grade shop class and positioned themselves next to the sweetest, most easily manipulated boy in the room. Actually, it's not a mystery how it happened at all. Sonnet always got what she wanted.

At first, Kenner ignored her; this strange and unpredictable lower classman. She repulsed and frightened him. He would come home and tell us at dinner about this girl who sat beside him in shop, always flirting and putting her hand on his thigh. Mother was horrified. "What kind of a girl from a good family does that?"

"The kind who are always trouble," Father commented from behind his paper.

Kyan never said a word.

All of those years trailing behind Rosabel and me, he didn't seem to mind when we made all the decisions. He never argued with Mother or Kyan when they snapped at him to do a chore or finish something they had started. Kenner just nodded his head and got to work, like the good little soldier he was. We had all trained him to be the follower and thought he would go about the rest of his life happily trailing behind the right person.

Sonnet was relentless in her pursuit. She showed up every morning at his locker and somehow managed to be there at the end of the day as well. Mysteriously, she reached his locker before the release bells in the middle school had rung.

She would bat her eyes and say ridiculous things like "you hunky love" and "my beautiful beast" as she stroked the front of his shirt. Our Sparrow had never been noticed before. When other guys noticed he was getting attention from a girl, his status rose. He was a delicate butter sculpture in her burning hot fingers and, as such, he melted quickly in the presence of her charms.

"We shouldn't judge, Robin," Rosabel would start during lunch time. "You don't know her true heart."

"Well, I've heard about some kid named Jackson that she left so scarred he doesn't even speak anymore," I protested.

"She says weird things to her teachers," I continued. "She calls them 'dear' and 'sweetheart' and they don't seem to flinch." I shook my head. "Can you imagine if we did that? If I was to say that to Mr. Halbert, I'd be doing make-up science until I turned nineteen." I fantasized for just a moment that Mr. Halbert wouldn't be completely repulsed by my advances.

"I choose to believe she's good. You should too. She makes your brother happy," Rosabel said softly. I could never win an argument when it came to someone's character, since Rosabel always believed the best.

I decided I would start researching Sonnet and find the most horrifying stories. I would bring them to Rosabel; it didn't seem to matter to Kenner. Somehow, I would convince her that Sonnet was capable of anything. If she knew, she would fix things for him like she always did for me.

"She has someone clean out her locker once a week, you know," I said triumphantly. This information had come through a long chain of informants, each swearing they had more to tell.

"Well, that in itself isn't a bad thing..." Rosabel protested, delicately biting into the egg salad sandwich made from the eggs I had given her last week.

"It sure is if they only clean it so that Sonnet won't go to the principal about a party they had while their parents were out of town at a funeral."

Rosabel took in a sharp breath, causing her to choke on her sandwich. I patted between her shoulder blades and took note they were becoming increasingly bony.

The food situation in her home was getting much worse. I didn't want Mother to know as she always found some way to make it seem more shameful for Rosabel than for her parents. So, instead, I found ways to sneak more things into my lunch bag. Mother must've had an idea, as one day she suggested I put extra apples in my bag in case there was a "someone" who needed it.

"That's blackmail, Robin!" she sputtered.

"Oh, that's not all." I leaned forward, delighting in her horror. "She has a whole network of people doing things for her. Have you ever noticed..." I looked around just to be sure we were still alone. "Have you ever noticed how the lunch people always bring her a salad from the refrigerator?" I knew she hadn't. I was the only one waiting for bad things to happen. "Apparently one of the lunch ladies sells food from the freezer before school for cash. Sonnet caught her. Now, its gourmet food every day so she'll keep her mouth shut."

Rosabel frowned and leaned back. Not the reaction I was expecting. "How can that be true? I think this is pure gossip. She would've been arrested."

I smiled. "That would normally be the case," I said confidently. "If there were any adults who knew about it." It hadn't taken me long to get this out of Jimmy Larsen, who wanted Rosabel to meet him at the movie theater on Friday.

"There are people here at school who spread the word. Jim... they help her find people who are interested in buying it. Thousands of dollars-worth of whatever that stuff is, stolen from the cafeteria deep freeze and she's been getting away with it. That is, until Sonnet somehow found out. Now, this lunch lady brings gourmet food every day for Sonnet. And who knows what else."

We sat in silence for a moment, each pondering the larger implication of this news. I hadn't realized before saying it out loud that Sonnet wasn't just mean, she was powerful. She had somehow discovered a way to control everyone – not only students but also adults in the school – from the whimpering freshman boy to her teachers and the lunch lady. What was she planning for our Kenner?

"We have to figure out how to end this," Rosabel said softly, putting another warm hand on mine. "I know our little Sparrow is smitten, but he is a gentle soul, and gentle souls, unlike all the rest, can be shattered permanently."

Finally, she got it. Sonnet could destroy his confidence and then he would never be able to date again, or maybe even function. "What should we do?" I asked. "Is there some way to make him decide he wants to end this, without it seeming like it's our idea?"

Rosabel pursed her lips into a model-perfect pout, the

way she always did when she had a serious thought. "We need to research this further and pick a few things she's done... just a few..." She tapped her leg. "And then sit down and talk to him about it, you know, to show him we care. Then we will pull back and let him think about it for a while. I'm sure he'll decide to do the right thing."

She wanted the best for him just as much as I did. As much as I wanted to believe she knew my brother inside out, this didn't sound nearly dramatic enough. I wasn't at all sure he would do the right thing. He had never made such a monumental decision without someone in his life telling him firmly what was to be done. He still asked Mother every morning if the outfit he chose for the day was appropriate.

"What if he doesn't believe us?" I asked. "Shouldn't we have a backup plan, like maybe burning her at the stake or something? What if he thinks we're somehow turning against him? What do we do if he decides WE are the enemy?"

Rosabel shook her head. "He won't. She doesn't have anything to use against him yet. We'll explain how lucky he is that he can leave before she can hurt him. He'll be grateful to know, I'm sure of it. We'll never have to worry about that girl again." She looked at me and smiled. The one she used to make everything better. "It will all turn out okay. I promise," she said. "Our Sparrow has a good head on his shoulders."

She was the glue that held us together. Never, up to that point in time, had I ever doubted her ability to fix my life or Kenner's. There is no explanation then, for why, in this one, horrible instance, she was so completely wrong.

Chapter Eighteen

SANDY SALTS
2012

"T HAT'S JUST AWFUL, Dee... but..."
"Yes, I 'spect you should know the whole story.
I should sit." She takes the tea kettle from the stove and
pours cold water into her glass. "Oh, for heaven sake's..."

"Here." I take the glass over to the sink. "Let me make
you some tea while you talk."

"We did lots of camping back then," Dee sighs. "Sometimes we didn't have a home and lived in our old camper.
That way they could call livin' in the woods 'camping' when
it was just actual livin'. Anyway, we were just outside of
town – in the only cluster of trees for 200 miles. It was a
holiday so there was lots of folks out there. My mother sent
me to the community bathroom to wash up. I was always
afraid of that place, so I did it real fast. We were going to
have supper when I got back and then my brother would
play his guitar for us. He was taking lessons.

"As I was leaving the shower room that was the wash-
room, I met this nice lady who told me I was a beauty. She
must've needed someone to talk to because on and on she
went. About the beauty pageants she won and how her own
daughter wouldn't do any even when she begged. I knew I
would be in trouble for taking so long, and my legs were

shaking from being cold and wet. Finally, she took a breath and I said that my folks were sick and I needed to hurry back. That's the only thing I could think of on short notice."

I hand Dee her cup of chamomile tea and sit down with mine.

"I wasn't too smart..." she continues. "Dilly-dallyin' like that. By the time I got back to the trailer, I was in big trouble. They'd sent my brother out to find me and now we would have to wait for him to have supper and it was already cold. Almost an hour we sat around. Finally, my daddy went to see what became of him. He was nowhere to be found." Dee picks furiously at her teeth for a moment and then continues.

"When Daddy did come back, we realized it must be serious. Everybody in that campground searched that night and the next day. There was no trace of him. No one had even seen him leave our camper." She leans back and drapes her arm behind her chair. "So, there I was again, bein' the reason somethin' horrible happened to our family. My mother said it so often, 'It's not *your* fault, Deeloriandra,' that I knew she meant it was. They didn't really live much after that. I graduated from high school and then they died of grief. Their only child was gone, really. 'Cause I didn't count." She sniffs a little, but no real tears appear on her face.

I reach over and rub her arm. "I'm so sorry, Dee. That's just horrible. And there was never any trace of him?"

"Oh, all sorts of kooks came out of the woodwork sayin' they knew just where he was. In a woodpile or behind a vacant house, or run off to join the circus. You know, the oddball type."

"It must just kill you. Can I ask... about your cat? Why he is named Gentry?"

Dee stares at me for a long, uncomfortable minute. "Well, isn't it obvious, girl?" She shakes her head. "So I can still talk to my Gentry every day. That's what keeps me sane. This'd be my third one since he left."

I decide instantly that I have to try and help. To give her something besides a revolving door of cats in her life. Maybe this is why I ended up in Sandy Salts?

Chapter Nineteen

I HAD STARTED having nightmares. The kind that left me soaked in sweat and breathless, unable to feel settled for several hours. I set my alarm to go off twice each night, and somehow knowing that I would be woken at specific times gave me the safety to sleep, even for a few hours.

They were always the same. Rosabel and I were walking home late at night, down the middle of the highway. Her father was coming home from the casino, drunk as usual. He was blinded by the light of an oncoming car and swerved. Usually I woke up before we were hit, but some nights I heard the thump of our bodies hitting his hood before I jerked myself into the present. I wanted to tell Rosabel so she could make sense of things as she always did. But there were much more important issues to deal with than my nightmares.

We made a plan to stage an intervention for Kenner the following Friday. It gave us time to compile a list of Sonnet's accomplishments, evil as they were. Once people started talking, they would point us in the direction of someone else who had been blackmailed by her. She didn't do any homework, buy her own clothes, or pay for a coffee. There was always someone she could manipulate because they had made two mistakes: first in committing whatever act they thought was completely private, and second, their misdeed was somehow recorded by Sonnet.

There were so many: the paperboy who hid his undelivered papers in his locker, the lunch lady and her black market sales, and poor Elena Campbell. Somehow, she was privy to all of that information.

Elena Campbell was a girl who couldn't stop running during PE class. It didn't matter what we were actually supposed to be doing, Elena was running. Volleyball? Elena ran around the perimeter of the court. Tag? Elena tagged as she went. At first, the PE teacher was annoyed because she just wouldn't stop, the way some people can't stop putting popcorn in their mouths, even when their mother bats it away and says, "Enough now, girl!" When the class came to an end, she kept on going, until he caught her and directed her to look him in the eye while he said sternly, "Class is over, Miss Campbell, do you understand?"

Someone – one of Rosabel's many followers – mentioned that there was some sinister reason Elena had to run all the time. It had nothing to do with fitness. This reason had everything to do with Sonnet.

We knew we had to track her down, somewhere outside of PE class. It turned out we had a hard time catching up to her because she ran between classes too. Outside of summer games in our fields, Rosabel didn't believe in running.

"Stand your ground, Robin," she always said. I didn't understand what that meant when we were late for class, but on this particular day, she did find a way to reach Elena's locker before the end of class.

By the time I got there, those two were in deep conversation. I could see Elena's face was twisted and she was uncomfortable with what Rosabel was saying, but as she always did, my friend gently rubbed her arm and calmed her down. Rosabel looked up as I approached and shook her head back and forth violently, warning me away from the sensitive situation.

I stood and pretended to look over my Modern Problems assignment, which by this point in the year was a real problem involving grocery shopping for a family of five with only $40 to spend for the week. Since Mother canned most everything whether it violated the laws of nature or not, this would not have been a hard assignment in my house. I was wishing I had paid attention in third-grade sign language lessons.

"She's going to talk to us." I looked up to see Rosabel, breathless, standing by my side. "It wasn't easy, but she agreed. She is afraid, the poor dear." She looked around, making sure no one was listening.

She leaned in close and whispered, "My house, after school. I promised her no one would know except you and me."

If it were a spy movie, someone sinister would have been lurking around the corner. It struck me as funny that I was actually expecting that they might. Some evil friend of Sonnet's just lying in wait to off us when the last bell of the day rang. I didn't dare share my thoughts with Rosabel. She wouldn't see the humor here, and rightly so.

It was a long day trying to concentrate on school and what this horrible, awful event might be. We didn't even speak on the bus, for fear one of us would say out loud what we were thinking: Sonnet was possibly so powerful there would be no way to stop her.

It seemed like forever until we were able to sit on Rosabel's porch drinking orange juice she had squeezed that morning. I could hear the sound of her mother snoring on the couch, probably not many hours removed from a gambling and drinking event that surpassed her daughter's daily needs in her mind.

With an abrupt thump, Elena jumped up on the porch from the side, something we weren't expecting.

"I ran to your barn first, to burn off some energy," she said quietly.

"Sit down, dear." Rosabel gestured to the wicker rocking chair. "Would you like some juice?"

Elena nodded. "Just a little, please."

As Rosabel poured, I tried to get to the heart of things without being too indelicate.

"You know that Sonnet is dating my brother, right?"

She nodded once more as she sipped her juice.

"And you probably know that she is the worst person in the world," I continued.

"Yup," she said, looking out over the brown grass littered with rusty machine parts.

"We need to save him," Rosabel continued for me. "We know you have been through so much, and you might be able to keep him from something just as awful."

"I know... it's just... hard." She looked toward her running shoes and a tear slipped down her cheek. She sat back up and wiped her face on the back of her hand. "No, you're right." She bounced her knee so violently that we could feel the vibration from the wood slats under our feet. "You have to know."

Rosabel went over and rubbed her soft hand over Elena's shoulders. "Take your time," she said.

Elena took a deep breath. "Well, it all started last summer. We used to see each other a lot at the library. She liked poetry and I liked anything having to do with sports. For some reason, we just hit it off." She pushed a piece of short, dark hair behind her ear.

"We started walking home together and just hanging out – watching movies and eating pizza. She was funny and so smart."

"Did she hurt you?" I asked, imagining this poor, innocent but muscular girl somehow being beaten by the waif that was Sonnet on an uncharacteristically energetic day.

"No, not in that sense. But one day she asked if she could spend the night at my house. I thought that was strange. She has this big beautiful home and I live in a kind of dumpy part of town. But I was okay with it. We were good friends by then."

I remembered the first time I had spent the night with Rosabel and how she had tried so hard to keep her ugly home life a secret. It must've been so difficult for her.

Elena switched her legs, stretching the bouncing one and setting the other one to work on the porch vibration. "I slept so well that night. Better than I have in a long time. I thought it was because we stayed up late watching movies, but now I wonder if she put something in my soda. Who knows. I woke up to her shaking my shoulders. She was completely dressed and had a big smile on her face."

I shuddered. Whatever was coming next was going to be bad.

"She explained to me that she couldn't sleep, so she went

down to my mom's computer to goof around. She said she was really sad that she found some things that concerned her. She acted real worried, like for my safety, so I asked what she was talking about." Elena began to shake all over now.

"She got onto my mom's financial software and found some receipts for hotel rooms."

I breathed a sigh of relief. "That's creepy that she looked at private stuff, but how will that help…"

"The reason she looked at the financial records was because she first looked through my mom's emails. She found some from my mom to… Mr. Randle, the PE teacher." She sat back, waiting for it all to sink in.

"How did she… What the…" I couldn't wrap my head around any of it.

"I'm not sure. She must be really good with passwords or something. I don't know how or why you decide to invade someone's privacy like that. At the time, I think I was just numb. I mean, I knew things weren't great with my parents, but mostly I was in shock."

"You poor dear. What did you do?" Rosabel rubbed her shoulders.

"I had no words… so she found some for me. She said that she knew how hard this would be on my dad, because he was fighting cancer at the time. My mom was a mess too, what with losing her own dad to cancer. Not to excuse it, but… that's why my mom did it. It would kill her if anyone knew. Sonnet promised not to tell a soul, but in return I would have to do some specific things for her."

"Oh, like do her homework? So many guys are doing that too," I said, folding my arms. "How does she even pass her grade-level test each year?"

"She passes the tests because I steal them." Elena looked straight ahead. "And I have to keep my ears open. Anytime I hear anything about anyone, no matter how small, I report to her. If she hasn't heard from me in a couple of days, she calls me up and reminds me what is at stake."

"So that is why you run all the time..." I started.

"I can't stand to look at that man – Mr. Randle. I have to keep going or I'll kill him. I really will." Both knees began to bounce and the porch actually started to shake. "Always keep moving, I say."

"This can't go on forever!" Rosabel protested.

"The running? It has to. I have to. If I sit still for too long and let my mind wander... I just have to keep moving or else I'll go crazy." Her legs bounced quicker, vibrating the porch so hard that our legs started to bounce as well.

"She has notebooks full of things on everyone." She nodded toward the one person I couldn't bear to see destroyed. "Even you, Rosabel!"

I sucked in my breath. "What?" I knew exactly what she could do to harm her. No – to destroy her.

My fists balled up and struck my knees with each upward motion from the boards on the porch. "We'll sneak into her house and get 'em all. We can do it when she is out with Kenner somewhere."

Rosabel had been quiet. "No. It isn't our purpose to go in and destroy her property. We have to save Kenner. That's always been our main goal here."

Sometimes her pureness and logic just infuriated me. It was no wonder that someone like Sonnet could so easily destroy her. There comes a time in life where you just have to jump in and do things, whether they look good on paper or not. This was one of those times.

"It's not just Kenner we're dealing with here. It's you. Didn't you hear her? She has things in a notebook on you!" Then I thought about the absurdity of that statement. What could she possibly have to threaten Rosabel with?

Rosabel shook her head. "I'm not in imminent danger. Your brother is."

"Does she have a notebook on Kenner? Why doesn't she keep all of this on a computer somewhere?" I looked over at Elena, shocked at the thought of this evil witch entering my house and pretending to like Mother's lemonade cookies while searching through our mail before Mother even set them on the table.

"She has a file cabinet in her bedroom. Alphabetized."

"Does she have anything about Robin... Keilah?" Rosabel asked.

"Not that I know of," Elena replied, her legs finally calming down.

I was at once relieved and depressed. I mattered so little that even the meanest girl in school didn't take notice.

"She doesn't keep it on the computer because it would be too easy for her parents to find. Her mom is some sort of computer programmer. Her parents think she is a genius. Files full of knowledge she has collected about things. They all have labels like, "Butterfly through Calendula. She finds it all insanely amusing. Someday, she'll run this entire town from that stupid file cabinet."

"I wonder what would happen if Kenner read the things she wrote about him," I said.

Elena shook her head. "She doesn't have anything on

him yet. That I know of." She bent forward and looked through the torn screen door, towards the large living room clock, a fancy piece with the name Medea Time Company engraved in the middle. It was something Rosabel's father had won on a bet and often bragged about; that he was the only person in the entire county to own such a fine time-piece.

"Crap. I have to get home and do my chores before I call her with my daily report." Elena jumped up and was off the porch, running for town before either of us could tell her goodbye.

We looked at each other for a minute. "This is unreal," I finally uttered.

Rosabel nodded and clasped her hands together. "It's not a story I would have written," she said. "We have to prove this to our little Sparrow before it's too late."

"How?" I asked.

"Like we always do. We'll feed him something he likes and tell him the truth. He'll believe us. We are more powerful because we have the truth on our side."

For the very first time, I didn't believe her.

The Kenner from our times playing in the barn was in the past. Maybe Rosabel thought he was still the same person, or maybe she just couldn't bring herself to believe he would be attracted to someone so bad.

"I'm going to talk to him this weekend," she said, taking a bite of her carrot, the only thing she found in her kitchen for lunch that day. "I'll tell him about my parents and how I know it's sometimes difficult to do the right thing when others around you can't."

"Are you sure? I mean... it's your private stuff." We

never spoke of the really bad things around Kenner. I wasn't sure he knew the extent of her misery and, for all those years, I didn't want him to. "You don't need to do this to save him, Rosabel," I said, not at all sure that she didn't.

"I'm sure. How can we call ourselves family if we aren't willing to give without hesitation?"

We had planned a pizza night, just the three of us. It would be like the old times, only instead of playing our game in a make-believe land, we would be forcing Kenner into a land that was very real and very frightening.

First, he had to ask for Sonnet's okay, to leave her alone on a Friday night. She agreed, reluctantly, as long as he would spend all day Saturday posing for a painting she was doing. I tried not to picture Kenner in some awkward pose, sweat dripping from his face because of the awful contortion of his limbs, while the monster gleefully painted away. Tried.

It would have worked out so well; the three of us laughing and remembering the good times we had together. At the end of the night, when we had laughed so hard chocolate milk came out my nose and probably Kenner's, we would sit him down and show him the paper. He would finally understand that we loved him enough to tell him what had happened, and what his future would be like.

Instead, Melanie went into labor with her baby. She and Kyan had decided they would have their first child, a daughter, by C-section the following Wednesday because Melanie wanted to make sure her daughter wasn't born during a full moon.

Meredyth Virginia Brownwell had different plans and I loved that about her from the start. All six pounds and four ounces of this auburn-haired beauty entered the world on a full-moon Friday, the planned date of Sonnet's reckoning, after a two-hour labor. Melanie barely made it to the hospital in time and was distressed she had not completed her full makeup and hair session before it became obvious she needed to leave or risk having the baby on the floor of her esthetician's shop.

Kenner, Rosabel, and I left our pizza on the floor and rushed to the hospital when Mother called to give us the news. Standing in her crowded hospital room, trying to admire my first little niece from afar, I felt a persistent tap on my back. I turned to see Sonnet, who had somehow discovered the news of Meredyth's birth before we had managed to notify all of our family members.

Kyan stood beside his wife with the edges of his mouth at an upward slant. It was the closest thing to a smile I had ever seen on his face.

Melanie had taken a disturbingly quick liking to Sonnet and, as soon as she saw her head in the doorway, she motioned for her to move forward through the crowd and see the baby. She pushed past me like I was another one of her frightened rabbits in the hallways of the school.

After Sonnet finished cooing over the baby, Melanie called for Kenner. Sonnet immediately wrapped her arm around his backside, squeezing his butt cheeks like she was checking for ripeness.

Now my view was blocked entirely. "Would you two please go over and feed Butter and Babs?" Those were Melanie's obnoxious Pomeranians who, up until that day had been the reason for her very existence. "You'll have to stay for a little bit to make sure they poopie before you go.

They get nervous when I'm not there."

I looked at Rosabel and we both stifled a giggle.

"Of course we will, doll." Sonnet smiled.

We had to postpone our talk with Kenner for another week, during which time we found another disturbing case of blackmail, this time involving Sonnet's father.

On Tuesday, Rosabel came to the bus with a crumpled-up piece of paper in her hands. I asked what it was and she only shook her head, like she didn't want to talk about it just yet. We met at our usual lunch spot and she slipped the paper under my brown paper bag and put her finger to her lips.

I pulled it out but left it sitting on the cement ledge, trying to glance down and read it without being too obvious.

She only told me of this one last week. Her daddy is stealing money from his own father. Having Sonnet sign the checks in her grandpa's handwriting. I'm only telling you this because I want you to understand how horrible she is. Not only doing this for her daddy, but also blackmailing him. She gets whatever she wants with this stolen money because her mother is never to know. Now you understand how none of us will ever be out from under her control. Especially not Kenner.

E

We thought she was this way because she was the apple of her father's eye. A rich daddy's girl who got her way in every aspect of life. Now we understood the depths of her manipulation. It wasn't just kids or teachers in our school, it included her family. Her playing field had no boundaries.

"I'm not sure we want to get in the middle of this," Rosabel said with a hesitation I had not heard in her voice before.

Suddenly I felt panicky. "But how do we get her away from Kenner? We're giving up on our Sparrow?"

"We'll confront him, just like we planned," she said, unpeeling her banana. "But we have to make certain the idea of the breakup comes directly from Kenner. He's the only one left who still has power because she has feelings for him."

I rolled a piece of my peanut butter and jelly into a ball in my hands. "He's not that strong, Rosabel. You know he isn't." I wanted to add that we so easily controlled his every move up until he entered high school. I wanted to remind her that he tried on dresses and ate funny concoctions willingly while under our control. But I didn't.

"I can convince him. You'll see," she said confidently.

We planned out our evening with all of Kenner's favorites: Canadian bacon and pineapple pizza, his favorite movies, *Robinson Crusoe on Mars* and *The Damned*, and then we waited. Sonnet was upset that he was going to waste an entire Saturday night on his sister yet again, but there was nothing she could do. I still had at least that much authority over him, pulling family rank. She always made a point of telling us when she came over for dinner that she thought family was so important and she just looooved how our family ate dinner together and blah blah blah.

It started out just as it always did, with Rosabel tickling him and telling him he looked like a magazine model and to keep his shirt on. We ate our pizza and joked about his favorite cheesy movies. We had our usual "who can make the best alien face" contest. And then it was time.

I pulled out my cell phone and opened the file I had, the one with the cases of blackmail that we knew he would care about. The list had grown to almost thirty. I handed it to Rosabel.

"These things all seem unrelated, Sparrow. But please listen until I finish. There is a common thread." She read them like she was doing a dramatic reading from Shakespeare, without ever mentioning who was behind it all.

Kenner shook his head when she mentioned his favorite teacher, Mr. Randle. He rubbed his hand furiously on his jeans as she told the story of Elena. And then when it came time to talk about Sonnet's father, Rosabel nodded to me.

"Well, Kenner... There is a guy we know who is writing checks on someone else's account..."

Suddenly my baby brother's face turned ashen. "I know who you're talking about. She told me it was all a misunderstanding."

"It isn't. She seeks out these situations. Maybe not her father, but who knows? She gets her hooks into people who least expect it and then she squeezes until they give in..."

"Are you talking about Sonnet? You think she did all of these things? And to her father? He asked her to sign those, but it was just because her grandfather was confused."

Rosabel took his hand in hers. "I know it's hard, Sparrow. You've grown fond of her. But it's not too late to unhook yourself. Before she finds a way to throw you into her bag of tricks."

Kenner jumped up. "I gotta go to the bathroom," he said. He ran quickly and slammed the door when he got there. We looked at each other, more than a little shocked that he would react in such a manner. At least he didn't discount the things we were saying. At least he understood how horrible she was and he could break up with her. We could get about the business of being the fun threesome we always were.

I banged on the door until he opened it. "It's ok, bud, we all make mistakes. Come sit down. We'll get this all figured out."

He opened the door and wiped the back of his hand on his chin, just like he did when he would get orange popsicle dribble on his chin as a little boy. I wanted to take him in my arms and tell him it would be all right. But we were so far beyond that.

Rosabel jumped up as he came back to the couch. "Are you okay? Do you need a cloth? Just catch your breath for a minute."

He sat down and put his head in his hands. "You don't understand." He started to weep.

"What is it, Sparrow?" Rosabel stroked his hair. "You can tell us anything!"

"She... we... It's too late." He let loose and cried harder than I had ever seen him cry, nestling his head into Rosabel's shoulder. She lightly stroked his neck as his muscular body heaved. I pictured her comforting the despondent children on her bedroom walls. She was created for this role.

"Tell us," she insisted.

"Last week, when we went over to feed the dogs. She said she didn't believe I loved her. The only way I could prove it to her was to..."

A cold chill went down my spine. "You slept with her?"

I gasped. The thought of my baby brother with Sonnet – or anyone – had, thankfully, never crossed my mind. I always imagined he would find a princess, someone as innocent and pure as he was.

"I had to. She was going to break up with me if I didn't," he sobbed.

"Shh... it's ok, Sparrow," Rosabel soothed. We exchanged worried glances.

"When we were getting ready to leave, she told me to remember that we slept in Kyan and Melanie's bed. If I didn't want her to tell them or our parents, then I was going to do what she wanted from now on." Kenner began to sob again, his shoulders shaking so hard it reminded me of his performance in *Romeo and Juliet,* when he forgot his lines and just started to cry.

There was nothing that could save him at this point, I realized. He was just as imprisoned as Elena. Soon he would be running in circles trying to escape the images of the awful things she would be forcing him to do.

I looked over at Rosabel's face, hoping to find solace. Instead, her buttermilk skin was pulled tight with worry. Part of me wanted to believe she was still capable of fixing anything. But the part of me that was starting to understand the real, grown-up world realized that there was nothing anyone could do for my little brother but comfort him.

"Maybe she'll move," I offered weakly.

"Her dad owns part of that bank," he replied between sobs. "She's not going anywhere."

Rosabel had gotten some tissues for him while we sat. He took them and buried his face in the middle. "We can fix this," she said soothingly.

I looked at her with disbelief. How could it possibly be fixed? There is no going back from sleeping with the devil.

"We'll find a way to destroy all of her files," she continued. "And then she'll have no proof. Kenner can be free."

"She doesn't need notebooks!" I half-yelled. "All she needs is big, stupid Melanie! And once she fills her ear with what really happened and then some, Kenner has no hope. Mother and Father will disown him once this gets around," I said firmly.

Rosabel looked at me with shock. I seldom disagreed with her.

"Our only hope is that Kenner can lie his way out of this," I said. We both looked at my little brother, so forlorn. His face appeared ten years older than it had just two weeks ago. He looked pleadingly at Rosabel.

"No, I realize that you can't lie, Sparrow," Rosabel said quietly. "It's just not in your nature." She got up and looked out the front window, where Kyan was pulling heavy pieces of equipment across the driveway in his dirty overalls.

"What else does she know?" she asked.

"What?" Kenner said, wiping his nose with the back of his hand. "I don't know what you mean."

"What else have you told her? About your family?"

"I haven't..."

I felt another wave of nausea. Like I had been dragged under the car all the way to the main road. "Oh, buddy... you didn't..."

"I've messed it up. I've messed it up so bad." He sobbed again.

Chapter Twenty

VANESSA WITHERS, REPORTER
2012

I WALK THROUGH the saloon doors and hear the sound of classical music coming from the back room. I sit down on one of the bar stools, not wanting to disturb Vanessa in any task she might be undertaking. She seems to perform so many at once.

She enters through the swinging doors, eyes half-closed, and her hand is in the air as if she were conducting a great symphony.

"Prokofiev, right?" I ask.

Vanessa jumps back, reminding me of Dee in her ability to change direction so abruptly.

"You scared me to death, girl."

"Sorry. It's the 'Cinderella Suite,' right? I remember it from the coffee shop I used to work in. The owner was a big fan." I remember the ridiculous poofy skirts and tall, cone-shaped hats she had us wear every Halloween, in keeping with the fairytale theme of the coffee shop.

"Yeah. I listen to keep myself calm. I drink a lot of caffeine to stay awake, but the downside is that I can be a little jittery. What can I do you for? Help you find a library book? Is there a package you need to be mailed back to Pepperville? Maybe a new shade of lipstick?"

I smile. "Thanks for remembering." No matter how much the people in Pepperville irritate me, it still feels good to have someone say it out loud like it's somewhere that really exists outside of my memories. "No packages today, thanks," I say. "I'm actually here to ask you some questions, as sort of the town historian."

Vanessa takes a stack of papers and moves them from the back counter to the front. "I'll do my best, but I don't know what I can tell you. We might have to dust off some of those actual books."

"I just want to tell you again that I really love those obituaries. They just come to life, so to speak."

Vanessa looks taken aback for a moment, but then she smiles. "Thanks, Keilah. It's something near and dear to my heart. My grandpa was such a great man..." She sits down on a stool facing me and puts her elbows up on the bar, where many a great story were likely told at one time over a whiskey.

"Everyone used to tell stories about his bravery during the war, and about how he built up the family business from nothing – just a main office that became the hub for three satellite locations we have today. Insurance, you know. Then when he died, there was practically nothing in the paper. When people like you and I go to look him up years from now, they'll do a search for Wenzeslaus Withers and the page will be blank. His whole amazing life lived with no evidence of it for generations to come."

She takes a sip of her coffee, one of several cups sitting around, and sits back on her stool. "I want everybody who passes in Sandy Salts to have their moment to shine. To show what they meant to the world and to have it on the front page of the *Salty Sun Times*. Don't you think everybody deserves that for one day?"

I nod, thinking of Father's bare-bones obituary. It told so little of who he was. When Kyan and Melanie's children, or their children's children, want to know how their farm came to be, they will only have the gossip of old-timers and the terse stories from their uptight parents to rely on. They'll never know about the real man. Maybe I don't have that answer either.

"You are so right, Vanessa. You have the most important job in Sandy Salts. I just never thought about it before. So much more important than working in a coffee shop." I sigh. The thought of going back to work tomorrow and confronting Nova makes my stomach twist and turn.

"You have an important job too, Keilah." Vanessa pulls three sugar packets from under the counter and rips and pours them into her drink. "Sorry, I'm trying to cut back. It's my sleep substitute."

I nod. "I used to drink my coffee full of creamer and other things until I started working in a coffee shop and became a 'purist'."

"You have customers in every day who will probably tell you their life stories. They wouldn't have anyone to talk to without you. Those two old-timers who play chess every day – Bart and Moses. What a great amount of information those two carry around. They have already given me full obituaries to run. I'd tell you but I have a signed statement that I won't release any information until they are gone, to protect the innocent." She winks. "And all of Nova's boyfriends – she'll have a full column. I bet that's a story within itself."

"I don't know how all of those men can stand Nova. There's only so far that 'pretty' can take you," I reply. "Especially... Phillip." I glance, just slightly, in her direction to see what her physical reaction will be. The way gossip works in this town, it won't be long before my night with Phillip becomes public information.

"Oh, I know," Vanessa agrees, without seeming to catch on to my sudden interest. "He is such a nice person. So good-looking. And a real stand-up guy. He's been on his own since high school." She looks at her coffee. "In and out of foster homes all of his childhood. Ended up here when he turned eighteen, long before I arrived."

"What?"

"Yeah, everyone felt kinda bad for him being so young and on his own. He worked at the construction company during the day and took emergency calls for the vet in the evenings. I think people were randomly dropping food at his doorstep for a while. Just to make sure he was still eating. Don't know how he got by without any help."

"Oh no. Poor Philip." No one in my family has ever worked more than one job at once. I didn't realize he had such a hard upbringing. It doesn't seem to fit the Phillip I know. Or at least knew for one night. "Why would he torture himself with Nova after all of that?" I say grouchily. "Doesn't he want to be around someone who will nurture him?"

Vanessa shrugs. "Probably," she says. "Nova's had her problems too. Her mom ran off when she was in grade school. With her dad's fishing buddy. It was a big scandal around town. Jack was caught completely off guard when he woke up one night to see his wife loading his favorite pickup with all of her belongings. He thought she might be sleep-walking until she told him she had been planning this for months. She didn't want to see him ever again and didn't even bother saying goodbye to Nova."

"If she had any human qualities, I might be feeling sorry for her about now. I just can't bring myself to that point," I mutter. "Sorry, I didn't mean to say that out loud."

"I don't think she's had any contact with her mother since. That's why everyone thinks she's so clingy, what with all of the boyfriends. Jack did his best, but he's not one for conversation or making one feel safe. Poor ol' Nova wants to make sure she has plenty to choose from so she's never alone again."

I still can't fathom why Phillip would want anything to do with her. They both came from tragedy and both experienced loss, but Phillip is a nice guy. At least that's how he seems from our very brief encounter.

"Oh, boy. We've gotten completely off track here and I've got to do an interview soon. What was it you wanted my help with?" Vanessa asks. I look up at the oversized clock and realize almost an hour has gone by.

"I wanted to ask you about Dee's family. About her brother. Do you know anything about her brother's kidnapping?"

Vanessa shakes her head. "Poor little Gentry. I'm afraid I don't have a lot of information on that. I can look through some old newspapers if you want. That was a big deal in its time as well. Everyone seems to know the general story, but not much for facts."

"Did they ever have any leads? Any people who might have been eyewitnesses? Surely someone saw something."

"You would think," Vanessa says. She chugs the rest of her coffee and sets a pile of books on the old bar to be re-shelved. "What I remember reading is that they talked to a few people staying at the campground. The whole group had a nice sing-along by the campfire the night before. Everybody remembered Gentry playing the guitar and playing it well. No one seemed to think things were out of place. The police questioned them all and then let everyone go along their merry way. The poor boy just disappeared with no trace."

"Can you look them up for me? The witnesses?" I ask. "I just want to know who was there. And the police records? How would I go about finding those?"

"You have some great reporter instincts." Vanessa smiles. "Unfortunately, the old police department building burned down in 1970. Bad wiring is what they settled on. All of the old records are gone."

My stomach sinks. I had really hoped I could come up with something new. Some way to brighten Dee's day and give her an idea of what happened to the real Gentry.

"Hey, don't be so glum, Keilah. There are lots of ways we can still search. Like I said, lots of old newspapers. I promise I'll do that for you this week. You can check out some *Sandy Salts: Year in Review* books if you like. You do have that shiny new card!"

Without waiting for my response, she heads to a section with lots of large reference books. She pulls several down and brings them over to me. "Here's about five years to get you started. Lots of obits in these." She winks. "Card, please."

SUDDENLY I FEEL a little silly that I've shared my fascination with her. I pull the library card from my purse and hand it to her. She scans the card and hands it back to me.

"Ok, thanks. I appreciate you helping me, I mean Dee."

Vanessa smiles broadly, revealing one broken tooth on the top I hadn't noticed before. "You're welcome. But I really do have to run..."

I jump off my stool. "Of course. Sorry I took up so much of your time."

Vanessa grabs her suitcase-sized purse and slings it over her shoulder, causing her short body to stand at a slant. "Don't be silly. It's nice to have someone to talk to. We'll get together again soon and I'll get you that info."

"Great," I say, feeling hopeful I may have finally made a friend. I stand as she grabs her keys and turns off the lights.

"Follow me out? I have to lock up when I leave. Even though it's a small town, you never know who's lurking about." She pulls out a large key chain from her purse with at least fifty keys hanging on it. "Oh wait." She runs to the door and turns the sign from *Tie your horses in the front,* to *Mosey on. Back later.*

There was much to digest from this conversation. Phillip, the tragic hero. Trying to make a living for himself every day, going it alone until Nova came along. Somehow, she manipulated him, latching on to him and not letting go. Like a spider. Or Sonnet. *She is just like Sonnet.*

Did I sleep with Phillip because somehow his situation reminded me of Kenner's? Was I trying to make him feel better because I couldn't help my brother? Am I that sick?

AFTER I GET HOME, I peruse the books, finding pictures of all of the buildings still standing today. The obituaries don't hold a candle to Vanessa's colorful interpretations of life. The books are full of dry facts about the town – wheat harvest totals and who is on the town council. There is only a one-sentence mention of Gentry's disappearance. My mind drifts.

When I close the last book, I sit on my bed for almost a full hour, just thinking. I take the bag of Nova's things out of my closet, the ones Phillip brought to Jack's Beanery. They don't smell like Nova. It's Phillip's scent I drink in until I can't keep my eyes open any longer.

Chapter Twenty-One

THE NEXT DAY and the day after Kenner's big confession, we avoided eye contact in the halls. Rosabel and I ate lunch in silence, only speaking when the subject of an assignment in Earth Science came up. When we ran out of things to say, I would turn and allow her to braid my hair until the bell rang, summoning us back to class. That was our silent connection when all else failed. Kenner wouldn't even acknowledge us when he saw us, as Sonnet hung on his arm and giggled about something only she found amusing.

It had been a week or so of our non-conversation before it became so painfully obvious that our parents even caught on. We were sitting at the table and they were discussing the price of wheat, as they always did, when Mother looked up and said sharply, "You two need to get this straightened out right quick."

I almost didn't catch what she was saying. I was smashing my sweet potatoes with the back of my fork, pretending they were Sonnet's head. I was lost in my misery. "Huh?" I asked, surprised either of them had the energy to notice.

"Fix it. Both of you. I'm darned tired of it," Father said.

"There's nothin' wrong." Kenner didn't bother looking at either of them. He got up to take his plate to the kitchen, but Mother stood and put her finger in the air.

"Tut, tut now, boy. Sit and listen to your father," she said. "And you too, Keilah. No more of this poutin' like you're five."

I resisted the urge to cross my arms, but sunk down in my chair nonetheless.

"Now you hear me," Father began, as if he were on the way to a long lecture that neither of us would retain. "You listen good. I don't know what kind of nonsense has been going on between the two of you, but it has to stop. Someday it's going to be you three runnin' this place and I don't want personal problems to be the downfall of our farm. Family has to stick together. Get it out and be done."

I had never before considered myself to be a viable option for farm operations. I didn't want to be a part of this place. Sure, I'd like to come visit, but actually running it? No, that was Kyan's job.

"I'm sorry," Kenner burst out. "I'm sorry for everything." He got up from the table and ran to his room, away from our father, who had always had little tolerance for men who showed emotion.

"Well, what in the heavens?" Mother furrowed her brow. "What has gotten into that boy?" Her eyes quickly came to rest on me.

It would be so much easier to make something up. "It's me," I said. "I've been teasing him at school because he... can't do math like I can." It was true that I had become quite good, thanks to all of Rosabel's would-be suitors and no thanks to Kyan's years of half-trying to help. "I tease him all day," I said weakly, "whenever I see him in the halls."

"You can be a real spiteful little gal, but I never thought

you would torture your brother," Mother said sadly. She gathered the leftover food on the table. Usually what she thought meant little to me, but today, my heart hurt.

"Apologize to your brother," Father said. "And let this be the end of it. We Brownwells support our own." He leaned back in his chair, taking the stock market page with him.

I was lost without my best friend's words and my brother's jokes. That was all I had to anchor myself to the world. It suddenly dawned on me that, if I propped up Kenner, I wouldn't be trying to ride through life on a flat tire. The better he felt, the more chance the three of us had of working through things together.

I knocked on his door. "Kenner? Let me in, Sparrow."

"Come on," he said quietly. I opened the door and saw him sitting on the edge of his bed. I hadn't really looked at his face for a few weeks, but I could see that he hadn't been sleeping well. We always used to tease him about the big, puffy eyes he got after a good night's sleep. Now the underside was flat and dark.

"We have to figure out how to get through this," I said, sitting down beside him. "You and I are best buds and this can't ruin it."

"I know," he said, wiping his nose with the back of his hand. "But I can't get over the fact that I've destroyed this family. There's no way out."

"Yes, there is," I said. "There is absolutely a way out."

Kenner cocked his head to the side. "What?"

"I'm not running this farm, in any way shape or form, and I'm pretty sure you don't want to be Kyan's hired hand for the rest of your life."

"Nope. He only talks when he wants to tell me how stupid I am."

"Well then, right now, let's come up with a plan. To get away from all of it." I sat up straight. "We'll run away. Just the two of us. We can find someplace to hide for a while, 'til she moves on to some other poor sucker."

"What? We can't just run out…"

"No, we won't run out. This will take some time to research. But we'll find the perfect place. You'll save up your money from the farm and I'll get a job. And then one day, without much notice, we'll tell everybody we're leaving. To hell with Sonnet and all of them." I smiled at my brother, confident that he would go along with my plan.

"I'm not sure. I mean… I want to, but… running out on Father like that…" Kenner sat back on his elbows. "I'll really have to think about this. I see what you're saying, but…"

"Don't you want a chance to do something besides work on somebody else's farm? Don't you want to be able to take a breath without Sonnet sucking half of it in first?"

"Well, what about Rosabel? And her orphanage?"

What about Rosabel? Would she agree to go with us? Leave her plans behind? "She wants me to find… the moon. That's what she's always saying. We're doing this just as much for her as for us."

Kenner thought for a moment. "What do you mean, 'the moon'? I'm not goin' to college."

I smiled. "You remember, don't you? The list I made in the sixth grade of things I wanted to do. I wanted to go to the moon. Well, actually, I wanted more to pee in a space suit and see what happened. But Rosabel really latched onto the moon part of that statement."

Kenner shook his head. "I still don't get it."

"She's been bugging me to go. She wants me to find myself, find my moon. Wherever that would be. And you'll find someone fabulous." I grinned. "Someone smart and funny and good enough to be your girlfriend."

"And we'd just take off? Like that?"

"Just like that. But let's not tell Rosabel about it until we know for sure what we're doing, until we've got a real plan in place." I wanted to make it up to him for all the times I hadn't been able to solve our problems. I was always running to Rosabel for help and, this time, I would fix things myself. For once, I would be the heroic one.

We went back to school the following Monday and, to the outside world, nothing had changed. Sonnet met Kenner at the bus and took his hand firmly in hers. Rosabel pretended as if they didn't exist and walked by my side to class. But Kenner and I had a plan to save him; for the first time we had made a major life-changing decision and we hadn't included the third spoke to our wheel.

Chapter Twenty-Two

SANDY SALTS
2012

T HE TWO OLD MEN play outside, no matter the weather, five days a week. The Jack's Beanery staples are in the middle of an intense game of chess, one that requires no words. Instead, they communicate through a series of grunts each one seems to understand. I walk cautiously up the steps of the polished log front porch of the coffee shop. I'm not afraid of Bart and Moses, but certainly, if Nova senses my presence, she'll put me to work, day off or not.

"Hello there, miss," Bart says, without looking up from the board. "Already got my coffee. Not as good as the days you're here to make it."

"Thank you, Bart. I appreciate hearing that. And good morning to you, Moses."

"Mmmmhmmm."

I pull up a chair, unintentionally making a cringeworthy, loud sound as I scoot it closer to their table. "I was wondering if I could ask you both some questions about the history of Sandy Salts."

"Well, you know my great-grandfather was at the signin' of the proclamation. Said fourteen people died that day from the homemade liquor and rotten egg salad. Darned shame they didn't understand the fermentation process. Guess that thinned out the confused ones, though," Bart says. "Your move, or didn't you hear me?" He looks across the table at his partner. Each stare with equal intensity at the all-weather chess board Jack had carved from an old maple tree he cut down to build the coffee shop.

"Don't yell." Moses folds his hands in front of him. "Won't make me move any quicker."

"Well, I was thinking more about something specific. A big kidnapping that happened in the park outside of town."

Moses perks up and looks directly at me. "How'd you hear 'bout that one? Happened quite a long time ago. Doubt you were even born."

"Dee, my landlord. It was her brother and..."

"Oh yes. Little Gentry, wasn't it? Quite a big thing for a few weeks. Summer of '55 Bart leans back in his seat and crosses his arms over his large belly.

Moses shakes his head. "Then it was like the whole town just forgot. Moved on to other news. That was the year we got the new grocery store, remember?"

"And the dry cleaners. Don't forget about that."

I take a deep breath. "Well, I was more interested in the investigation. Do you remember if they had any suspects? Was there someone in town, or maybe someone traveling through they might have had their eyes on?"

"Nope. None come to mind. Oh, here and there you'd hear a rumor. But nobody they saw fit to bring in for questioning. Isn't that right, Moses? Or am I thinkin' of that murder that happened in the back of the cat food plant?"

Moses leans back in his chair and crosses his arms, to match his partner, over a considerably smaller stomach. "Don't recall anyone under suspicion. You always wonder, though, with that highway runnin' right through town. Any ol' drifter could've snatched the boy and taken off for parts unknown. We wouldn't be any the wiser."

"That's what I was thinking," I say hesitantly. "Someone just stopping in town for a couple of days and they happened to see an opportunity."

Moses hunches forward and motions for me to come closer. I lean in, so close I can smell the coffee on his breath.

"I'll tell you what the rumor was, though, and I think this might have just a bit of truth to it... That family of his was a bunch of grifters. Made their money off gambling and stealing from way back. Even the rich ones were the unsavory types. Just better at their games."

I think about Dee, good and kind Dee. There is not a dishonest bone in her body. "They all aren't like that! Dee is wonderful."

"No, that Dee's a good egg," Bart says. "Don't get yourself all worked up." He pats my back. "She just got mixed in with the wrong type is all, when it came to her husband. I'm talking about her folks in particular. They didn't meet a person they didn't swindle somehow. Always had someone on the hook for something."

My mind starts to swirl. I can't believe that her own family might be responsible. "So, what was the rumor? What happened to Gentry?"

Moses studies my face. "This sure has you twisted up, doesn't it, honey?"

"I'm just worried about Dee is all."

Moses smiles. "It wasn't her fault. Most likely her folks worked this all out ahead of time. Sold the boy in some kind of deal they thought would make them famous and rich."

"What? I don't understand."

"Runnin' all of those games got tiresome and they figured they could work out a big one. They got a little cocky from those small wins and set about to hook a big fish. That's what all the locals thought, anyway."

"But... but how would they think this could make them rich? I don't get it."

"There was a fund set up to help the family in crisis, you know. It's coming back to me now. I helped at a bake sale to raise money for her folks. The whole town pitched in, one way or another. Don't think anyone ever thought about where the money was going. Just tugged at everybody's heart that some little feller was missing," Bart said. "And the newspapers were all over them. Every time you turned around the mother was doing another interview with some reporter from Timbuktu. They had money pouring in from all over the country." Bart looks like he is transported back to his boyhood. He shakes his head in disgust. "Never saw that woman shed a tear."

"What kind of a person...?"

"So, time goes by, and there are more interviews and no real searchin' on the part of the family. Folks started putting two and two together. The boy had some talent, they were always putting a hat out when he played. What if these ne'er-do-wells decided to get some real money for him? They could sell the boy and make a big production of things, then go pick up their boy when they sucked all they could outta folks. Except the other party played even dirtier than them and just took off with the boy, never to be seen again."

I can't imagine that Dee's parents would be so callous. I think about everything she's said about her brother, how they idolized him and put him out as their showpiece. To think that it was less about pride and more about making him a commodity is quite sickening. There is no way I can tell Dee about this. Absolutely no way. She is just an innocent in this story.

"Nobody ever found anything? No sightings of him anywhere? And the parents just... gave up? That was all? I can't imagine that would be it."

Moses looks at me with kindness in his eyes. "You and I, Keilah, we aren't like that type. That's why you can't imagine. They didn't have no attachment to anything. Could be they thought they'd sent their boy off to the high life somewhere better. Or they just didn't want to be bothered."

Moses shrugs his shoulders. "After a few months, we all just went about our business. Life goes on, you know. The family was quiet and we all kind of forgot."

"You want to know the real strange thing?" Bart shakes his finger at me. "Changed their appearances shortly after. Cut the girl's long hair real short and the lot of them dyed their hair real funny, a light color. I remember my ma talkin' about that one. She said, 'Son, only folks with somethin' to hide change who they are.' That stuck with me."

"Even the police? They didn't think something was strange about this?" I ask. I notice out of the corner of my eye that Moses had moved the pieces around on the board, ever-so-carefully, as Bart was talking. He winks at me as I'm trying to keep my attention focused on Bart.

"We only had two policemen at the time. It was well known they both liked to gamble. Probably lost their shirts to those two swindlers in some game of..."

We're interrupted by the all-too-familiar screeching from

inside the coffee shop. "Lorraine! Did you forget the latte on this last order? It's milk and coffee, not rocket science! Go take a break somewhere! I can't stand the sight of your face anymore!"

Moses shakes his head. "You'd better high tail it outta here if you don't want to be in her sights."

I smile. "Thanks to both of you for your help!" I scramble off the porch in three big steps.

Ever since Dee told me the story of her brother's kidnapping, I had this nagging feeling that there was more to it. It was too horrible to imagine Gentry being carted off to a life even more awful than the one he was living. Maybe, instead, he had been whisked away by some well-intentioned person, thinking they had just saved him from certain misery.

I have to help her. This is such a huge loss in her life and I can't just sit – knowing how it feels to lose someone so precious – and do nothing. If I can put this to rest somehow for her, maybe she can be happy just being who she is and not always looking for the next "shook up".

Chapter Twenty-Three

MOTHER PROMISED SHE WOULD BUY me a prom dress if I went. Translation: please go to prom so I'm not embarrassed to have you as a daughter. It was a real rite of passage in Pepperville to attend the prom, preferably with a well-dressed date. Those who stayed home were somehow damaged and thought to be headed towards a dead-end life with no hope for meaningful employment or family.

For years, she reminded me, "Proper girls from proper homes attend all the big events at school." I hated going anywhere without Rosabel, so mostly I stayed in my room, much to Mother's embarrassment. I missed every dance, football game, and social club, until now.

I saw a great opportunity. Without telling her that we had already found dates, Mother and I came to an agreement: I would attend prom for a month's worth of chore-free living and a side of beef for Rosabel's freezer. This checked two boxes. First, I was able to help Rosabel out in a small way, and second, I could pretend, just for one night, that I was the kind of daughter Mother really wanted.

As hard as it was for me to admit, I really wanted to go to prom. It usually didn't bother me staying home during school activities. Rosabel didn't like them and I agreed they weren't worth the stress. There was just something so urgent about being a part of high school energy once before it ended.

I could have committed social suicide and offered to go to prom with my brother. At least I could try, even though that was considered a worse faux pas than staying home on prom night. Then I remembered Kenner was completely under Sonnet's control. He would readily agree to go with me and then she would, in her sweetest voice, inform him that he would not be attending prom with his sister. He would put his head down and sheepishly admit it was a stupid idea.

I felt a little guilty for forcing Rosabel to go. "Sometimes unpleasant things need to be done. As a means to an end," she repeated several times.

Rosabel was not able to afford a fancy dress. I knew she could whip something up in a heartbeat, but all of those supplies cost money. Being so resourceful, she probably could have found what she needed if she had felt any enthusiasm about the event. I thought about re-negotiating my deal with Mother, but then I remembered Rosabel's thin body and I couldn't bear the thought of her going hungry.

We both went into Cup of Dreams, the new coffee shop with a fairytale theme, and filled out job applications. We really just wanted to make enough money to buy ourselves beautiful prom dresses, but we told the owner that we were planning to stay through high school.

I told Mother I would pay for my own prom dress too, so that Rosabel wouldn't feel bad. Our first week at Cup of Dreams was full of picky customers with specialty drinks called "Sit on a Cloud Latte" and "Marry me, Princess

Mocha" and lots of do-overs. No matter what, Rosabel could smooth over any accident with her smile and a gentle pat on the back. We started to fall into the groove and we liked what we did. Mary Anne, the owner, graciously agreed to schedule us at the same time so we could walk together.

When Father found out I was working, he was so pleased that he bought me a little hatchback car to get us to and from work. I had a work permit, not a real license, but it meant Kyan didn't have to drive me. Kyan was upset that I was spending my time and energy somewhere other than the farm, but Father reminded him that I was developing skills (like counting change and dealing with customers) that would come in handy when I learned how to do the bookwork for the farm.

In six short weeks, we had saved up enough to buy our dresses at the discounted Glass Slipper Formals. We wanted them to match, but because I was shockingly pale and her skin was the color of peaches, we had to get different colors. Mine was a navy blue, fitted tightly around my waist with a big bow in the back. Rosabel's identically-patterned dress was done in watermelon; she looked like royalty.

Since Melanie had gone to three months of beauty school, she agreed to fix our hair and even coerced Kyan to take our pictures. Mother wanted to make us a fancy dinner, fitting of our fine attire. Father rented a limousine and paid his hired man extra to come in on his day off and drive us.

The night of the prom, Mother made us a fancy dinner of braised short ribs and some sort of green mush. The vegetable concoction was a show of support for Sonnet, who had become a vegetarian the week before. Despite our meat-centric life, Mother wanted her to feel at home. Dessert, a canned cherry-topped cheesecake, sat alongside the leaf-etched champagne glasses we only used for special occasions.

We all sat very seriously at the long, Macassar Ebony table in our dining room. Every time we had a new guest, the formality of the big room seemed to swallow up each personality as our guests sat for the first time, taking in the antler-shaped chandelier, containing thirty-one lighted prongs and the endless, shiny table. They often hesitated before sitting on the plush seats and stared, in awe, at the spectacle surrounding them. Everyone, that is, except Sonnet.

As Charles and Gage surveyed the room from floor to ceiling, Sonnet pulled out a chair and sat down, hands folded on the table. She made a quick jerk of her head in Kenner's direction and he quickly moved to her side.

Sonnet had fittingly decided to go to prom dressed as an evil stepmother. She took several black slips, sewed them together, and added tiny doll heads, smeared with red lipstick, to the skirt. Her lipstick matched the dolls'. On her head, she placed some sort of black, feathery hat that looked strangely similar to something Kyan had shot on a hunting expedition just a week before. I took some comfort in Mother's abject horror. It was nice to be the "good" child for a change.

Sonnet said nothing during our polite back-and-forth, refusing to make eye contact with anyone except Mother and Kenner. As she spoke, her arm sat protectively over the top of Kenner's chair as she gazed off in space, like she had somewhere else she would rather be. Kenner pushed a glazed cherry around his plate until she took her fork and, with an impatient sigh, stabbed the cherry and ate it.

Mother seemed quite taken with Gage, batting her eyes and acting like she was the one on her first official date. Several times she patted his hand and called him "young man". She offered him seconds and then thirds of everything she made, and even brought out her last jar of Grandma's Top-Secret Recipe Marmalade for his particular usage.

After the obligatory living room pictures, we all piled into the limousine for the long, uncomfortable ride to the high school. Rosabel refused to look at Sonnet for the entire ride. Sonnet refused to look at anyone but Kenner. The two of them giggled over things only they found funny. Gage and Charles didn't understand what a tinderbox they were sitting on. I stared at the ceiling, wishing we would hit a bump hard enough that it would cause Sonnet's dress babies to bang into something and go flying over her head. Gage tried, unsuccessfully, to make small talk. We were all relieved to step out and go our separate ways.

I waved at Rosabel and Charles, feeling a twinge of jealousy as he took her hand and they headed to the dance floor. I didn't want to lose the bond she and I had to some boy she had just met. Despite the fact that she had turned away every other potential relationship up to this point, I still had anxiety over the idea that one day she might find someone to occupy her time—someone other than me.

Gage and I had fun dancing and talking and soon I forgot there had been anyone else with us. We sat by ourselves and didn't run out of conversation for a good hour. As the night wore on, Gage showed me the flask he had snuck in and we decided to go into the teacher's lounge and try some of his mother's homemade gin. He was cute and funny and way more interesting than anything happening at the dance anyway.

I hadn't had any alcohol since the days in Rosabel's house when her parents would be out for the evening and we experimented with whatever we found in their liquor cabinet. It didn't take long for that familiar, dizzy, fuzzy feeling to resurface. We laid down on the floor when we thought we heard someone walking by, and suddenly my hands were finding places on Gage that, even with two brothers, I barely knew existed.

I remember the sweet smell of his mother's gin on his breath. His soft, welcoming lips. His kiss on my neck. There was no one making me stop. No one telling me to be a good girl, or do what was right. It was just me, Gage, and our high school hormones.

I fell asleep, not in his arms but beside them, on the floor of the teacher's lounge. So did he. The next thing I remember, Gage was patting my face.

"Keilah! The dance is over! We've got to get back home before you get in trouble!" he whispered.

"Huh?" I replied sleepily. It took a minute for everything to come into focus. I stumbled to my feet, pulled down my dress, and looked up at the clock. It said eleven fifty-five. I felt a little dizzy, but I knew I'd better keep moving because whatever was going on in my head was nothing compared to what would be happening to the rest of me after coming home this late.

We both ran outside, not caring at that point who saw us and what questions they may have had. The limousine Father had provided was gone and Rosabel and Kenner were nowhere in sight. I didn't worry about getting home, as any number of people would be willing to give me a ride. I was more concerned about how I would explain being late.

It only took a matter of minutes to find a classmate in the parking lot who agreed to give us a ride, provided I had a good email address for Rosabel I would be willing to share. Since I had also become quite good at setting up fake addresses for her, it was an easy trade.

Any discomfort I was feeling on the ride to the dance was multiplied by fifty when it was just the two of us together for the long ride out to our farm. The strange twisting emotions of being with a boy for the first time and knowing how much trouble I would be in for my late arrival made my stomach hurt. Or maybe it was too much cheese-cake and homemade liquor.

Gage tried to make small talk, but I resisted with a shrug of my shoulders. I couldn't concentrate on him now. Even though he had been my first, something that should have been a momentous experience in my life, I had more pressing issues on my mind: like where Rosabel had gone and what she must be thinking right about now.

That was nothing, though, compared to the thought of Kyan and Melanie sitting up in our living room waiting for me. Melanie didn't like to be up past eleven as it made her age prematurely. Mother would have gone to bed early at Kyan and Melanie's home while she was taking care of the girls, and would surely be up with them in the morning. Melanie would have far less to worry about than I did.

Kyan would be angry and insulting, and who knows what kind of insinuations he would make. It would be humiliating and, somewhere in the process, I would have to offer an explanation of just what had happened. Secretly I would be thinking that for this one night only, the negative things he said about me were all true.

I turned to poor Gage, fidgeting in his seat. "My brother is going to be so mad. Things are going to get really rough for you," I said simply. "I hesitate to think what he'll do to me. That's what he does when people don't follow his rules. So, you and I – we need to come up with a good story."

Gage swallowed hard. "I'll go in with you. I can explain... I can tell him I caused you to be late."

"I wouldn't do that to you." I patted his arm. "Just help me think of something."

"Okay..." He paused, thinking as hard as his alcohol-muddled brain would allow. "Once, I told my dad I was out with the guys after a game. I was really sitting in the library, with one of the special-ed kids eating pizza and playing a board game." He shrugged his shoulders and smiled.

I stared at him, not believing someone of the opposite sex could be that kind of good – almost Rosabel-like in character. "That's just great," I snapped. "I'll tell him I was doing something noble on prom night. He'll buy that. And then he'll give me a big ol' pat on the back and the keys to the nice truck."

We rode the rest of the way in silence. I had to come up with something, but my mind simply would not let me concentrate on more than Rosabel. I was also still afraid to be out late at night. The nightmares about Rosabel's father now included cattle in the middle of the road.

When we arrived at the farm, I stepped out, relieved to see the yard light and porch light were both still on. At least Kyan hadn't shut them off to make me stumble to the door in the dark. I suddenly realized there was no ride for Gage. I made a second promise for the night, a face-to-face after school meeting with Rosabel if our driver would somehow get Gage back to Charles.

As I stumbled out of the pickup, Gage grabbed my arm. "Wait!" he said.

"I have to go!" I said dismissively, then realized he was leaning in to kiss me. I let his lips brush mine lightly before turning my face away. At that moment, emotions, cheesecake, and alcohol came to a head. All over Mother's Peaches and Cream rose bush.

"I'm so sorry..." I mumbled, wiping my mouth on the sleeve of my dress.

"You're gonna be ok?"

I could feel dribbles running down my face. "Uh huh."

I tiptoed in the door to a dark entryway. The only light still on was the one shining over the portrait of the One-Armed Man's stern mother, Millie. I glanced at the clock over the mantel in the family room – it was 12:45. I made it to the second step before I heard something.

"Keilah? You back?" It was Melanie's sleepy voice.

"I just came down to grab my shoe. Forgot it on the stairs earlier," I said, hoping Melanie had been asleep long enough to be really confused.

"Oh. Kyan went over to check on the girls. Your mom called and said Merydith got up with a fever. What time is it? Your brother came home hours ago."

"I got busy... playing a game in the library and eating pizza. Alternative prom activities," I muttered. I pulled my coat tightly around my soiled dress.

"Ok, goodnight." She yawned. "Can't be up too long or I'll be puffy in the morning." She never turned on the light to check the time or seemed to notice that I still had my coat on.

The next day I woke up with a smile on my face. I had someone who wanted to be with me because I was me. Rosabel had been nowhere in sight all evening long. Gage only danced with me. Only touched me. I was exhilarated, flattered, and... ashamed? No, I wasn't ashamed. For once, the spotlight shone on me. Then I remembered I had thrown up after my first real goodnight kiss.

I hesitated to call Rosabel. Things might be different. We had something big between us now. Last night I hadn't as much worried about where she was as about what this would do to our relationship. Could she even understand, or would she hate me for being so reckless?

Finally, I took out my phone and called her number. She asked me to come over as soon as I could. I took a shower and put on makeup and my best brown t-shirt. Everything looked the same. But it wasn't.

"Did you have fun, Robin?" she asked without any hint of emotion. We were sitting on her porch, where just a week earlier we had discussed our jobs and how boring life had become in our small town. Two different people.

I studied her face. I didn't want to say something that would hurt her. Somehow Rosabel knowing I had slept with Gage was an even more shameful thought than the possibility of Mother or Father knowing.

"It was all right." I stuffed a big piece of orange peel muffin into my mouth, suddenly feeling ravenous. "Did you?"

"Charles wants to come up with Gage next week and go to a movie," she said, without acknowledging my question.

My heart leaped. "That would be so much fun! We could go out to eat first, and then…"

"I told him no. He escorted me to prom so that I could confront Sonnet. That's all I really needed from him," she said quietly, as she wrapped her arms around her middle. "What else were you going to say?"

"You confronted Sonnet? Without even telling me?" Never before in our relationship had she gone behind my back.

Rosabel took in a deep breath and let it out slowly.

"Well… don't leave me in suspense. What happened?"

"First, I want you to know that I didn't want to tell you ahead of time because you would've felt obligated to join me. This was my worry, not yours."

"Oh, Rosabel, you shouldn't have…."

"Shh…" She put her hand in the air in protest. "Let me finish."

She took a long sip of her water and then set it down on the porch, looking around for several minutes before continuing. "I asked her if I could talk to her about Kenner while I was dancing with Charles. She didn't want to, but when Kenner went to get punch, I whispered in her ear that I knew things."

I wiped the muffin crumbs on my leg. "What did you say?"

"I told her about everything we had uncovered. She had to know that eyes were watching her as well. She seemed shocked. At first, I thought she got it." Rosabel leaned forward and picked at her shoelaces. "Even when I told her she needed to leave Kenner alone, or I would play her game of blackmail."

That was just not something Rosabel, at any time in her life, would have done. Perhaps I had underestimated her loyalty to us and the fact that she valued our friendship above everything in her world.

"She started laughing, like someone out of the horror movies we've watched. She called me some names I'll not repeat. And then..." Rosabel hugged herself again and began rocking slowly. "And then, she told me about my father's bad checks. He has written many to the track, apparently. Her father paid them because he knew how close Kenner was to me. But he warned him never to do it again." Out of nowhere, she started sobbing.

I rubbed her back. "That's awful. I can imagine how that would be devastating if people found out. I don't blame you at all. You tried."

She continued to sob. "No, she was so much worse than I imagined. She has access to secrets that no one should know. Somehow, she has found ways to reach into everyone's soul and tear apart the one thing that can't be healed."

"What do we do now? About Sonnet?" I never knew her to have such deep feelings for her father. She always seemed to be ashamed of his incessant drinking. Maybe I had been misinterpreting the situation our entire lives.

"We do nothing. There is nothing we can say or do to keep her away from Kenner, I'm afraid." She took a tissue out of her pocket and blew her nose delicately.

Suddenly my evening with Gage seemed so frivolous. I was mindlessly groping a complete stranger, the first boy to show any interest in me, while Rosabel was, as usual, doing something noble, trying to fix problems in my family. In the process, she was confronted with something so horrible that it crushed her gentle spirit.

Rosabel continued to sob and I felt awkward that I had no way to comfort her. I was used to being the person in need of assurance. The longer we sat, the more I wondered if there was another piece to the story.

"You said she tore apart your soul. Is there something else, besides your father?"

She looked up at me and shook her head furiously. "I can't," she said.

"It's ok. You don't have to tell me now. We'll talk about it when you feel better." I pulled her in close, as she had done with me hundreds of times.

The biggest, most gigantic regret of my life is that I never asked her again.

Chapter Twenty-Four

SANDY SALTS
2012

A FTER MY CONVERSATION with Bart and Moses, I decide to take a walk down to visit Dee. The little lady I had seen crossing the highway on my very first day in town is coming down the street. She grasps a clear bag of bread and bananas in one hand and an umbrella in the other. "Hey, Mrs. Shorty!" I call, waving vigorously. She glances at me and nods, offering me a slight smile. In the next instant, she steps out into the buzzing traffic, without so much as a sideways glance. Miraculously, she makes it across; all of her grocery items remain intact.

Thinking of Dee and her brother brought up issues I have with my own. I'm starting to worry about Kenner; that perhaps there *is* something going on with him other than the move. He rarely answers my calls. Mother says he spends all his time with Sonnet, and Kyan has trouble getting him to do his work before he leaves for the day. It's something that feels heavy on my shoulders, adding to the worry I have each day about dealing with Nova.

When I arrive at the Salty Gas 'n' Snack, it's surprisingly busy. Dee isn't her usual calm-and-in-control self, instead seeming flustered and confused.

"What do you want? Pizza sticks? I can't remember if I

stocked those," she says softly.

The twenty-something wearing the battered Cubs hat sighs loudly. "This is a bunch of BS. What DO you have, lady?"

"C'mon, man. I ain't got all day," the next person in line barks.

"I'll go check, Dee."

She looks up from the cash register, mouthing the words *Thank you.*

"She'll check for you, young man." She smooths her lavender smock and then squeezes the corners of her mouth, nervously. "Can you step aside and I'll help the next customer while she's looking?"

I find the pizza sticks on a different shelf and quickly deliver them. I make a few slushies and, in a matter of a few minutes, we have cleared out the line and no one new has pulled up outside to get gas.

"I'll tell you, Keilah, that was just too much for one old lady. I was trying to clean out the coffee maker and the next thing you know, the customers were lined up from here to the next county. This job may be gettin' too hairy for one old lady." She reaches into her pocket and grabs her Practically Purple lipstick to re-apply. "How 'bout you? Are you making good use of your day off?"

"I've been thinking a lot about what you said last night. About your brother and everything."

Dee has migrated over to the space around the coffee maker, setting things on another counter so she can clean the area. She stops for a moment and stares at me.

"I shouldn't have told you all of that. It's over and done. In the long ago past," she says firmly.

I touch her shoulder like Rosabel did mine many times. "Dee, you are my only friend here. I would be completely miserable if it weren't for you." My voice is a little shaky. I don't want to think too hard. "I wouldn't be able to handle Nova or being alone or... anything otherwise. Now it's my turn." She puts her frail arm around my waist and hands me the wadded-up Kleenex that has been in her jacket pocket for who knows how many days. I take it without fear.

"Ok, dearie. You're right." She pats me with her free hand. "What is it you want to know?"

I blow my nose and try to distract myself from the tears. "I want to know... what was it that you said happened right before you realized your brother was missing again?"

"Well, I went into that smelly bathroom. I was trying to hurry so I didn't have to spend much time in that dirty place with odd sounds, you know. That's when the lady came up and started telling me her god-darned life story about..."

"No, before that," I say impatiently. "What happened while you were on your way to wash your hands? Did you see anybody? Other people camping who might have seemed suspicious?"

Dee crosses her arms. "How in the world should I re-member that? It was so many years ago and I wouldn't have been thinkin'..."

"What about the people you had already met in the campground? Were there people your family made friends with?"

She smiles. "Oh, we always made friends with strangers. Everywhere we went. My folks wanted to show off Gentry for all of his talents and see if they would throw a few dollars in the hat. 'Play your guitar for these people, Gentry.

Sing a song for those folks, boy.' Always with a big grin on his face." She put her hand up to her mouth, looking like she was going in to pick her teeth. "I remember the night before, 'round the campfire. There was a man who seemed real interested. He thought Gentry was the real bee's knees... Said he collected wild animals. Took 'em in when they was abused."

The hairs on the back of my neck stand up. "What? Could he have taken your brother?"

Dee frowns. "What are you thinkin', girlie? That the kidnapper sat right there during campfire time and sized us up? That's too many mystery books is what that is."

I bite my lip, trying not to let any critical words come out. "Well, was he the same man? The one they thought might have taken your brother?"

She shakes her head. "No. I would've remembered that. Honestly, why would you think I'd know anything that far back... I don't remember anything really..."

"Well, it was worth a try... Just want to help..."

"Only remember the other things because the policeman asked so many times. Almost like they expected one little girl to do their detective work." She pulls one wisp of hair from her face that had somehow escaped the hairspray that morning.

"Do you remember his name?"

"Who? Mr. Campfire? C'mon, Keilah. Do you remember the name of every warm body you've ever met? I can barely remember to put my brassiere on face-forward every morning. That's enough of this talk for now." Dee pushes the heavy coffee maker away from the back of the wall. "Come help me with this real quick."

I stay a while longer, half-listening to her stories of polka dances and conquests she's made in that middle-of-a-cornfield dance hall. In my head, I'm trying to bring together the image of the One-Armed Man, a kind and generous soul with that of a hardened kidnapper. Is this completely crazy?

I stop on the way home to pick up ingredients to make spaghetti casserole, like Mother always did in the winter. It was filled with processed cheese and canned soups and completely unhealthy, but it felt like a warm, comfortable blanket. I hope Dee will like it, even if my cooking can't possibly compare to hers.

After I finish mixing all the ingredients and top with the *pièce de résistance*, the crushed potato chips, I slide it in the oven and wait for the cheesy goodness to cook.

Since Nova wanted the weekend off to spend with her new boyfriend, I won't be able to go to the library, where there is actually internet, until Tuesday. This is going to nag at me until I find some answers. I hate to bug Vanessa when she isn't working, since she has so many jobs and so little free time. I decide to call Mother, despite the fact I missed a rather big event in our family.

"Mother?" I ask the normal dead air that follows three rings of our family phone. My family has always expected those calling to state their business immediately.

"Keilah. You missed Melanie's annual party," said the all-too-familiar, deep voice of judgment on the other end of the line.

"I know. I'm sorry, Kyan. Just busy with work and it's a long way and I am banished..."

"Family is always more important. You know that. Practically broke Mother's heart. Just a card was all that was needed."

I sigh. There is no winning this battle, even though I know that Mother's concern was less about my presence and more about what the neighbors said.

"You're right," I say, knowing this was the only way to end this. "I should have been there. Can I speak to Mother? Is she there?"

"Hold on."

I'll have to approach this carefully or Mother will shut me down before I begin. The history of the farm is wrapped in memories of Father and that wound is still wide open.

"Y-ello? This is Georgina." I smirk to myself, thinking how ridiculous it is that Kyan couldn't even tell Mother it was me calling.

"Mother? How are you?"

"Well as can be expected."

I steady myself for a lengthy list of ailments, but instead, she sits quietly on the other end before asking, "You're still writin' in that notebook like you're s'posed to? Sure wish you'd've agreed to see that counselor more than twice 'fore you left."

Just tell your story, Keilah. That will help with those dark spaces in your memory.

"I'm sorry I missed the party."

"There are other things goin' on besides the party. Your brother doesn't have his head on straight."

Normally I would remind her that she has mentioned this in our previous two conversations. "I know." It can't be easy for him to prepare in secret. That's what I've decided was the reason for his sudden distance. "He's going through some stuff." I'm grateful for once that Mother takes so little interest in what I have to say, and doesn't press for details.

"I was wondering if you could help me with something. It's about the farm history."

"Oh?" She seems surprised. "Well, I'll do my best. It was your father who really had all of that in his head. And Kyan. If I don't know, he will."

I doubt very much that Kyan will be interested in real conversation. "Well, the One-Armed Man... do we know where he went when he left the farm?"

"I think the sale of the farm went through the spring of 1937. You know he ran off real quick. Not much time to say goodbye..."

"I know that. I just wondered if we had an idea where he settled after he left."

"Well, I don't... Come to think of it, he did send your grandfather a letter. It was shortly after we got married. 'Parently he kept up with the paper, getting it sent in the mail I s'pose."

"Yes... and what did it say?" I asked impatiently.

"Let me think..." There is dead air, leaving me to wonder if she has drifted off to sleep.

"Mother? Still there?"

"He asked about the family and the upkeep of the place... If we were takin' nice care of the Mem'ry Garden. That sort of thing. Sent us a glass vase. Shaped like an elephant."

"But did he mention where he was? Or what he might be doing? Just anything about..."

"Why would that matter?" Mother snaps.

"I'm doing some... research. The lady I live with is very interested in Pepperville history. She thought the story of our place seemed really unique." I've barely mentioned the farm to anyone. The memories I do have are too painful.

"Oh... I see." Her voice softens. "Isn't that nice of her. Well, let me go through that trunk with your grandfather's things after my bridge club and I'll see if we kept that letter."

I let out a loud sigh. "When will that be?"

"Oh, this evening I 'spect. I was goin' to make a lemon cake for dinner at Kyan's tomorrow, and maybe pull the outdated canned tomatoes from the shelf. Is it real important to know soon?"

"Yes, it is, Mother! There are things that I need... want to figure out. Just as soon as you can. After bridge."

"Well, I s'pose I can make some time before I go. You seem all worked up and that always gives you the face pimples. I can call you back at this number?"

"Yes, Mother."

I sit on Dee's grape-and-tan living room couch and take in the room around me. Now that I know about her horrible past, it all seems to make sense. She wanted to create her own little fantasy world filled with her favorite colors. Her cartoonish style of decorating and living is more about hiding from her pain than about being different.

I lay my head on a burnt orange pillow, the same one that acted as a prop during my wild night with Nova's boyfriend, and promise myself I'll only nap for a minute. Phillip's face and his sweet, musky smell envelope my head. The next thing I know, the oven timer is going off. It's been almost thirty minutes.

Dee's oven and Mother's obviously cook at different temperatures; my casserole shows the telltale signs of an overly-crisped potato chip topping. I grab a blue paisley oven mitt and retrieve my masterpiece. Mother would have thrown out something this pathetic and given us canned peaches and bread for dinner. I'm not as picky.

The moment I close the oven door, my phone buzzes. I drop the mitt and run over to the couch, where my phone sunk between two cushions. When I finally wedge my hand in the right area, feeling bits of Dee's midnight snacks along the way, I see that I have a message from Phillip. Mother is calling and she won't call again.

"Mother? Are you still there?"

"What on earth took you so long? You knew I would call back."

"I've been making your spaghetti casserole," I say quickly. "I had to clean my hands before I could answer."

"Oh? Good that you're doin' some of the cookin'."

"So... what did you find? Was there any information I could use?"

I hear her unfolding paper, and then Kyan in the background, probably grumbling about her wasting her time on the phone with me when she could be kissing his feet or combing his hair. Doesn't he ever go home to his own family?

"Here it is... Let's see... '*My Dearest Harlen, I hope this finds you well...*'"

"You don't have to read the whole thing, Mother. Just the part about where he is and what he might be doing." I don't mean to be impatient.

"Ok, well... How's the little family... keeping the barn painted... kitchen table... Here's what you need."

We sit in silence for a moment. I want to reach through the phone and grab that piece of paper myself.

"Yes, it sounds like he traveled the Midwest, from trees to rocks to nothing of note at all... More about the farm... Oh, here. *'I have decided to settle in the South, where my animals and I can live in peace. Have found a nice young man to help with the feeding and care.'"*

My stomach sinks. A young man – like Dee's missing brother?

"Anything else, Mother?"

"Just to contact this Mr. Fortner in Connecticut if he had any more questions about the farm. That was his relation. Cousin, I think I remember."

"No, that's about it. What were you wantin' to find out again?"

I sigh. I can't tell Mother about my suspicions. She wouldn't believe me anyway. "Do you have contact information for the cousin?"

"No. We heard tell around town the cousin had died some time ago. Don't remember for sure why I know that. So that poor man was without a single relation. Not even a lady friend to keep him company."

It was foolish to think that he would have confessed more to my grandfather than anyone else.

"What was his name again?"

"Dmitri Baransky. Strange sort of name. S' that about it? I promised Kyan I'd bring dinner over tonight. Melanie has a headache."

More often than not, Mother puts her casserole dish and a loaf of bread in a little red wagon and pulls it down our driveway and over to Kyan's house. Her grandchildren have come to think of their grandmother as their cook and housekeeper.

"Oh, one more thing. Can you tell me the postmark on the envelope?"

I hear Kyan once more, grumbling in the background.

"I'm just about done, son," Mother replies in a syrupy voice she never uses to address me or Kenner.

"Let's see.... Fort Smith, Arkansas, looks like," she says.

"Thanks, Mother. I appreciate your help."

"Time to get that roast out of the oven."

She hangs up the phone before I have a chance to tell her anything about my life or my job.

I have time to create a rosy salad before Dee arrives, using cucumbers and tomatoes from her little year-round hothouse in the back yard and raspberries for a nice vinaigrette. I find some candles in one of her endless drawers in the kitchen and set them in the middle of the table, with two fuchsia placemats and mismatched water glasses to garnish the table. *Home Style* magazine it is not. But it looks like Dee.

I hear her humming before she walks in the door, an unidentifiable tune from her time. Probably something my parents would have listened to if they hadn't been so against listening to anything enjoyable.

She opens the door and jumps back, obviously startled by the scene. Normally she is the one preparing the food, comforting me after a miserable day with Nova.

"Well, I'll be gosh-danged, Keilah! You gave me a start. What's all this about?" She sets her purse on the couch and takes off her jacket.

"I just thought it was time I made dinner for a change. I can't cook like you, but I can give you a little taste of my home."

Dee glances at my overly-baked casserole and salad and tears come to her eyes. She puts her hand to her chest. "This is the nicest thing anyone has done for me in... oh, I don't know how long."

I pull the chair out and she sits down. I try not to stare eagerly while she dishes up the food.

"What... is this exactly? Lookin' as wonderful as it does."

"Take a bite first," I say.

She studies her fork for a moment before slipping it into her tiny mouth. "I don't think I've ever tasted this kind of cheese before. It's got a real smooth taste. My, this is impressive. Real good meal, Keilah."

"Do you like it?' I ask again.

"Oh yes, ma'am. Good stuff." She takes more on her plate and eats until the casserole dish is half empty. I hope she doesn't explode on my account.

I'm pleased with myself, even though I know she is just being nice. I had never seen Dee eat something from a box or bag and I'm pretty sure those crushed-up potato chips are the first she has ever sampled.

It's time to ask her about Gentry. I have to be delicate. She doesn't need more pain.

"Dee... do you have any photos of your brother? I'm just curious."

She stops chewing the extra potato chip topping she has scooped onto her plate. "I don't think so. We didn't do much in the way of pictures unless they were goin' to be used to swindle someone. We got some pictures taken to give to Uncle Delorian though. That was the only time I remember."

"Can I see? After dinner?" I ask, adding, "If it's not too much trouble."

"You don't have to wait for all of that. It's just sitting over there by Gentry's perch on the window." She gestures to the window sill full of miniature salt shakers and teacups, and in the corner, an unassuming family photo.

I hop up and grab the picture, forgetting my plan to stay calm and not make her suspicious of my actions. It is the picture I noticed on my first day. Right in plain sight. I pick up the black and white photo, framed in silver, spray-painted bottle caps. Young Dee is sitting on the floor with her hair in long, brown ringlets and straight bangs. She has a big bow that consumes most of her head. Her print dress is spread out neatly on the floor around her. She is a beautiful child with large eyes and a distinctly sad face.

Her parents sit sternly, in chairs to each side of her. They look like they could be siblings – each with the same smirk and curly, dark hair. Her Mother wears dark lipstick and a large-brimmed hat cocked to the side. Her father is in a suit that looks like it is a size too big, his curls slicked down at the center part.

Standing in between the chairs is Gentry. He is smiling a broad smile that displays a hole where his front tooth should be. His curly hair is combed over to the side and he is wearing suspenders to hold up his knee-length shorts. His happy demeanor seems out of place in this already sad and disconnected family.

"You were so beautiful, Dee. Just like a doll." I bring the picture over to the table and hold it up to her face to see if there are still remnants of this little girl in current Dee. The look of a survivor in those beautiful eyes has not changed a bit.

"Oh, I suppose…" She blushes. She gets up and starts to clear the dishes.

I put my arm on hers. "I'll do that. I'm treating you tonight."

"Now that don't seem right, after all your hard work," she protests. Nevertheless, she sits back down and looks at the picture again. "I think this was taken a good six months before we lost him."

"It must've been quite a big deal in a town this size." I clean the food off the dishes. I'm thinking about how everyone seemed to know the story of the One-Armed Man (the public story, anyway), even though they never talked about it unless they were in the museum looking at his picture.

"Everybody knew, that's for sure. People assumed it was my folks who were lazy and didn't watch my brother. Even though all of the kids in town – from poor to rich – played outside from dawn 'til dark without any adult supervision."

"I know. I think it makes people feel better to have someone to blame, no matter how irrational. If they can place the fault on someone else, then something that terrible will never happen to them." I try not to remind myself of Rosabel's death, how one little unruly child was the focus of all of my anger. It wasn't his fault. It was her father's. He had been the one who caused…

"I spent a long time thinking I made him disappear." Dee sighs. "That I had these powers that I pretended to have when I was playing in the yard. He was irritatin' and I was jealous of his attention from my folks. And then, one day, *poof,* he was gone. I thought, just like my folks had said, it was my fault."

I shake my head, not knowing what to say. How awful to grow up with such a burden on her shoulders. I knew my parents didn't exactly appreciate my being there, as I wasn't Kyan and I certainly wasn't the extra farm hand Kenner was groomed to be. But at least I had Rosabel. She shielded me from everything bad and each day I grew to appreciate her more and more. I didn't have to shoulder that kind of blame.

"Always thought if I could just find his bones and bury them, right beside my folks, then I could say, 'Y' see there? I lost him, but I brought him home for eternity.'"

I want so badly to be the one to do that for her. For once in my life, I want to be the hero. I tried once to be the hero and I failed miserably. But this is a new life in a new place.

"So... who was the gentleman you went home with the other night? Someone I should know about?"

Dee touches her hair. "Oh, Donald? The 'old buzzard', I call him. Always comes sniffin' around when he thinks his other prospects are dead in the water."

"Yeah, Donald..." I say absent-mindedly.

"Well, he is quite the lover. He can do things men half his age don't even attempt..."

I drift off, trying to remember if our local librarian in Pepperville had offered any further information on the One-Armed Man when she gave tours. She seemed to tell the same story my family did, of his innovation and bravery.

"Don't you think, Keilah?"

"What? I'm sorry, Dee, I missed it..."

"I said it was about time you found yourself a young man." She is winking hard.

At first, I'm confused. She must've found out about Phillip. I blush. "How did you... I don't know what you're talking about..."

"Oh, don't be a prude. He came by the Salty Gas 'n' Snacks to tell me. Like a true gentleman who doesn't just use your place like a brothel."

I am furious. It doesn't take long in this small town for word to get around about anything. If he told Dee, it won't be long before Nova finds out. That must be why he called.

"He shouldn't have told you! I was drunk and I should never have done that." The words don't match what I'm thinking. I don't regret anything that happened that night. Just that it had to be with Nova's boyfriend.

"Well, he's awfully cute. He always visits with me an extra-long time after he gets his gas. Always thought he would be a good catch. Don't think you need to feel ashamed at all."

This isn't a conversation I've ever had with someone out of my age group. But Dee isn't like any older person I encountered before.

"You gonna see him again? I can leave, you know, for the night, if you want some time for more hooty too..."

"I don't know... He's kind of Nova's property." Saying that out loud makes my chest fall with a thud.

Dee spins around in her chair and stares at me. "But he seems to suit you. More 'n that crazy gal. I don't think you should give it all up just yet."

I've never been in this situation. No one, not even Rosabel, has ever talked to me seriously about boys... men. Kenner just turned his back even though I'm quite positive he heard through the grapevine about all my one-night stands. And Mother's only concern was that I didn't find someone that would embarrass the family – someone without standing in the community.

"I'm tired, Dee. I'm going to bed."

"Well, you think on it. He's the one for you, Keilah. I'm never wrong about these things."

"Good night, Dee."

"Night there, Keilah. And thank you for the smooth cheesy goodness. Nobody has done something like that for me in a long time." She stops and turns around.

"You know, once I really started thinkin' about it, there was one more thing I remember about that man at the campfire. He definitely had lots of wavy brown hair and a beautiful face. Heck, I would've gone with him if he'd asked." She chuckles. "And the poor thing, he just had the one arm."

Chapter Twenty-Five

M Y JUNIOR YEAR, Father decided it was time I learn the basics of business. Because Sonnet had become a fixture at our dinner table, he thought it was a great idea to ask her father to take me under his wing at the bank and teach me the basics of accounting.

Albert Crandell readily agreed to help with my education but, at the time, he was spending a lot of his day out of the office on "special" work projects. I heard people gossip at the bank that he was having multiple affairs. I kept hoping someone would follow him and use that information to blackmail Sonnet.

One day one of the guys doing her homework did follow Albert to a run-down house outside of town. He waited several hours for Albert to emerge, and when he did, he looked disheveled. That person thought that would be enough information to scare Sonnet into leaving him alone.

Instead, Sonnet laughed in his face. Sonnet told him she already knew exactly what her father was doing. And how did he think she got her summer trip to New York City?

No one else had the nerve to follow someone as power-ful as Albert. He was as influential as his daughter, but on an adult level. I was a little scared to be in his office every day.

A tall man with Sonnet's long nose and thin wisps of dark hair over the top of a mostly bald head and square, gold-framed glasses, he commanded attention whenever he was in the room. The perfectly white teeth he displayed as he told his many stories about travels across the globe were mesmerizing. He had a different suit for each day of the week and gold rings on every finger. Father only wore his wedding ring on Sundays and told Mother more than once that it didn't seem right for a man to wear "baubles".

My first day, I showed up in my best dress (Rosabel insisted that she make me a new one) and a notebook in my hand. I expected he would instruct me for hours as I struggled to stay focused. Instead, he sat me next to his secretary's computer and patted my back. "Stella, show this fine young lady how I do my personal books. I'll be back in an hour."

It was very easy. I opened each bill and entered the amount needed to be paid for each business into the computer. The secretary printed out the checks and placed them on Albert's desk to be signed. It took us all of two hours.

One day I came in and Stella's desk was empty. The picture of her Bichon Frise, Booger, was gone and her scented candles were in the trash. I didn't know what to do at first, so I sat in her chair and imagined my life as an adult, coming into an office like this one every day and staring at the dark faux-wood paneling until five p.m.

Albert finally came in, adjusting his Thursday suit and

smoothing his hair.

"Stella has decided she can find greener pastures." He snickered. "We'll see."

I was hoping he didn't think I would do the rest of her job. I was still working at the coffee shop and I wasn't going to give that up for a non-paying job with creepy Sonnet's creepier father.

"From now on, you can do the books by yourself. You've done them long enough to know how it works, right?"

I nodded. It wasn't that hard. I just couldn't believe a man as important as Albert Crandall would trust me with something so personal. I came in twice a month and worked from a new computer Albert bought and set up in the corner of his new secretary's office. He never looked at the checks other than to sign them.

The job was so easy I got bored and one afternoon after Albert was gone, I opened his desk drawer to see what a man like that kept close. There were hundreds of keys. I began trying them in the drawers to his file cabinets, a few each day I was alone. Finally, one turned. I opened the drawer and then closed it again quickly.

As senior year drew closer, Rosabel talked about college. I didn't have any ideas about anything. Mother and Father only talked about my working for the farm and I didn't want to have to formulate a life plan for myself.

"We'll go to the junior college here, Robin. You and I, and then Sparrow will join us when he is old enough. You need an education for whatever comes next."

I shrugged. "What would I even study?"

"You'll take the basics for business. That will help you

with your farm work, and then when the time comes to spread your wings, you can take that knowledge with you. To your moon."

She always knew best.

Rosabel was a little girl with grown-up worries. From the age of five on, her parents discussed their finances with her. They wanted her to be aware of how much money they had so she didn't go off "half-cocked" and "spend like a Kennedy". If they were too drunk to buy groceries, I let her come to take what she needed from our kitchen.

They did create a college account for her, with little bits from their gambling winnings. They had started it back when they lived in Texas and reminded her frequently that this money would put her through college. They boasted that at one point the account contained three thousand dollars.

She was always so proud that her folks had done that. I think it was the one way in her entire life that they showed her they loved her, so she held on to that like a prized stuffed animal. Rosabel did have one crooked tooth. Top right. She asked her parents about it right after I got my braces. They said they didn't want to waste that kind of money when it could be going into her college account instead. They noted that lots of famous people had crooked teeth, including Mother Teresa.

One day, Rosabel visited me at the bank with tears in her eyes.

"I'm so sorry to bother you at work," she sobbed.

It was shocking to see this normally light and happy soul so distressed. "Let's go out in back. We'll have some privacy there." I guided her out the back door and down the rickety stairs to the alley behind the bank.

"What's going on?"

Rosabel took a hankie she had made and embroidered (with an R) from her purse and delicately blew her nose. "I went to the college today. I wanted to see what classes were available for the fall. They showed me the catalog and offered a summer course in child development. When I went to pay, the card I used wouldn't go through."

A cold feeling ran from my feet to my throat.

"I thought there had to be some mistake. So I went home and asked. It's all gone. All of it. You know where."

Rumor had it that Rosabel's father had almost run someone off the road on his way home from the track. He didn't even bother hiding it anymore. Suddenly I felt very guilty. It wasn't her fault she had to live like that – stepping over empty bottles and dirty dishes. I had been so lucky. Even if my parents didn't seem too interested in me, at least they made sure I never needed a thing.

"I'll take care of this. I'm going to make sure you start your orphanage on schedule. Don't worry."

I knew what I had to do. I went right home and begged Mother to put her through college. "We have enough money. Just think of what it would mean to her."

Mother shook her head. "We're not in the business of paying bills for others."

"But she's always been like another kid in this family. You know how horrible her life has been!"

I thought her face softened just a bit.

It was at that unfortunate moment that Kyan came into the room. There was no winning this argument with him involved.

"What's goin' on here?" he asked Mother.

"Keilah thinks we should fund her friend's college. The parents drank it all away." Mother clicked her tongue in disgust as if somehow this had been Rosabel's doing. "Not too smart."

"Then where does it stop? People will be lined up at the door wantin' us to pay their mortgages next," Kyan said, with his trademark sneer. "No sireee."

Mother nodded in agreement.

Tears streamed down my face. Kenner and I were nothing like them. "Don't you remember that we got this place practically for free? That grandfather got a handout to start his farm? Why can't we help someone else the same way?"

"You and your friend spent all your time playin' in the barn while Father and I were out makin' something of this place. We worked hard to make it what it is today. If you weren't such a spoiled brat you'd understand! I ain't got time for this nonsense." Kyan stormed out, slamming the screen door as he left.

I looked at Mother hopefully. Surely, she could find some generosity in her heart for Rosabel.

"Your brother is right, Katherine. Rosabel will get her education. She'll just have to work for it like everyone else."

That night I thought about all the times Rosabel had saved me. Ever since I met her, she had been my protector. It was my turn to fix things.

Chapter Twenty-Six

SANDY SALTS
2012

New York Register, 1934

Martin Baranski, age 45, was found dead this morning in an alley behind his apartment building. Martin was a successful banker on Wall Street for over 20 years. Alongside his father, he built up a business that survived the Big Crash and has continued to prosper. His colleagues will remember him fondly. Martin is survived by his dedicated wife of 19 years, Millie Sanderson Baranski, and an adopted son, Dmitri. No services will be held.

"That's really all I see here for Dmitri Baransky," Vanessa says, turning the screen back around after she lets me read the obituary of the One-Armed Man's father. "Your family friend is a man of mystery."

Vanessa generously agreed to open the library on a Sunday to help me in my search, when I could stand the mystery no longer. I want to find the fate of the One-Armed Man and put to rest my crazy thoughts about his involvement in Gentry's kidnapping once and for all. I was hoping the circumstances surrounding his father's death would provide some information. "There's nothing else? How can that be?"

Vanessa shakes her head. "You could do a public records search and see what comes up. That'll cost a little bit and, since he was older, he might not have a lot of information out there. Maybe he went by a different name?"

I remember my conversation with Mother and the letter he wrote to our family. "What about Fortner? Maybe Dmitri Fortner? His cousin had that last name."

"Hold on. That will take a few more minutes. Not the greatest internet in these old buildings."

I sit down on one of the bar stools and look around at the beautiful woodwork. It reminds me of my home. It always made me feel safe and secure knowing that someone had taken the time to stain and polish those beautiful railings and trims with such detail. It was a foundation, a bit of structure for Brownwell Farm and my world. I try to think about the type of person who would so lovingly craft such a masterpiece, to keep himself safe and secure, taking such pride in its creation. He doesn't sound like a kidnapper. I may have put this all together in my head simply for my convenience.

"Ok. This is interesting. Come take a look."

Vanessa turns the screen around again to show me the result of her search. An interview entitled "Locals Who Give Back" features a photo of someone who looks very similar to the One-Armed Man, sitting on a couch next to a young boy of ten or so. It is dated March 5th, 1946. My insides twist into knots.

"Do you want me to print it off?" Vanessa asked. "There's one more here too. An obituary."

"Print them both," I say, turning my back so she can't watch the color drain from my face.

I don't want to stand there with Vanessa watching as I read the article. I still feel like my family secrets should be guarded. "Thanks for doing that. I know you're busy with the mail and all."

Vanessa hands me the papers and smiles. "No problem. You've got your hands full with Nova. You can call me if you ever want to just go and hang out. Maybe vent a little."

"I'll see you at Dee's tomorrow night, right? Book club?"

I don't want to be anywhere near this bizarre book club, but I have no alternative place to exist during those hours. "Sure. I'll see you there."

AFTER WORK THE NEXT DAY, I open the back door and the scents of fresh chocolate chip cookies and cheap wine fill my nostrils. I hear women giggling and whispering in Dee's living room and realize it is the unavoidable meeting of the Salty Sinners Book Club.

For a few minutes, I stand by the back door, hoping they will soon become engrossed in their discussion and I'll sneak up the stairs to my bedroom unnoticed. From my vantage point, I can count at least eight heads in the other room.

A woman I recognize as a beautician from the shop on Main Street stands up. "Bow your heads, please. Dear Lord, please guide us as we discuss our readings today. Make our time educational, stimulating for those who need it, and worthy of the calories. Amen."

"*Amen.*"

"Ok, ladies, show of hands – how many finished reading *Handy Dan*?" Vanessa asks.

Seven hands pop up.

"Ok, great. Before we get to the juicy stuff," the room erupts in laughter, "I want to talk about the serious plot points in this story."

A lone hand persists.

Vanessa sighs. "Okay, go ahead."

"I had a question about them Ben Wa balls? Could a lady use a marble? And... I guess this is two questions... It don't seem logical that Dan could handle that while he's workin' his power tools."

"In a minute, Verla. I want to talk about the emotional issues Dan faced in dealing with his father's suicide first. Does anyone want to start?"

Dee stands up, her exceptionally tall hair wobbling. "I can surely understand his problems with his father. Ol' Mr. Fisher was just as closed off."

Several people mutter. "That alcoholic thing. It's bad news. Can understand why the father killed himself. I'd be ashamed too if I'd made a big show like that in front of my kids."

I grab three cookies and decide to make my move through the living room as silently as possible, but I'm not quick enough.

"Oh, Keilah! You joinin' us?"

The ladies all turn to stare at me. Everyone but Vanessa looks to be Dee's age. "Sit yourself, girl." Dee pats the folding chair next to her. "We're missin' a few today."

"I didn't read the book." I maneuver myself closer to the stairs.

"Well, you may have had some experiences to contribute," Vanessa pipes up, cocking her head to the side. The other ladies laugh, some covering their mouths.

"I..." There is a room full of judgemental faces, all women. Just like Mother. It feels like I'm back in Pepperville and everyone knows something but me. *Don't dwell on things, Katherine. You're down in the dumps because you think things need to be rehashed. No one wants to hear 'bout ugly events a second time. Just get on with your life and leave it at that.* A memory is bubbling to the surface I hadn't seen coming. "The only person I know who was an alcoholic was my best friend's dad. He was horrible. He ran her over and then killed himself. I guess that's all I know about that." I don't know why that just fell out, but for the first time, I've told people what has been pushed down inside for five years. Complete strangers. The words that tear at my insides every day. Tears begin to pour down my face, but I don't want to put on a show for these people. I turn around, facing the stairway so that I can wipe my face with my sleeve. The room becomes incredibly quiet.

Dee finally breaks the silence. "Gosh, I didn't know that one, Keilah. Seems like we coulda discussed that in private first."

"I can't imagine your pain," Vanessa adds softly.

"No, you can't." I am trying to disguise my sobs with coughs, so they think I choked on a cookie and not these horrible words I've spoken for the first time. "Rosabel's life ended because her father was a useless drunk who didn't care who he hurt," I continue, speaking to the worn, orange carpet on the stairwell. Now that it's coming out, I can't seem to stop it. I wish Gentry were sitting in his usual spot so I could look into his eyes and connect with his kind kitty soul. "He was on his way home from the track, like always. Ran her over. Then he killed himself like the coward he was before her funeral."

Someone in the room gasps.

It feels so good to let this out. But why did it have to happen in front of the Salty Sinners?

"I'm... not sure what to say. You never... in all our talks..." Dee's voice wavers. "You shoulda told me. You don't need to carry all of that, girl."

One of the ladies, I think her name is Ida, gets up and starts rubbing my back with a thick, warm hand. "You poor, poor thing," she says soothingly. I can smell cheap wine and the lavender caramels Dee made yesterday on her breath. "What you must've gone through. Losing your friend like that."

"No one wanted to talk about it. I felt so alone. She was my world." The tears keep coming and I'm not sure I want them to stop.

Another woman, I don't know her name, gets up and puts her arms around the two of us. And then another. I sob for a few more minutes in the comfort of the huddle of strangers, until the wound is covered again, this time by a blanket of peace. I wipe my nose on my sleeve one more time, realizing full well they are all watching. I turn around and face the rest of the women who now look at me with concern. Or is it pity? I feel completely drained. Thankfully there is a loud, booming sound coming from the driveway. Dee goes over and pulls the pale lavender curtain back.

"Phillip's truck. That's Keilah's boyfriend," she announces.

I realize that the makeup I took care to apply today must be all over my collar by now. I don't care. "He's not my boyfriend! I barely know him!" I say, more to the rest of the room than Dee. I don't want any of this making its way back to Nova.

"Well, whoever he is, you'd better high tail it on out there, 'fore he heads in here and we all know your business," Verla says, chuckling softly.

"Verla's right," Dee says. "Get on out."

I look through the window to see Phillip, dressed in a slim-fitting pair of jeans and a plaid button-up shirt, hopping down from his obscenely tall pickup. More handsome than I remember.

I meet him at the door, just as he's putting his hand on the knob.

"Keilah? Can we talk? You ok? Your face looks a little... weird."

"In your pickup. Too many nosy women inside."

Phillip pushes the newspapers to the floor and pulls me up to the seat beside him. I try to ignore the spark of electricity that goes up my arm as he touches it.

"I've been thinking about you. You're probably having a hard time understanding the Nova thing. It's just real complicated..."

I put my hand up. "Before you say anything else, you need to know that I used you. For the exact same irritating, blonde reason." I smile. "I have a habit of doing that, unfortunately."

Philip puts an arm behind us and looks out the window. His beautiful blond hair is tucked neatly behind his ear and a hint of a beard frames his face. He looks a little sad.

"So what do we do now?" he asks.

"I... don't..."

He drums his fingers on the steering wheel. "Look, you're different from people I meet around here. I'd like to see where this goes if you don't have someone else waiting for you back home."

I turn abruptly towards him. I don't know how to respond. No one's ever said those words to me and meant it in a positive way. Kyan always told me that I wasn't like anyone else, but he meant that as a warning, that I should stay out of the public eye.

"What about Nova? Are you really done with her? Is she ever really done with you?" I try not to think about his sad history and how alone he must feel.

Phillip smiles. "Here's what you don't know about her. I was her rebound guy."

"She does a lot of that rebounding stuff. Maybe you don't realize how long that list is..."

Phillip shakes his head. "You don't get it. She got married right out of high school – to a real abusive guy. Put her in the hospital twice."

I'm shocked to think of Nova in that position. She is a force to be reckoned with, just like her father.

"I can't imagine. She seems so strong and all..."

"Well, she wasn't. She was head-over-heels crazy for this guy and she decided she would do anything to keep him. That included keeping her bruises a secret from her daddy. I took her to the hospital both times. We drove thirty miles to the next town so none of the busybodies here would tell her family." Phillip sighs and leans back in his seat. "That went on for almost a year. When she left him, she told her daddy she was cheating, with me. Couldn't stand him knowing she had let herself get beaten every day, she told me. She still loved him so much that she didn't want Jack to take him into a field and shoot him like a wild animal."

Jack would not have tolerated anyone harming his girl. In this small town, he was an influential man. If he decided to get rid of that husband like a used rag, no one would say a thing.

"What happened to him? The husband? And why you?"

"He took off. I heard Las Vegas. Just the idea that his wife was with someone else, even though he knew it wasn't true, was probably too much for his ego.

"Hard to believe, but she was so funny. Every day on my break I went in to get coffee. She always made me feel better when I was pushing through one job, knowing I still had an entire shift ahead of me somewhere else. Like a mid-day refresher. She trusted me with her secrets and I wanted to help her."

"How could you... Nova had a sense of humor?"

"We made a deal to have this fake relationship to keep her safe. Nova and I had this understanding for a long time. Then one night we... things went to a different level."

I blush. The thought of Phillip with someone else bothers me more than it should. He isn't mine.

"I never had real feelings for her, other than sympathy until that night. I thought we were exclusive at that point. Then I started hearing about other guys and I thought, 'Okay, we never really made this official.' I was fine when she decided to be with other guys, for the most part. Until I found out it wasn't just one guy at a time and it wasn't just a casual thing. Then it really started to bother me. Kinda felt like I'd been used."

He places his hand on my knee. It seems like such an awkward thing to do with someone you've only really known one night. But I don't move it.

"I realized this was going nowhere. I wasn't mad so much about the other guys as what it meant for me. Making me a laughing stock for putting my life on hold that whole time. She doesn't need me anymore. She is divorced and can live her own life now. And, finally, I can live mine."

I nod.

"So... like I said before, Keilah, I want to see you again. See where this goes. I haven't stopped thinking about you since the other night. You ok with that?"

More than ok. "I do think you're a great guy, Phillip." I rub my forehead. Suddenly I have this overwhelming urge to pick my teeth. "I'm a bit of a mess. I don't know if you want that. I... just..."

"You wouldn't be interesting if you were perfect."

"No, I don't think you understand. I have to get these puzzle pieces in order. We have to tell Nova, for one thing... Actually, YOU have to tell Nova."

Similar to our last encounter, I reach out and pull him close. Maybe it's too much time away from people who are familiar, from the hugs I got every day from my customers back home. I need human contact. I push his face into my neck. His arms wind around my back and rub, up and down. He gently kisses the nape of my neck and I pull him closer.

Suddenly, I begin to shake, like I had that day at Jack's Beanery. I sit up quickly. "I'm sorry. I have baggage like you can't believe."

Phillip leans forward to brush my shared cookie crumbs from his shirt. "What's going on?"

I tell him about Gentry and Dmitri. I tell him about Rosabel's life and death, the same words that poured out in Dee's living room. Time disappears and the book club ladies begin filtering out. They are staring at me and Phillip.

"I've got to go. I... thank you for listening. Send me a text when you've straightened things out with Nova." I reach over and kiss him one last time.

I do my best to hop to the ground gracefully. I still don't understand what a person like Phillip would see in me. I've always been like the wallpaper on the wall. There, but not significant. Phillip is more a center-of-the-room kind of person.

It's at that very moment that I realize there is still a big hollow section where Rosabel used to be. Dee is great for conversation, but I never know when she'll get up and throw things. Phillip is the first person to just sit and listen without judgment. I want to thank him for that. I turn around but his truck is already gone.

I run into the house, this time not caring what anyone says on my way by. My heart feels almost light. I even slam the door shut, without worry that Gentry will be jumpy. For now, my focus should be the investigation into Dmitri's life so that I don't have any more outbursts like the one that just occurred.

Begonia Springs Journal, May 1950
Locals Who Give Back

Dmitri Fortner of Peachtree has been sharing his love of animals with the community for ten years. Thrice yearly he opens up his farm of exotic animals, all captured from the wilds of Africa, to the delight of the townsfolk. The cost of admission is donated to the children's ward of the local hospital.

The Local Order of Benevolent Men president settled in Georgia with his young ward, Colin Fortner, ten years ago. Colin was abandoned by unfit parents and soon taken in by Mr. Fortner. Our LOCAL WHO GIVES BACK hero didn't stop there. Soon he found a way to help the indigent, bringing boys from the State Home for Foundlings to his place on weekends to help with basic upkeep. Over the years, Our LOCAL WHO GIVES BACK has fostered many young boys and taught them about the care of wild animals. It is rare not to find young boys running here and there on his property.

Dmitri is himself a child of misfortune. After both of his parents died of illness, he was fostered and adopted by a wealthy socialite and her husband in New York. When both adopted parents passed, he vowed to use his inheritance to make others happy.

Our LOCAL HERO put all his misery aside so that he could help others, and that he has. In addition to his zoo time caring for young boys, Dmitri also finds time to visit inmates at the local penitentiary and plays tambourine for the city band.

Chapter Twenty-Seven

I KNEW THAT Albert had an account with Pepperville Appliance and Pizzeria. His wife liked to purchase new appliances every year because she wanted her kitchen to be updated in the latest colors. Sonnet always ordered pizza and charged it to her father, so I wrote checks to them once a month.

I decided that if I told Albert they wanted to be paid twice a month, I could take one of those checks and put it into my savings account for Rosabel's college. He had taken to signing a pile of blank checks so that I could print them off whenever I had the chance and mail them. For a bank manager, he paid very little attention to his own account.

It wasn't like real stealing. He was a wealthy man who wouldn't miss the money. His daughter was taking advantage of every kid in school in some way or another. This was a way to give a little back to the community. Like forcing him to give to charity.

I told Rosabel that Mother and Father had set up a scholarship fund. They didn't like people to know their business, so they didn't make this information public. She wasn't to say anything to them.

"But I must thank them for this great gift!" she protested. "What can I do?"

"Just make them one of your pies and leave it on the table. They'll be so happy to have something like that."

The next day, a peach pie, still sizzling, appeared on the grand Macassar Ebony table.

My family was used to Rosabel's kindness and didn't say anything beyond, "That's thoughtful of the girl."

I went to Pepperville Junior College and prepaid for Rosabel's fall semester with the money I took out of my savings.

We planned two classes together: American History and Beginning Literature. As with everything else in her life, Rosabel approached her classes with joy and exuberance. Every day after class we would meet in the student cafeteria and talk about what we learned over a shared sparkling water.

"I would have loved living in the early 1900s. Just to be around the country when brilliant minds were moving it forward. Charlie Chaplin and Thomas Edison – can you imagine being in a room with minds like that?" she asked excitedly.

I pinched up my face. "Really? So many layers of clothing. And stinky things, like outhouses."

Rosabel shook her head. "You're not seeing the bigger picture." Sometimes I felt like she was way too evolved to still waste her time on someone as simple-minded as me.

"I suppose," I said. "Everybody probably smelled so you were used to it..."

"And besides," she continued, "if I just painted my parents with a broad brush, the way others do, I wouldn't be able to appreciate them for the wonderful people they are.

Look at where I am! With such humble means, they managed to save enough to put me through college!"

"They saved and then lost, Rosabel. They aren't any good..." I turned away quickly. I didn't want to see the look of pain on her face. No matter how I tried, I was never a good person like her. I let out a puff of air and turned back around.

"I'm really glad you're here. I can't wait until you open your orphanage. Kenner and I will be right there." Another reason to feel guilty: my stupid idea to leave with Kenner. I had regretted the very next day making that statement.

"Remember your list? From sixth grade? Those are the things you need to accomplish."

I laughed. Then I looked at her face. "You're serious? I don't know what I did with that thing."

Rosabel's face was somber. "You don't have it because it's in my drawer. In my Folder of Life."

I couldn't believe it meant that much to her. "You didn't have to keep that..."

"Children are humans in the most honest form. You'll go back to look at your list and discover it's really who you are meant to be."

I shook my head. Even though she was brilliant and almost perfect, there were times when her idealized view of the world was just a bit off. This was one of those times. But I said nothing.

We walked outside together, feeling a rare bit of winter sun on our faces. "Do you want to study together for the finals tonight?" I asked.

She nodded.

"I have to pick up some things from the cleaner for

Mother and then I can…"

"It was a dog."

"What?" I asked, turning my body to avoid the sharp wind hitting my face.

"They bet my college money on a dog. Named Whatsitsname."

"Oh… Rosabel…"

She started laughing, which startled me. "It's funny, isn't it Robin?"

"I'm not sure…"

"That they thought the animal without an actual name was the best way to spend all of my college money."

I gave a half-hearted chuckle. "Yes, it is."

"I mean, if they spent my money on a dog named Lucky, then I would have at least lost it all to luck."

"Or Fate," I added. "To lose it all to Fate would be kind of hilarious."

We laughed together, back in our old rhythm.

"Work hard next semester and make some life plans," she said, suddenly serious.

I wasn't failing my classes, but I wasn't excelling either. "I don't have any life plans. I'm going to help you. That's all I know," I replied. It was safe, wrapping my future in hers. Maybe Kenner could shake Sonnet and we could just stay here forever. There was no way I could be the failure Kyan expected as long as Rosabel was by my side.

"You need to spread your wings a bit. You can do anything, you know."

I didn't.

"Do you know why I always wanted to go to the moon?" I asked. "I thought it would be so wonderful to be somewhere quiet and peaceful. But even more, so I could sit and observe life without actually having to live it."

She smiled. "That was then. There is so much for you to see. You'll find your moon here on Earth. Just wait. You'll be so busy observing one day that you'll look up and realize that you ARE actually living it."

I didn't realize how wonderful life was until the day Father called me into his office.

"We need to talk about your creative accounting, Keilah."

Chapter Twenty-Eight

SANDY SALTS

2012

Begonia Springs Journal, June 10, 1960

Dmitri Fortner, age 66, died yesterday of what some say was a broken heart. His young ward, Colin Fortner, had passed just six months prior. A beloved member of the community, he leaves behind a legacy of volunteerism and true selflessness that will never be forgotten. Dmitri's generosity extended to other locals down on their luck as well; he helped as a volunteer fireman and delivered meals as a part of the Meals for the Mending program. In addition, any poor soul down on his luck or without family could count on a turkey delivery courtesy of Mr. Fortner and his son every Thanksgiving.

Mr. Fortner will also be remembered for his wondrous zoo of exotic animals. He shared his large "pets" with the community during the annual Big Cats for Charity Dinner. As with everything, Dmitri was generous in allowing the community to see his animals while enjoying an evening of entertainment, all for the benefit of the local Home for Wayward Youth. "All I want is to make others happy," he told his friends repeatedly.

Please plan to attend his celebration of life this Saturday, at 2 pm at the county fairgrounds. A large crowd is expected, so plan for the weather as you may be standing in line.

At first, I thought Vanessa had given me the wrong obituary. I study the large picture on the other page and, sure enough, it is the same One-Armed Man whose large portrait hangs in the Pepperville Farm and Ranch Museum, his long wavy hair now grey with age. His face looks unnaturally smooth with just a few wrinkles beside his eyes. He still has an engaging smile and piercing blue eyes. He has certainly become a pillar in his community. Almost too perfect.

Gentry's disappearance pops back into my head. *Only people who have something to hide change their identities. Don't they?* Dmitri Baransky, the One-Armed Man who made a quick exit from Pepperville after his mother's death, became Dmitri Fortner seemingly overnight. He offered my grandfather this incredible gift, his entire world, only to steal a piece from someone else's? It didn't make sense.

What if, instead of just feeling guilty about what his animal had done, he also wanted to leave before another secret came to light? Kenner and I would camp out in the backyard on those warm summer nights and tell each other horror stories about Millie.

"What if she had a knife in her purse? That she was going to use to stab the One-Armed Man and live in our house?" Kenner made dramatic streams of light on the side of the tent. *"And then just like, whoosh, he came up behind her and got her first?"*

"Yeah!" I said excitedly. *"Like that movie Psycho. She*

was going to keep him in the attic forever. But he found out and killed her first."

"*Right here – where we're sleeping!*" We squealed in unison.

Mother hated that we talked about Millie. She was a constant presence but a subject that was off-limits. "You children quit gosspin' about others and get to bed. Don't need to be spreadin' nonsense all over town, y' hear?"

"You are thinking the worst of someone who gave you their best, Robin." That's what Rosabel would say. And then to add salt to my wound, she would add, "What is it in your life that is causing you to take out your pain on someone else?"

Maybe after all of this, what he really, truly wanted was to make amends. Perhaps taking Gentry and trying to give him a better life was his "I'm sorry". And my misery? Nova, for one. Each day I come home from work with so much tension in my shoulders you can practically bounce a quarter off my shoulder blades. I would actually enjoy my job if it weren't for that. I need to nap on things and see what happens.

I dream of Dmitri reinventing himself in Sandy Salts, just as I had. Shocking Nova with his animals and charming Dee with his smile. He is familiar and comforting, a piece of home transplanted to Sandy Salts. Suddenly his tiger appears out of nowhere, bouncing to the back of the shop where Lorraine always stands, checking her phone. He consumes her in one gulp, seemingly unnoticed by everyone but me.

I awake with a start, realizing I'm alone in the dark, with the curtains shut. In all of the years since Rosabel's death, I've always left the curtains slightly open, to keep a sliver of light, maybe of hope, coming into my room. Even though the nightmares that used to plague me have gone, I feel like they too will return without the light. To go to sleep without it feels like I've given up on living. Hurriedly, I open them to the dusty, orange sunset that is a daily display in Sandy Salts.

I go downstairs to see what kind of leftover baked goods from yesterday are lying around and find a note on the counter:

Off to the dance. Hoping to meet up with Stanley. No gas and lots of moves. I'll tell you about that one later.

PS – Want to hear more about your friend and her father. Shoulda mentioned that before now.

Dee

Maybe Vanessa is up for more conversation.

Hey, just wondering if you could help me find more information on Dmitri Fortner. Anything at all. Thanks. Keilah.

I'm halfway through the whole-wheat applesauce donuts with maple drizzle when my phone buzzes.

Meet me at the Sandy Bar and Grill. I've already started ☺

I tense up. It's been two years since I've stepped foot inside a real bar. When I fell into that hole after Rosabel's death, it was the only place I could go to escape the stares of everyone in town. Even Father's friends who frequented the bar pretended like I didn't exist when I sat down beside them on a bar stool. It was a relief to feel anonymous. I could be like everyone else in town.

Then it had become an ugly crutch, and my drinking became less of a hobby and more of a need each and every day. It wasn't something I did for fun, it was something I did in place of it.

Today is certainly a different day. In a different town. I pull a comb through my hair without bothering to use a mirror and head off to meet Vanessa. I can smell the grease from the grill before I walk in the door.

I look around the dimly-lit room as the familiar feeling of hopelessness creeps in. The space is filled with others trying to forget their lives and I think briefly about turning around and leaving before I spot Vanessa in the corner booth. She waves and raises her drink, something blue with a big umbrella in it.

"Thanks for meeting me." I slide across the duct-taped seat.

"What do you want? I'm buying." She smiles. "This thing," she points down at the swimming pool of ice and alcohol in front of her, "is really... bad. But after about ten minutes, I seemed to stop caring."

I notice there is another glass equal in size sitting empty beside it. I shake my head. "No thanks. I had a little more than I needed the other night and made some questionable choices."

"Oh... I get it." Vanessa winks. "We've all been there." She stirs her drink with her straw and then takes a long sip. "I gotta ask you – what's with your friend? Her dad killed her? That's some messed up stuff."

"Yeah. She stopped to help this couple with a flat tire. The kids were running around on the road and Rosabel tried to keep them contained while the parents changed the tire." I start shaking but pull my arms across my chest, hoping she wouldn't notice. "Out of nowhere, this drunk driver, Rosabel's dad, plows right into her."

"That's bizarre and so tragic. And then he ended it all? Out of guilt? Wow."

I nod, pulling my arms in tighter.

"Well, if you ever need to talk, I mean in-depth, let me know. So, was that on your mind tonight, or something else? You look like you have the weight of the world on your shoulders."

Dee. Gentry. The One-Armed Man. Kenner. Phillip. Yes, it feels like the entire world.

"I just want your opinion on something," I say. Slowly, I tell her the story of Dee's brother and what Bart and Moses told me. Then I read her the obituary and tell her everything I know about the One-Armed Man. Telling Phillip and now Vanessa the secret of our farm seems wrong but so freeing. No more secrets. I want to tell her more. About my mistakes. But I don't want to scare her away.

"So, what do you think? Am I right to be suspicious? It's a strange coincidence, right?"

"Well... it could be this inappropriately-named drink talking, but I definitely think there is more to the story of your Dmitri. That obit is very telling. Not a lot of back story there. Hold on a sec..." Vanessa leans back in the booth and closes her eyes. "That's really hitting me now. I don't drink much, and now I remember why. Really counterproductive to the gallon of coffee I drink every morning."

I shove my water to her side of the table. "Here, drink this. I know from experience you don't want to be dehydrated." She leans forward and takes several big slurps, half of it landing on her shirt.

She sits up straight, but her eyes are looking droopy. "Okay, that's better... Where was I?... Oh yeah... When there is someone, like a drifter who just happens to be in town and their jig is up, if you know what I'm saying, I figure I should give them a respectable goodbye. I've written some great stories about people, but I always make them vague. 'John so-and-so had been in town for a few months and was a businessman.' Something like that. This guy... well, this guy was somebody important. We should've had an entire account of his life. His big cats... obvious... obi... obviously, there should have been something about this son that was so important he couldn't go on."

"So, what do you think happened?" I'm getting anxious, knowing Vanessa's behavior all too well. Soon she'll be slurring her words and I'll have to get her home before something really messy happens.

"I think... I think..." Her eyelids flutter. "I think that your man Dmitri wrote out a detailed obit before he died. So much easier when they do it for you..." Her head slumps onto the table. I look over at the bar and motion for the bartender to help me.

I dig through her purse until I find her wallet and her address as a man at the bar, who I remember for his daily caramel latte with an extra shot, offers to help me get her home. It is so much nicer being on the sober end of things.

After we tuck her into bed, I turn to leave and notice her

walls are covered in a variety of obituaries she's collected. I glance at the ones featuring prominent politicians like John F. Kennedy and Ronald Reagan. To the side are peacemakers like Gandhi. In between those obituaries are the regular folks – people who have accomplished great things on a smaller scale. There's a lady who rescued cats from bad homes and a man who gave every penny he made to buy band instruments for children. Amazingly, she has collected them from all over the world.

"Not that lipstick shade. You'll look like a two-dollar hooker," Vanessa murmurs before rolling over. I decide it won't hurt anything if I stay for a while and read more of her walls. If she needs to get to the bathroom in a hurry, she won't make it by herself through the heaps of clothes. She may be the master of her day but she sure hasn't figured laundry into her schedule.

Some of the stories really move me. The things people have accomplished in their lives is amazing. From traveling the world to helping others with no expectation of return. My Rosabel's obituary would have found its way to Vanessa's wall, had she lived long enough to accomplish her goals. These are her people. I shiver.

I decide to give it fifteen minutes longer before I leave. Vanessa hasn't moved in a while and I've found a trash can to set beside her. She'll be fine. I'll have to ask her about all of these obituaries tomorrow.

On the bottom row of the wall containing the obits of Audrey Hepburn and Indira Gandhi, something catches my eye. There is a half-page photo of a young man with the words, PAID OBIT over the top:

Colin Fortner, age 25

Young Colin succumbed to injuries he sustained from a car-pedestrian accident. A true gentleman with musical genius far beyond his tragic few years, Colin often entertained sick children in the local hospital with his ukulele and his beautiful tenor voice. "The gifts you're given are meant to be shared," he would often tell his legions of friends and fans.

Colin was orphaned at a young age and spent his formative years as the ward of Dmitri Fortner. He excelled at Brookner Academy for Young Men and, upon graduation, began teaching others his joy for music. When he wasn't entertaining at the local VFW, he also gave tours of Fortner Farm, where young children stood in awe as he talked to the wild beasts. Brilliant, funny, and immensely gifted, he will be missed most especially by father and mentor, Dmitri Fortner.

Chapter Twenty-Nine

JOURNAL – PEPPERVILLE
2006

"**I** DON'T KNOW what got into you. You weren't raised to steal from others. I can understand once or twice, seein' how much you can get away with. Young folk always have to try dumb things. But you did this for months."

It was actually over a year.

"I've taken care of our debts to the Crandalls. I'll be takin' the debt out of your savings as well. Keilah, I just don't know what to say. You've disappointed me more than I can put into words."

I should have told him I was doing it for Rosabel. Helping her in a way he and Mother should have. I wanted him to know that I didn't take anything for myself. I just took enough to pay her tuition and no more. I was trying to repay her for all the years she had helped me. She inspired me to help her. If they really loved me, they would have wanted to show her their appreciation as well.

She brought pies and muffins and beautiful tablecloths to thank them. But they never noticed. It was something she would do anyway, and they had grown so accustomed to her bringing delicious sweets and smells into our kitchen that they didn't think anything of it when they came with more regularity. More than once she wanted to write them a heartfelt note of thanks for the secret scholarship. I reminded her that Mother and Father were very private and something like that would make them feel embarrassed.

"I'll make them proud, Robin. I might even name my orphanage after your family. 'The Brownwell Home for Special Children.'"

It seemed ironic to name something after people who couldn't muster interest for more than one child. "Don't do that, Rosabel. Give it a name that makes people smile. But thank you."

All these things should have been discussed with Father that snowy day in his office, as I swiveled nervously in the leather guest chair. Instead, I chose to stay silent. I wanted him to understand without my verbalizing. To see into my soul just as Rosabel had all those years ago and realize that I was someone special just trying to do good things in the world.

"Of course, you won't go back to the bank. I offered Mr. Crandell a written apology from you. He said no. You're lucky he's not goin' to take it to the police. He's had a run-in with the chief or else he would have, I'm sure. Makes things real awkward, what with his daughter datin' your brother. I think you'll be grounded for a month or two, other than the hours that you're working at the coffee shop."

I nodded.

"And you won't mention a word of this to your mother. No one else needs to hear 'bout what happened. It would just embarrass her to know she had a daughter like this. She's always thought... Well, on top of that, she would worry her bridge club might find out. No, we'll keep things just between us. That's what's best for the family."

I looked at him one last time with my brows raised. A hopeful look, that he would see the real me. Just like the One-Armed Man and my Rosabel, I was a person who helped others. He stared at me with hurt in his face. "Anything you want to say?"

"No." I started to get up and then I sat back down. "Father, I found the letter. Our letter. The one Grandpa wrote about the One-Armed Man."

Father's back stiffened. "What're you doin' in my private things? How many more problems you gonna cause?"

"It was in... I was... looking something up for Mr. Crandall and I found all sorts of photocopied letters and documents. All in a file in his desk. There was a sticky note on the top with your name. That's why I read it."

He leaned forward and rested his chin in his hand. "So you know." He stared at me for a long time and then drew in a deep breath. "That was with my will. In my safety deposit box. Planned to have that read after my death."

"It said... It said that you were supposed to destroy it after you read it." I was risking further punishment by challenging him, but I wanted to know.

"Seemed too important – a handwritten letter and all. Just wanted you and your brothers to find out after I was gone. We're good, upstandin' people. Your grandpa and I worked hard to make this farm what it is today. We earned everything we have now. That one event don't define us, horrible as it is. I just didn't want you knowin' this young. Children shouldn't have to bear that bur..."

"I already knew, at least I had an idea. Kyan used to scare us when we were little by telling us there was a dead lady in the back yard. He said her hands crawled out of Mother's begonia bush every Halloween. That's how I learned what the word 'dismembered' meant."

Father shook his head. "He heard me talkin' to your mother one night. Made him promise never to speak of it. Thought he knew better than to talk about it with young ones."

"What happened to him? Do you know? Did the One-Armed Man go on to have a good life?"

He sighed. "He sent one letter to Grandpa, sounded like things were ok. Other 'n that, we didn't hear a thing. It was better that way."

I had almost forgotten why I was sitting in his office, with us carrying on an almost-normal conversation. I was hoping Father had forgotten as well. That I had disgraced him and our entire family by stealing for Rosabel.

"Seems there are things that need my attention at the bank. You were right to tell me. I s'pect you know the words in that letter don't leave this family."

I looked at the floor, bracing for the rest.

"But nothin' changes the fact that you stole from your employer. Almost ruined the family's good name. People expect more of those who have more – you know that. I thought you were a better girl than that."

I gulped.

"D' ya have anything else?"

I looked up at him, searching his face for some connection. Something to affirm our kinship and assure me we would grow as father and daughter. I found nothing. "No, Father."

He squinted for a moment. "Then you're free to go."

That night at dinner, Mother told a long story about the pair of dead deer she found beside the road. Father and I pushed our food around our plates. Kenner had brought Sonnet home for dinner, but they both decided they weren't hungry, which meant they spent the dinner hour giggling in the living room until we were done so they could take the leftovers to his bedroom.

"My word, it feels like someone died. Was it someone we knew, Kenneth? I don't recall seein' that in the paper today."

"It was a long day. I'm goin' to head up." Father got up from the table and left. I looked at his face one more time, to see if he had any signs of anger. His mouth was tight and pulled down at the corners.

"Are you sick? I was thinkin' you seemed off today. I have a real sense about these things." Mother gathered the sherbet dishes from the table.

Father paused for a moment, looking me dead in the eyes. It was the last time in his life he ever locked eyes with me. "You're never wrong about folks, that's for sure."

Chapter Thirty

FAREWELL
2007

"**K**EILAH, REMEMBER THAT YOU have to look beyond the outhouses to see the beautiful landscape."

That was the unimportant thing Rosabel said to me that morning, the last time I would ever speak to her on the phone, or anywhere. It's funny how you expect something profound out of the last conversation, not a patient reminder. "But such-and-such always acts like every question is directed just towards him," I had protested before the phone disconnected unexpectedly.

I had two finals and then I was going to study for a third. She had to work in the coffee shop, or rather was "lucky as a bird in a two-story birdhouse" to make lattes and mochas all day. We were going to meet at 4 p.m., as we always did. Sometimes we went to her house and sat on her porch for hours, just talking.

When I told her that the "scholarship" she had been receiving wouldn't continue for her sophomore year, she shrugged her shoulders and said, "I've been so fortunate to have this year. I'll get some loans, or I'll save up and do it with my own money. Don't worry, Robin. Things work out the way they should."

Father had not taken the money out of my savings account yet. I wasn't sure if this was some kind of test, to see if I would try and remove it on my own as someone of my character would do, or if he had forgotten. It was so tempting to use it to pay for another year of Rosabel's school. But I didn't.

Kenner was going to start college in the fall, a fact she found very amusing.

"Sparrow and Robin in college together? Who will be the taskmaster?"

We laughed about that, even though we knew that, in reality, Kenner's mind was not his own. He was so controlled by Sonnet, who was still in high school, that he wouldn't dare sign up for any classes without her approval. Rosabel could find the solution to any problem in our world, except for the problem that was Sonnet.

That morning had gone just as they all had. I went to my finals just wanting to get through them and move on. Another semester, another few months closer to finishing my degree. And then... I didn't know what came next. I finished the first exam and headed to The Abyss, a sunken lounge area where all the students met up between classes.

No sooner had I sat down then I heard people whispering around me. I tried to think about what I had done. Father wouldn't have told. But it was a small town and people found out whether it came by public announcement or by whispers. I tried to remember Rosabel's admonition from that morning, and forget about the sounds around me while I studied.

After several minutes of hearing my name being whispered, I lost my tolerance. "Whatever you have to say, SAY IT!" I yelled. The entire lounge area fell silent. I packed up my books, ready to leave school early and go home. I could tolerate Kyan's sideways why-are-you-here-and-not-working-somewhere looks for the afternoon if I had to.

"We're so sorry, Keilah. We just heard."

I looked at the group of them, all with sad faces and the uncomfortable air of being in the room when someone is about to get the worst news of their life.

"What? Did something happen to Mother? Is it Kenner?" My mind was racing with horrific possibilities.

One older student, who had played the bass drum in band with me both semesters, put her arm around me, and sat on the edge of my chair, uncomfortably close. "Your friend. Rosabel."

I couldn't comprehend. What could happen to her? She was the best person in the whole world. I always believed there was some kind of invisible protective shield around her at all times as a reward for her good deeds. "Is she sick?" I asked.

The woman shook her head. "No. I'm afraid it's much worse than that. There was an accident this morning out on the highway. Pickup and pedestrian."

No, no, no. This wasn't happening. Not to me. I felt chills going down my back, the kind I usually got right before some terrible illness.

"It... was bad."

"Will someone take me to the hospital?" I asked. They all froze in place, like my voice wasn't making an actual sound. They were sucking the air – my air – out of the room. "Will any of you... Forget it. I'll just get there myself."

I got up, my books and purse falling to the floor as I headed for the door. I couldn't stand these faces staring at me anymore. Someone followed me. I only know that because magically my purse ended up beside me as I collapsed on the grass outside, my head touching the ground, my hands grasping for something, anything to hold on to.

"Maybe you should call someone..." a disconnected voice said.

All of me, everything that I knew to be Keilah Brownwell up to that point in my life, came spilling out onto that grass. As much as I had in this world, from physical things to the reflection I saw in the mirror each day, they were all held together in a neatly-constructed basket, formed from the personality and guidance of one person. All of the memories and instruction and years of love and laughter oozed out of the gaping wound this news had caused, leaving nothing inside of me but dark, empty space.

I don't know how long I spent on that lawn, but it seemed dark when I heard Kyan's cold voice. "Stand up now, Katherine. Quit makin' a scene," he demanded. I couldn't.

Finally, he scooped me up like a sack of grain and put me in the back seat of his car. We rode the thirty-minute drive home in silence. I had no thoughts to think, no words to say. I guess Kyan didn't either. When we arrived at our farm, he took me in and put me on the couch. I didn't see him again until the funeral.

Mother came into the room, her heavy feet an unwelcome sound. "Brought you some milk and leftover squash casserole." I turned my face to the couch, wanting her to leave me alone.

She patted my hip. "Come on, now. You need to eat

something. Or get up to your room," she said gruffly.

"Leave me, please," I said with someone else's voice – someone still alive on the inside.

"You hear the whole story?" she asked, pushing as much of her body against me as would fit.

I didn't reply.

"I called Virgil Jacobs, from the sheriff's office. He told me she stopped to help some family. They were having car trouble on the side of the road and the kids were runnin' wild on the side of the highway. She pulled over to help with the kids while they waited for the tow truck."

I could see Rosabel doing just such a thing. Naughty kids running amok on the highway was a situation made just for her. But it should have ended with them giving her a reward – several hundred dollars she would have put towards her education. We would be meeting for dinner right now and laughing at the absurdity of it all. The emptiness inside me was beginning to fill with pain.

"She sat with them in the car for a bit," Mother continued, oblivious to my suffering. "Then the couple started to argue about one thing or another. One of the kids got upset and went out to see what the ruckus was about. That's when Rosabel went chasin' after him."

I couldn't take it anymore. I tried to find music in my head – any song I could play to drown this out. *Gotta Dance. Gotta sing, gotta dance.* Only one, wildly inappropriate song left inside my brain.

"Little boy just darted right out there. Course she went after him. Didn't look for cars herself."

There was no way to block this out. The images. The thought of my friend giving her life for a child. As awful as it sounded, it seemed exactly as her death should be.

Mother patted my leg. "You'll feel better in the morning. Can't entirely blame her. Tragedy is what it is."

I turned and looked at her, for just a moment trying to understand how she could be so heartless. She didn't know how to communicate with me. This was all she had to give. Mother at her most basic. There was no way I would feel better by morning. Or any morning.

"I'm going to bed now," I said.

"That's right. Get some rest."

As I willed my feet up the stairs one at a time, I could hear murmurs of conversation from the kitchen. Mother and Father, discussing the day's horror. It was odd for him to be home in the evening before he had chatted with Kyan about the day's accomplishments. I hoped he had come home to comfort me, so I paused on the step, waiting for gratification that never came.

"She'll come through it, just give her time."

"Things happen. No rhyme or reason…"

Nothing about this was fixable in my mind, but I didn't have the energy to go back down and tell them. My bed never felt quite as good. The dark of my bedroom was a relief. I could hide away and pretend I was someone else. Someone who knew how to live without half of their soul.

My door opened a crack. "Keilah?" It was Kenner. "Can I lay down here with you?" His voice sounded cracked and hoarse.

"Mmmm…" I groaned.

He laid down on top of my covers, just like he did when we were young and were planning our next story in our little kingdom. Unlike those times, when his hair smelled of baby shampoo and little boy sweat, he smelled of cigarette smoke. One of Sonnet's many bad habits. Normally that smell alone would have caused me to push him away. But tonight, I needed something that felt familiar.

"I can't believe it – any of it," he said. "I can't believe she's gone."

I rolled over and pulled his arm around me.

"Don't blame him. He did his best."

My mind clicked. Rosabel's father. That stupid drunk. He had almost run over several people around town on his way home from the bar. It was bound to happen. "A father is supposed to take care of his child. No matter what."

I couldn't tell him that it was my punishment for daring to think I could help her. I couldn't say anything. I just needed to be.

Chapter Thirty-One

SANDY SALTS
2012

H E'S STRIKING, this Colin Fortner. His hair is dark and wavy, similar to Dmitri's, and he has big, brown eyes. His upper torso is draped over a guitar and his two dimples frame a perfect smile. It may be another time and place, but I would recognize that face, those eyes anywhere.

"He ate tacos in his spare time," Vanessa murmurs. One leg comes out from under the covers and hit the floor with a thud. Soon she is snoring – a deep, rhythmic *hhhnaaah!* that reminds me of the times Mother would nap on the couch and Kenner and I would giggle on the stairs at her strange sounds.

I look at her and suddenly feel suspicious. Was she playing me (and the entire town of Sandy Salts) this whole time? Did she know all along what had happened to Dee's brother? I envision this scenario in my head, one of Vanessa coming to this small town to write for the newspaper and discovering she can manipulate them all. She pulls their strings by keeping the answer to this mystery to herself. She could quite possibly be a higher-functioning version of Sonnet and I've fallen easily into her trap.

Expect the best from people, Robin. Rarely will you be disappointed.

I know by now that Rosabel's words don't always apply to real life. The kids who shoved me behind her back were always nice to her face. Sonnet was a disappointment from beginning to end. It was a hard day when I had to come to terms with the fact that my Rosabel couldn't solve every problem or fix every person. But didn't she bring me here, to Sandy Salts, to meet Vanessa? Didn't she want me to help Dee find her brother and end this mystery once and for all? To help someone in a way I couldn't help her?

I remove Colin's obituary from the wall and check on Vanessa one more time before I leave. As I reach for the front doorknob, I notice a large typed paper she's taped to the wall. "Live today like it's your last. Make others feel like you know it's theirs."

I pull the door shut and wrap my coat tightly around myself, bracing for the unforgiving, sharp wind. As I walk nervously down the three blocks to Dee's house, I think about the Vanessa I know from my short time in Sandy Salts. She isn't someone who would purposely hurt Dee. She is the first – and only – person to treat me like a friend. It is such a weird coincidence, though, her finding that obituary out of the thousands she had most likely accessed.

I toss and turn all night, trying to put the pieces together in my head. They just don't fit. I keep coming back to Dmitri, the kind person who wanted nothing more than to better those around him. Why would he take a child? Or buy one? If he had known how poor Dee's world would be without her one-and-only brother, surely, he would have reconsidered.

When the alarm goes off, I've been experiencing the only solid sleep of the entire night. I throw my pillow in the general direction of the clock, hoping it will stop the infernal beeping on its own and I can go back to my rest.

After finding the least irritable clothing to put on my sluggish body, I'm surprised to hear Dee clattering around in the kitchen. As I get closer, I recognize the smell of her chocolate-chocolate chip muffins baking. I'm not expecting to see her this morning and it is bothering me. Of all the mornings to have her underfoot in the kitchen, this is the absolute worst.

"Mornin' Keilah. How'd ya sleep?" Dee says all-too perkily.

"Awful. Worse than awful. I...."

"You remember I told you about Stanley? Well, I told him straight away I was looking for a shook up and..."

"It's 'hook up', Dee. And I don't want to know," I say grumpily.

"Well, that's fine. But that Stanley – ooh la la! He's got the moves, let me tell you. I called my boss and told him I wasn't comin' in this morning. Let him cover for once. Gonna do some stretching and then see where things lead." She smiles and winks at me.

"Oh... he's here?" Suddenly I feel like I need a shower.

Dee nods vigorously. "Told him to stay put. Cause I'm gonna..."

I put my hand up. "I get it. I'll just head out early. I have some things I need to do anyway."

"Oh sure, honey. We can talk later. I'll have lots to tell you."

I turn and walk out the door without acknowledging her. I dread the inevitable rehash of her experiences. They will be followed by teeth-picking and awkward silence on my part.

Since I have extra time to walk to work today, I move slowly, breathing in the dry air and appreciating the big oddly-shaped rocks. It is nothing like Pepperville. The exact opposite, in fact. I have come to appreciate that, even though it lacks the green rolling hills of home, there is a certain beauty to this landscape.

The One-Armed Man – Dmitri must've had the very same feeling; leaving behind our farm for brand new scenery. Everything was different. The majority of the people in my hometown never left, never knew something different existed beyond our familiar buildings and faces. I'm lucky, really, being able to see this for myself. And maybe Dmitri just wanted to offer the same experience to a small boy in need, one with an uncertain future in Sandy Salts.

How will I tell Dee if this is truly Gentry's death I've found on Vanessa's wall? Will she be receptive? Will she appreciate the fact that someone tried to help Gentry, or feel resentful?

During a quick break in the morning rush, I go out to the front porch where Bart and Moses are involved in their usual game of chess. I give them a brief history of my search, ignoring their frowns, and then show them the obituary, hoping for a big reaction.

Bart shrugs his shoulders. "Doesn't look familiar to me," he says, returning quickly to his game.

"The eyes, though! They look exactly like Dee!" I protest.

Moses put his hand up before I even moved to his side of the table. "Concentrating."

I let out a big sigh.

As I head back inside, Nova motions to me. I ignore her and clean tables. Soon I hear the heavy sound of her footsteps behind me.

"Keilah! Are you deaf or just too dense to respond when someone speaks?"

I spin around. "I didn't get any sleep last night and I don't have time for your..."

"I can tell you didn't sleep," Nova interrupts.

I'm surprised that she would take that much notice of my appearance.

"It looks like you just rolled out of bed and stumbled in. Good god. Did you even run a brush through that nest on your head?" She pauses for a minute to shake her head before grabbing the dirty dishes from the next table over.

I put my hand to my hair and realize that I haven't, in fact, brushed it at all. I blush, at a loss for words, for once.

"I... was busy, and then..."

"I'm staying all day today. Daddy said he might stop by to check on me. Why don't you go get that mess cut and styled? Let a professional try and fix... that." She waves vaguely at my head without looking up.

I haven't gotten my hair styled since I came to town. Nova is probably right about the benefits of a good haircut. I hate to admit it to her, but for once she knows what she's talking about.

"Thanks, Nova. That's very kind..."

"Kind has nothing to do with it. You're embarrassing me. I don't want the customers thinking you're growing crops in that thing," she snaps.

I remember the beauty shop on Main Street, the one I

had entered my first day in town. Those women made me feel so uncomfortable. I'm a different person now, a stronger person. It's time to put on my Rosabel hat and think the best of people.

"I need my hair cut," I say to the C-shaped woman from the Salty Sinners Book Club. She comes around the counter and attempts to run her fingers through my hair. Her long nails get stuck and no amount of coaxing seems to loosen the grip of my angry ginger curls.

"Caroline? Bring me some deep conditioner please," she calls out. "Don't worry, honey." She pats my arm with her free hand. "This happens all the time."

For the second time today, I try not to be embarrassed by my lack of attention to my appearance. Mother would be completely horrified by this scenario. There was a time when I would have been almost giddy sharing this with her, emphasizing the public shame I was bringing upon the family.

"Lots and lots of split ends. How long's it been for you, Keilah? S'pose Jack keeps you so busy at that coffee shop that you don't have the time to get over here. I could put some highlights in for you too."

I shake my head. "No, thanks. Just a trim."

The other stylist appears with a tub of cream and the two of them set about to free one long set of nails from the hostage situation created on top of my head.

"There now," she says, after what seems like an eternity.

"I'm sorry. It's been a rough few days and I..." I begin.

"Happens more'n you'd think. Especially with all the wind we get. Never you mind. Just find yourself a seat." She points me to a black swivel chair. "Be just a minute while I get a cape from the dryer."

I try avoiding my reflection in the mirror. If my current look is bad enough to attract Nova's attention and snag an unsuspecting beautician, I certainly don't want to stare at it. In the corner of the mirror, I notice lots of small pictures. Several look to be from her childhood, about the same time as Dee's. An idea pops into my head as the stylist returns with the cape.

"Never introduced myself. Bev here. What did you say we're doin' today?" She whips the black plastic around my neck and fastens it with surprising ease, given the unusual length of her nails.

"Just a trim. So that Nova thinks I actually put some effort into it."

"Okay, hon. Lean back and let me wash this first and then we'll see what we can do." Bev puts on thick, rubber gloves and massages my head with shampoo. "Sure is a shame 'bout your friend. I've been thinkin' about that ever since our meeting."

I ignore her statement; I'm not in a mood to bring up Rosabel. "Did you grow up with Dee? I noticed your pictures and they remind me of the ones Dee has sitting around."

"Ummhmmm. We were classmates." She tips my chair upright and rubs my head with a discolored towel. "Sure was a sad thing, what happened with her brother and all."

I reach for my purse and find the obituary. "I want you to look at this picture." I hand the carefully folded paper over. "Tell me what you see."

Bev studies the page for a bit. "Nice-looking young man," she says dismissively.

"Don't you see Gentry's eyes? Tell me I'm not crazy to think that's him!" I plead. Bev takes the paper from my hand again and studies it.

"I s'pose that could be him. He liked his guitar." She sets the paper down and starts combing out my hair. "It could be lots of people."

My lack of sleep and frustration have built to an uncomfortable level. "What is wrong with you people? That's Gentry. I know it is!"

"Caroline!" Bev yells. "Get over here and look at this picture. See if it looks like Dee's brother to you."

The other beautician who also attended book club, Verla, picks up the paper and studies it carefully. "It could be," she says quietly. "Definitely looks similar. Lots of people do, I'm sure."

Tears are streaming down my face now. I need some confirmation from someone before I approach Dee. I'm starting to wonder if I'm really crazy. That this has all been some kind of hallucination.

"I... just... wanted... to help... Dee," I sob.

Bev puts her comb down and pats my shoulder. That is all it takes to unleash the flood of information from my sleep-deprived brain. I tell them everything about the One-Armed Man and the farm and how Rosabel has brought me here for a purpose. I just can't seem to stop this flow of information, no matter what the situation.

The two women nod and cluck their tongues in the appropriate places. When I finish, Bev swirls the chair around so that I'm facing her.

"I can tell this is important to you, Keilah." She sighs. "I'm just gonna be real honest. Nobody here wants to dig up yesterday's garbage."

I don't understand at first. "Do you believe me then?" I ask, trying to push down any remaining emotions.

The lady under the hairdryer, whom I haven't even noticed until this very moment, stands up and pokes at her curlers as she walks over to me. "Look, you gotta understand, that family was a mess. Everybody knew it. Dee's lucky they didn't sell her."

The room becomes quiet, except for the hum of the hair dryer.

"SO, YOU ALL KNEW? Like the entire town? I thought it was just Bart and Moses. How could everybody know and not do anything?"

"What were we gonna do? Go get the boy back to live with that family again?" Bev asks, rubbing the comb in her hand. "At least this way he had a 50/50 chance of a good life. From what you say, it sounds like things turned out pretty darn nice."

"Luckier than me," Verla says.

"You know it," dryer lady chimes in.

"Shouldn't Dee know what happened to her brother? Don't you think that would bring her some peace?" I think about the tears she shed telling me the story of his disappearance. The thought of the entire town she has known her whole life being in on her deception is almost too much.

"Dee's moved on. You've found where Gentry or Colin or whoever landed and that's just fine. But I wouldn't take it any further. She's had enough." Bev clears her throat, as though she is putting a verbal period at the end of this conversation.

Caroline nods in agreement.

The rest of my haircut is done in uncomfortable silence. The mask of this quaint little town has been removed today and I see these small people for what they are: gossips. Everyone loves spinning a good yarn but no one wanted to actually solve the mystery. It isn't the ending to the story that fits. Rosabel would keep going until Dee knew the truth.

When Bev removes the cape and hands me a mirror, I'm surprised by the reflection. This is a new Keilah – maybe even attractive.

I send Vanessa a text: *Need to ask you about an obit. Can you come in for coffee?*

Sure. Give me ten. ☺

Chapter Thirty-Two

EULOGY
2007

I SLEPT SOUNDLY for the first time in years. It didn't feel right. On the second worst day of my entire life, I woke up with a pimple in the middle of my forehead, something I must've deserved for a full eight hours unconscious. Later, I would be standing up in front of everyone who loved my friend almost as much as I did, telling them how much she meant to me, and they wouldn't be able to think of anything but the protruding pus sack positioned directly above my eyebrows. There had been no obituary; that was something her parents were incapable of creating. I thought it was because they couldn't bear to see her life on paper. Neither of them possessed the ability to feel shame over the way they had treated her. Instead, they allowed someone in the art department to create flyers using her senior picture, the one I had taken because her parents refused to pay for a professional photographer. Her lovely face was surrounded by daisies, the time and date of the funeral printed at the bottom.

The basketball court of the community center was full; most of Pepperville had encountered Rosabel at one time or another. Daisies and wildflowers lined the front of the space. Students from the college, some of her friends and some people she touched just by her mere presence, made poster board signs of affection. "You'll never be forgotten" and "The kindest soul to grace our planet" sat beside "Rosabel – you rock!" and "A hot babe we were lucky to know".

Rosabel's mother insisted I sit in the front row with the family. I couldn't stand the idea of sitting next to her father. Just the thought of him being there repulsed me. I knew he would be drunk, despite what had occurred. They both would. They were the worst example of what parents should be and I didn't want anyone thinking I condoned them calling themselves her mother and father. When the time came, I slid my folding chair as far away as I could without committing to the second row.

It turned out I didn't have to worry, as her father only showed up briefly, swaying in the back of the room. I sat tensely waiting to see what he would do next. Before Alfie Bastien finished singing the chorus of "You are my Sunshine," her father had found the door handle and let himself out. Rosabel would have winked at me, as if it were a minor infraction he had committed. I was glad she didn't have to be there to witness it.

It was just four days later that he was found at the cemetery with one bullet to his temple. Everyone surmised he was so filled with guilt over his daughter's death that he wanted to be with her in the afterlife from that day on. But instead of killing himself on his daughter's grave, he stumbled to the grave of Father Seamus Farrington, who had just passed due to undiagnosed cancer. Instead of his grieving widow, or even a friend like me finding his pathetic, cold body, it was two nuns out to show their respect who discovered him.

Most of my family was in attendance: Kyan, Melanie,

the girls, Kenner and Sonnet. Normally, Sonnet's parents would attend a service of such social significance, handing out bank-branded magnets to mourners as they left. But ever since I told Father about the photocopied letter, Albert made a point of avoiding my parents. We moved our large account to a bank thirty miles away.

Mother said she would help in the kitchen with the after-funeral brunch, so she couldn't attend. I was hoping she was feeling guilty about not helping Rosabel with college. She had taken over raising Kenner and me, leaving Mother free to do her clubs and gardening. I wanted Mother to think about how much she owed Rosabel. Father didn't come either.

A local country group offered to play a selection of Rosabel's favorite songs. Her mother didn't object, and even came up with a list of songs. The only time I remembered hearing any of them was when she and her drunk friends woke us up in the middle of the night to make breakfast for them and they all sang off-key while squeezing Rosabel's behind.

When it came time for me to stand up and give a eulogy, I rose on shaky legs. I felt my forehead, hoping by some miracle it had returned to a regular shape. It hadn't. I couldn't focus on my broken looks. I was already in enough pieces.

After showing her favorite pressed flowers and reading some of the scenes from our kingdom, I uncrumpled her list from 6th grade, the one containing all the things she wanted to accomplish. The roadmap not for her short life, but for the future her no-good father cheated her out of. It had been in my pocket ever since going to her house. I started with a shaky voice:

"Children are who we are in our truest form. This was my Rosabel.

"Number one: give someone inspiration. Number two..." I paused as I read her simple words to myself. *Buy my parents a decent home. So they can be proud of who they are.* I just couldn't. "Buy someone deserving a home. Number three: create an orphanage for unwanted children. Number four: blank space." My eyes filled with tears. "Because... because everyone must have some room for unexpected..." The sobs came fast and hard. "Things. Unexpected things."

I started to mumble. "Can't hear you in the back!" someone shouted. I looked up, through my tears. My body dissolved into tremors. I knew I had to get through somehow.

"Help my Robin..." They didn't seem to understand how hard I was trying. To be someone standing on her own for the first time and failing miserably. "Get to the... moon." My voice and body faltered. My legs buckled and I fell to the floor. The next thing I remembered was seeing Kenner's face above mine.

"You all right, sis? You've done a lot of crazy stuff, but I've never seen you pass out like that before. You got a good bump to the noggin."

"This is all Rosabel wanted from life," I whispered.

I heard Mother's voice. "It's just a bump. Looks worse than it is."

I put my hand to my forehead, remembering the pimple that sat imposingly in that spot just a few hours earlier. Now it was a flat, bloody mess. I smiled, silently thanking

Rosabel for pushing that embarrassing pimple right into the gym floor.

I opened my eyes wider and now I could see Kyan giving me his standard look of disgust. On his right side stood Patty, Rosabel's aunt. A sick feeling came over me.

"I know what you did," I said, remembering what I found in my friend's room.

Kenner helped me into a sitting position. "You're not feelin' right, Keilah. Let's get you somethin' to drink." Someone brought a plastic cup from the kitchen filled to the brim with cold water and my brother tried to put it in my still shaky hand.

"I know what you did!" I said louder, pushing the water to the floor as I pointed my finger at Patty. "You are an awful human!" For the second time in so many days, it was like the words came from somewhere else. "You don't deserve to live! Anyone who does that to a child doesn't deserve to live!"

Patty turned away from me, squeezing her elbows.

"Tell them what you did! Tell them!" I screamed.

Mother looked away and turned around, leaving me to fend for myself in what she surely thought was a predestined public disgracing of our family.

I could hear Melanie's voice from the chairs in front of me, but her face was blurred. "Go up there! Go up there and make her stop embarrassing us!"

I wanted them all to know how much she had suffered. My poor, sweet Rosabel, who only wanted to make life better for others. It was at that moment I felt a hand on my shoulder, one I still hoped was the comforting grip of my best friend. Instead, it was Kenner, using his strong arms to pull me up to my feet. "C'mon, Keilah. Let's get you out of here."

I was still wobbly and not at all sure I could move if I wanted. The band hurriedly started to play their version of "Try a Little Kindness" as my brothers carried me out, one holding my arms and the other my legs.

"Oh, God. Oh, God. Make her stop! She's nuts," Melanie shouted.

Someone went to the podium and asked everyone to file into the rec room for cookies and punch.

Somehow Kyan ended up behind us, ordering Kenner to shut me in the bathroom. He gave Kenner strict instructions not to let me out for any reason until everyone was gone. By the time I had my senses about me and had regained control of my own voice, I couldn't hear many people still milling about.

I thought for a minute about the time I shut myself in the bathroom after my nose exploded all over my cooking demonstration. My life could have ended right there. I would have been fine with that. Things hadn't exactly gone well up to that point. But Rosabel had been on the other side of that door. She had always been on the other side of my darkness, waiting patiently for me to see the light.

"Bud? Please let me out. I'm fine now. I really am," I begged.

"Kyan said..."

"I won't hurt anyone. I just had a minute of crazy."

Kenner chuckled. "A minute? Keilah, you haven't been right since this happened. Can't say I blame you. But you have to get a handle on yourself."

I wanted to scream that I wasn't the one with the problem. Kenner was acting like he hadn't just lost the most significant person of his entire childhood. Why wasn't he screaming? That's what I wanted to say. But I didn't. I was back in control.

"I know. I won't. I promise. If I go nuts again, Kyan can lock me back up." I used my sweetest voice. A minute later, the door opened. Kenner looked at me as if he wanted to simultaneously punch and hug me. He decided on the latter.

"You've had me worried, sis. It's a hard time for all of us, you know." He laid his head on my shoulder. I felt some tears run down the back of my shirt.

I wished Sonnet could have been there watching us, seething that he still loved me enough to show me affection publicly. She didn't own all of him. "I know, Sparrow. It's not going to be easy for us to move ahead. I never thought I'd have to live my life without her."

"You just can't blame anyone else. She was the one who ran out…"

Kyan appeared out of nowhere. He pointed a beefy finger into Kenner's chest. "You let her out?" Without waiting for an answer, he turned to me. "You gonna behave like a human now?"

I smiled. He was always true to his character. "Yes, I promise, Kyan. Like a human."

"Well, then. Mother needs your help finishing up the dishes in the kitchen."

I took some deep breaths and headed to find Mother. She looked up as I entered the room but said nothing. Someone handed me an apron and directed me to another sink full of dirty plates. No one spoke to me as I did the dishes. It was as if I wasn't the only person in the room who hadn't just lost her everything. It was surreal. I felt a tap on my shoulder. I turned around to see Patty standing beside me.

"I need to go out for a smoke. Care to join me?"

I nodded. I wiped my hands on my apron and tried to catch Mother's gaze, but she refused to look at me. It was probably for the better.

I followed Patty silently as we headed out the back door and sat on the bumper of someone's car, where she pulled a cigarette out of her purse and then stopped, putting her other arm around my back. I leaned as far as I could in the opposite direction. She patted my back before giving up completely and standing up.

"How long have you known?" she asked quietly.

"Since yesterday. Found it when I went through her things."

She sighed. "I was hoping she didn't know."

"Well, she did. She lived most of her life knowing." Anger welled inside me once more. "What kind of awful person runs away from her own baby?"

Chapter Thirty-Three

SANDY SALTS
2012

I'M SITTING ON the curb in front of Jack's Beanery. Nova's nonsense has pushed me past my normally high tolerance level. Her "generosity" in giving me time off to get my hair fixed only extended two hours. When Vanessa arrived to talk, I was in the back restocking and Nova told her I was already gone. That set the tone for today, then things got worse.

I made plans to meet Vanessa during her lunch hour, which was usually a slow time for the coffee shop. Like everything else, it didn't work out as planned. Instead, I decided to text her, but it turns out her phone isn't working.

Kenner will shake his head when I explain how Nova's tripping over the overflowing trash this afternoon turned into an event of significance. Things started off wrong when Lorraine didn't show up for work. When Lorraine has an illness or a doctor's appointment, she automatically assumes we knew she would be gone. Nova made some humiliating remark once that Lorraine must think her sparse calendar automatically syncs with ours, and when it tries, our calendars don't take it seriously. Lorraine never responded so it's possible she thought that to be true and gave up trying to tell her cousin anything.

Some days we survive without an extra pair of hands, but on this morning, a bus full of basketball players came in. We were slammed with customers, both regular and new, and only had two pairs of hands working to make their drinks. The regulars were somewhat bent out of shape that their needs were not put ahead of these strangers passing through. Moses even came inside, grabbing a washcloth before he began wiping down tables. He didn't want the "home folks" worrying that we were too busy to remove crumbs.

Nova, who on a good day doesn't handle cranky customers well, became quite agitated. "Keilah!" she squawked. "Why is there an extra steamed milk sitting here?"

I've learned to tune her out by playing music in my head, the silly oldies Rosabel and I used to put on while we danced around her living room.

"Keilah! Are there no more chocolate chip scones? Didn't you make enough for a Friday?"

Just let me hear some of that rock and roll music...

"Keilah! Didn't you get more bread from the freezer?"

Any old way you choose it...

"We don't HAVE soy milk, sir. Our HELP never went out and bought any yesterday, even though she had absolutely nothing else to remember!"

There's a backbeat, you can't lose it....

By the end of the morning, Nova was hoarse and I was reveling in her misery. Her squawks became muted whines. Eventually, the customers slowed down and, as the morning drug into the afternoon, things calmed down a bit, so I started to clean. I was happy to look up and see it was almost time for Nova's early release. I didn't see any of her boyfriends waiting outside, which concerned me, but sometimes they only drove up at the last minute.

Suddenly, I heard screaming from the back room. My first thought was that Nova must have done something to my possessions again, but I've been very careful to lock them up every day since the last horrible incident. Beyond my own personal things, I have no stake in whatever happens in the back of someone else's business. I'm blissfully ignorant.

After a few more minutes, she screams again. The two remaining customers look at me with an "aren't you going to do something?" look. I sigh.

Before walking to the back, I grab the tub of dirty cups and plates that need to be washed. At least that'll give me something to do while Nova is berating me. I push the door open with my rear, and as I turn around to face her, I almost drop the tub in shock.

Nova is lying on the floor, arms and legs straight out to the side. Her considerably thick makeup is washing down her cheeks in dark rows as her large chest heaves up and down like an angry ocean forcing its hefty waves up to shore. The trash is lying on its side, an empty sugar bag spilling the remaining remnants over Nova's leg.

"Tucker hasn't scrubbed the floor yet this week. Your hair will be stuck when you try to get up." I turn to set the dishes in the sink, trying hard not to laugh. I know my enjoyment will only make this situation worse for both of us.

Nova let out little sobs. I said nothing while I loaded the dishes into the dishwasher. For a few blissful minutes, there was silence. Then, abruptly, Nova let out another scream. So piercing I thought my eardrums would rupture.

Something snaps in me. "What in the... Nova, for heaven's sake, get up and stop acting like you're five!" I turn around and face her with my arms crossed. "Get up, now!" I feel like I'm channeling Mother and I don't like it one bit.

We stare at each other for a few long, uncomfortable minutes. I can always call Phillip and make him heave her over his shoulder.

"Can you... help me?" she finally asks in a baby voice that makes me cringe.

"Give me your hand." I yank her up hard enough that she lets out an "oomph" on the way. Several dark-rooted hairs clung to the floor, working in harmony with the spilled sugar to create a hair and sugar outline reminiscent of a crime scene.

"Can you tell me what in the hell is worth all of this? There are customers out there scared to death." I resist the urge to shake my finger at her, the way she had done to me countless times.

She starts to let out little sobs again. "It's a guy thing. You wouldn't understand."

"Try me."

"Well, this guy I know, Phillip, he called a while ago and told me he didn't want to see me again. We've been together for like forever."

Chills ran down my spine. "Oh really? Did he say why?" I thought he had taken care of this long ago. Then I remember Nova's things are still in my closet.

"Some... stupid... woman..." She devolves into a full-on cry.

"Does this woman have a name? And weren't you pretty much broken up with him anyway?"

Nova stops crying and looks at me through strands of sticky hair. "How would you know about anything that goes on in my life?"

"You've mentioned him a few times, that Phillip guy." I hope she doesn't notice me blushing.

"Oh. Well, we weren't totally together. But guys just don't break up with me like that. They usually come crawling to Daddy and ask his permission. Because... Daddy is protective of me. They know why. You wouldn't understand."

I shake my head. Part of me feels flattered that Phillip would go to such lengths for me, knowing the consequences. The other part, however, feels a little sick that I could fall for any man who had, on any level, felt an attraction to Nova.

"I mean, this is all so rude. He told me he couldn't even call me anymore. I thought we had a deal. I'm going to have Daddy call his boss. That's number one..." Nova brushes off the front of her pants and assesses her makeup in the mirror on her locker door. "Number two, if he wants to keep that job after his boss hears that he stole from them, he'll have to make a full confession, starting with the name of that bitch and how long this has been going on."

I am a little stunned by this accusation. Low, even for Nova. "Are you sure he is stealing?"

"It doesn't matter. He has to learn his lesson. That's not how you treat a lady," Nova says matter-of-factly. She found her makeup bag and applies its contents furiously to her flushed face.

This was the time. If I was anything like Rosabel, I'd tell Nova that I'm the other woman in this non-love triangle.

Instead, I stand silently. All I can think of is the mess I've created for this poor man and myself.

"Well, don't stand there and look stupid. We've got lots to do before we lock up. Those poor customers have been sitting up front wondering what mudhole swallowed you up." She snaps her lipstick palate shut and dusts her face with a thick powder.

I begin shaking, first silently, and then my teeth rattle. I haven't felt this deeply since Rosabel's death. I'm not sure if it is from Nova's hate or Phillip's kindness, or maybe the strange combination of the two in one small room. I focus my attention on my limbs, willing them to move towards my locker, where I grab my coat and purse. "I have to leave. You'll have to lock up today."

I move through the back door in one brisk movement, before Nova has a chance to argue with me. The only thing on my mind is talking to Kenner. He could help me sort this out. Thank goodness he'll be here soon to be my sounding board. Between the two of us, we'll work out my problems with Phillip and Nova, and maybe even solve the mystery of Gentry's disappearance. I'm already starting to feel better. I rifle through my purse until I find my phone. My breathing begins to return to normal.

Normally, this is the time of day when he is finishing up with whatever equipment he is fixing and gathering his oily rags for the day. He doesn't like to be bothered, but today I need him more than he needs to follow his routine. I take Colin's wrinkled obituary from my purse and stare at it while I wait for him to answer.

I can't wait until my brother is here by my side; every day we'll laugh about Nova's antics. There is so much now to tell him, to figure out. Maybe he'll even find Vanessa attractive and we can see where things lead. There will be no more blackmail.

Sonnet can't hold the death of the One-Armed Man's mother over Kenner's head if he's not there to torture every day. She'll be too afraid of Kyan to try and manipulate him, so at least that bit of ugliness will end. It won't be a moment too soon when that family is finally out of our lives for good.

"'Lo?"

I can tell he's stressed and probably a little irritated with me. "Sorry, bud. I just needed to get this off my chest. It's been a rough day and, for now, I have to make do with telling you everything over the phone…"

"Keilah? Been meanin' to call you." His voice is low. "Somethin's goin' on here."

My heart sinks. "Is it Mother?" I've been so centered on Colin… Gentry, that I haven't thought about my family. I couldn't take it if she was gone too. Even with all of our issues, she gave birth to me and I'm not ready to lose her.

"No, Mother's fine." There's an awkward pause. "It's not her I needed to talk to you about. It's me."

Now I'm panicked. I will really lose it if something is wrong with Kenner; this can't happen today.

"What is it? Are you sick? I'll come back in a heartbeat to help you. You know that, right? Forget about the stupid will. Are you ok?"

"No, I'm fine. I just… I need to tell you something and I don't want you to be mad."

A thousand things go through my head. Maybe he really is hurt. Or somehow, he has damaged some of the big, expensive tractors that Kyan is so proud of. Or... oh, no... My stomach lurches.

"You didn't..."

"Keilah, Sonnet and I got married two days ago. Just went to the courthouse and got it over with. Sonnet said she didn't want a big wedding anyway and we should save our money."

I start to sob. I've never been in a relationship long enough to be cheated on, but this must be what it feels like. Total betrayal. The one family member I have left in the world, the only one I can trust, has gone behind my back to cement his relationship with the most awful person I've ever met. "Did she blackmail you? About Tillie's death? I'm going to get to the bottom of that. There's so much you should know about the One-Armed... Dmitri..." I stop for a minute and an ugly thought crosses my mind. "Did you tell her you were moving?"

I can hear the wind echoing in the phone. "Oh, my God, you did! How long has she known?"

He sighs. "Just a few weeks. I had to tell her. I mean, we've been together since high school. I just had to, sis. It wasn't fair to her otherwise. She made me realize I didn't want to lose her..."

Just what Rosabel said would happen. Sonnet is a force like no other. "Oh, Kenner, we talked about this! I could've helped you escape! You don't really love her!" I feel like these words are just floating in the air with nowhere to go. Like nothing I say really matters.

"What d' you know about love? You've never been in a serious relationship before. This is real life. Gosh dang it, I wish you were the same Keilah I grew up with. She would've understood. I miss her."

These words sting even more deeply. I can hear Sonnet's judgment in them. "I can't help it if I've changed. My whole world turned upside down when she died, you know that! Why can't anyone in this family understand..." I think about the Kenner who sat on Rosabel's lap for hours. "You've changed too. Sonnet has sucked the life out of you and you can't even see it."

He is silent.

"So now, this is it? For the rest of your life? With someone who blackmails you?" The phone is still quiet. "Kenner? Are you still there?"

"You don't live in the real world, sis."

"You won't be moving here, will you? I suppose not. She wouldn't want you living somewhere she couldn't manage your every move." I take a deep breath, hoping that hurts him, just a little. "Rosabel wanted so much more for you – her Sparrow. You're just giving up that easily?"

"I gotta go, Keilah. I promised Sonnet we would eat dinner together and I have to get this machinery cleaned up first."

"Me too. Work and all." There is no point. In any of this. He is as much a stranger to me as anyone in Sandy Salts. I've never felt quite so helpless.

I want to smash my phone on the ground and never see his phone number or hear his voice again. I should have known. This is just as much my fault as his. Thinking I could win at her game. I've been too lost in my grief and I've let things slip away. I put my head in my hands and try to figure out what should happen next.

My job is a joke. I have to babysit a child every day,

dealing with her temper tantrums and degrading words. Now she's going to threaten Phillip; it's only a matter of time before the truth comes out. Why did I think I could have a relationship with someone like him? I can't talk to Dee about Gentry, at least not until I'm sure it's really him. I can't risk losing her too.

I walk around the same four blocks for what seems like hours. I can't go back in time. I truly thought that Rosabel would be here forever. When she died, I could barely order a pizza on my own. Now that I've finally been courageous enough to make a few decisions of my own, they've turned out to be horribly wrong. It seems I really wasn't qualified to sit at the helm of my own life. No need to find a middle name for someone unqualified for the rest of it.

Dee is the only person I haven't damaged. At least the only one that matters. Strange and lovely, perfectly normal and insane, she is my rock. The fact that she's always there at the end of my day, good or bad, mostly bad, brings me much more comfort than any thoughts of the farm. She hasn't seen my worst days and she sure hasn't seen my best. But right there in the middle, she sits and holds my hand like a second mother.

And Phillip? I don't understand why he would want someone like me. I've never allowed myself to consider him as a part of my future. It doesn't make sense that he would want to risk everything in his world to be with me. He probably doesn't understand how far Nova will go to hurt him.

I thought for so long that Rosabel was guiding my life. That somehow she had brought me here, through her words and her gentle nudging, to get me out of that terrible, five-year empty hole of darkness I lived in when she left. She always had a purpose for everything, including me.

Maybe she *is* still guiding my life. I doubted that she would continue to do that from the grave. I just haven't been listening for a while.

The wind dies down to a gentle breeze that lifts my hair and my spirit to a new place. I take a deep breath, feeling a new determination. Things suddenly feel clear.

Chapter Thirty-Four

"IT WASN'T ALWAYS so awful, I just wanted you to know that." Patty tapped the ashes from her cigarette on the car bumper. "When we first were married, he opened car doors for me and called me his princess. That's why we named our little love Rosabel. Like a fairytale character we created together. I wasn't supposed to have children. And frankly, as many hours as I put into work, I didn't think my body had the energy. She was a surprise. My Rosie."

I stared straight ahead. I wanted Patty to tell me that none of this was true. That the birth certificate, listing Patricia and Al Walton as Rosabel's real parents, was something she had made up, to pretend she had a better life waiting for her somewhere.

"Al lost his business, started drinking, the usual things you hear. But I still had my job at the hospital, so we thought we would be okay. I was gone all hours of the day and night, but my little Rosie had her daddy there, taking care of her. It worked out fine for a while."

"Don't do that – don't call her Rosie. Her name is Rosabel," I practically yelled at her. It was stupid, but I didn't want her to have any part of my friend, the baby she had thrown away. If she was going to pretend to care, she had to play by my rules.

Kyan came out the back door with a bag of trash. He paused when he saw us both standing there, his eyes narrowing into tiny slits. "Everything all right here?" he asked, more for Patty's benefit than mine.

Patty coughed a deep smoker's cough and smiled at him. "Everything's fine. Thank you so much for all you've..."

"Keilah, you smokin'?" He came closer and I could almost detect a gleeful note to his voice. How he would love to berate me for embarrassing him today.

"No, that's my smoke. Bad habit I just can't kick," Patty said. Kyan stared another minute and then turned and went in the back door of the building, letting the screen door slam shut.

"Not the friendliest sort, is he?" Patty asked.

I shrugged.

"Anyway, after Al lost his job, things got real bad. He could barely get out of bed and, when he did, he yelled and screamed at us both. I thought he was probably a nicer guy when I wasn't around, so I didn't worry about leaving my little Rosie... Rosabel... with him.

"She was about two, that night I came home from work and found her with lots of bruises. Al said he had just fallen asleep and she banged herself up without adult supervision. I hightailed it back to the hospital. Even though she looked mostly okay on the outside, other than the bruises, you know, I couldn't shake the feeling that something even worse had happened. I must've just known, had that mother's instinct, you know? It turns out he had been doing... things... to her for quite some time."

I felt like I was choking. "I need to... I may need some

air," I said, not knowing how to make that happen when I was already outside. I just sat down where I was and tried to take in deep breaths. Our wonderful lives together. *The beat-up porch where we planned our prom dates and life together. We sat for hours, just staring at the tall, green weeds in her yard and pretending her father would someday be sober enough to plant real grass and a garden.* It comforted me. I spent several minutes in this alternate universe, hiding safely in my memories.

"You need to hear it all," Penny's voice jolted me back to the present. "I want to tell you everything."

She was still standing beside me, hands on her bony hips. I got to my feet and brushed the gravel off my pants. Looking into her face, I could see Rosabel's eyes now – older, cloudier, and without the faraway, hopeful gaze I ached for.

"I think that's why I'm still here," I said tensely.

She moved a step closer, the strong odor of cigarette smoke and fried food becoming more prominent. I had to fight the urge to vomit.

"The hospital reported him. That was out of my hands. But he got a great lawyer and promised me he was going to be a new man when he came home. I didn't want to be alone. I had worked so hard my whole life to be attached to someone else. I couldn't imagine starting all over again."

My mouth dropped open. "You let him come back after he did those things? To your kid?"

Patty put her hand up in protest. "Wait. Just because I needed to be a 'we' didn't mean my little angel needed to suffer. I had eighteen months to figure it all out. To find someplace she could feel safe and I could just go on as a married woman. We all deserve a chance to be happy, right?"

I said nothing. There was no way she could be Rosabel's mother. She was as evil as anyone I had ever met. Sonnet could learn from her.

"My sister and her husband offered. They couldn't have kids of their own. They were doing so well in life at the time. They ran a feed store in a small town on the other side of the state. Had a nice house, sweet friends—the perfect set-up. Her husband seemed the most eager. He had always wanted kids. At first, they sent me pictures and letters every few months. My baby girl blossomed and grew, her chubby little cheeks and big smile filling the page. I could feel their love for her.

"After a few years, the letters slowed down. My sister said the feed store had closed and they were thinking of moving. She changed her number and didn't respond to my letters. Rumor in the family was that they filed for bankruptcy, that her husband had a drinking problem. The next thing I heard was that they had moved to Pepperville. I never heard anything directly from them again, until... this."

By then my face had to be as red as my hair. "And you never thought to contact her? When you knew her life was in danger? When you knew they couldn't parent a bug, let alone the most amazing person ever to walk this planet?"

Penny sighed. "I did what I thought was the best thing. It was pretty selfless, actually. I put her where I thought she would be safe. And by the time I had an idea that things weren't perfect, I had no legal rights to her. I couldn't take her back. She didn't even know who I was."

This was the thing with my Rosabel: she loved a good

story. She loved to make up wonderful people and places for us. From detailed gowns she created – meticulously sewing little beads and shiny buttons to them during an all-night session – to the lush, green landscape sculpted out of a putting green she found behind her barn – all were created to keep our kingdom safe from the Evil Ones. None more so than the castle, a haven for the lowly creatures as well as the royal families. Each detail was designed to that end, and it wasn't until her death that I understood why.

She never felt safe. She must've felt so scared her whole life, unsure why she felt out of place with the people who claimed to be her parents. Maybe she spent hours dreaming about the kind of loving people who tucked their beautiful princess into bed at night and told her she was their sun and moon.

And her love of children, her need to rescue them all, it had to stem from her horrible early life. That's what drove her each and every day. In a sick way, Patty and her awful husband were what drove Rosabel to get out of bed each morning. She wanted to make the world a better place because of them.

I went into her room before the funeral to find pieces of her life – something I could use to inspire me in the eulogy I was about to give. I didn't think I could do it. I wasn't as strong or as smart as she was. I had been created to be her sidekick, her steady-but-simple friend who did what she was told. But something in me said that if I found mementos of our life together the words would come.

In her bottom drawer, underneath the books of flowers she had pressed, flowers collected from my farm, I found it. I pushed aside her daisy-covered diary and found a black

piece of paper, folded neatly in half. It contained information that shocked me. Information I had hoped for all
along. I just didn't imagine her birth parents would be even
worse than the ones she spent her life trying to please.

The sticky-note on top, in Sonnet's handwriting, read:
Your real parents, darling. Sorry they didn't want you. She
must've been so pleased with herself to crush Rosabel with
the news. It must've happened on prom night, while I was
lusting after some guy I'd just met. The moment she needed
me the most.

"She never said a thing?" Patty asked, as if she were a
legendary creature, spoken of fondly. *We'll talk about it
later, Robin. When we can think about something besides
Kenner, or Sonnet, or Keilah's problems.*

"No, never. I didn't even know you existed. I guess she
didn't want to bring more ugliness into her life," I snapped.

"Always such a happy little baby, even when the fighting
happened. She just sat in her crib and smiled, like she didn't
have a care in the world."

I shuddered at the thought. My poor, beautiful Rosabel.

"What happened to Rosabel's father?"

"He died. Ten years ago. It was the alcohol, I think."

I was tired of smelling oily pavement and the stench of
cigarette smoke. "They were horrible parents. I just want
you to know. They didn't show her much love or kindness.
They even gambled away her college money. She should
have been miserable. But for some strange reason, she
wasn't. My Rosabel was a diamond. You had nothing to do
with it, but she was beautiful and sparkling every day of her
life."

Patty threw her cigarette to the ground and stomped it

with her foot. "I'm sure glad to know she had good people around her. It'll help me and my sister in our grief. Good meeting you, Keilah."

She turned and walked away. The wind whipped and my hair flew in front of my face, blocking my view for several minutes. When I finally pushed it out of my eyes, she was gone.

Chapter Thirty-Five

SANDY SALTS
2012

I START WALKING, then running over to the library, where Vanessa is just locking up for the day.

"Hey, Keilah. I was going to call you later. See if you want to repeat the other night?" She winks. "Just kidding. Sorry, I know that wasn't so much fun for you. Aren't you finished a little early?"

She lets out a miniature sneeze and her bags, all four of them, fall to the ground. I bend down to pick them up and tears spurt from my eyes like an out-of-control hydrant.

"What's going on, girl? Pull up a seat and let's talk." Vanessa lowers herself gently to the crumbling cement step. "I missed you this morning when I dropped off Dee's book club book. Sorry it didn't work for lunch."

I sink down, just missing the bag with her Avon supplies, and explain that I found Colin Fortner's obituary hanging in plain sight on her wall. "I think you've been playing me all along. How could you not have known?"

Vanessa furrows her brows and studies me. "You're from a farm, right?"

I nod, warily.

"I spent every August on my grandparents' farm. You know when you go out to pick the corn at the end of the summer, and the stalks are all above your head? There's not much you can see but the row in front of you. If something is going on in the next row, or across the field for that matter, you have no clue. You're just there, in your own little space, picking corn."

I'm starting to get irritated. "What does any of this have to do with Gentry? Or me, for that matter? I don't pick corn anymore." *Wipe your nose and hurry it up, lazy.*

Vanessa sighs. "Oh, girlfriend. I think you're in your own little space, picking your own ears of corn. How could I have known about your friend Mr. Fortner?"

I shake my head. "Gentry's missing photos. The obit photo. Hard to miss the likeness. I'm not as gullible as you think."

"I only heard rumors of Gentry. I never considered this a reason to get up in the morning the way you do. I just collect obits. That's it."

I stand up, my cheeks flushed with anger. "Well, I'm sorry I bugged you. I thought this might be kind of important. And unlike everyone else in this town, I'm here to help Dee. Sorry you aren't."

"Keilah, don't leave!" Vanessa stumbles to her feet. "I'm not telling you this isn't important. I'm just saying everyone here has kind of moved on. This story was painful to the community and they'd rather just close the book."

I start walking down the steps and then turn around. "Your problem is that you think that making up those stories about people counts as having a real life. It doesn't."

I let my words hang in the slight breeze for a moment before storming off. The closer I get to Dee's house, the guiltier I feel for saying those things to Vanessa. It isn't her fault she doesn't understand what this means to Dee.

All I have in this world is Dee. She has been there for me from the beginning. Instead of going back to apologize, I head up the hill to the grocery store. If I make some of Rosabel's brownies, Dee can appreciate that I baked for her and maybe it would soften the blow. I'll pat her arm and give her a warm smile, just like my Rosabel would have done.

I'll tell her everything I learned. I don't have all the answers, but at least she can see a picture of her brother as an adult. To see what a fine man he turned out to be. The entire town will owe me a debt of gratitude for all I've done to find their lost little boy.

I select a brownie mix, the only dusty, blue box on that shelf. When I get to the checkout, the tall woman with a name tag stating she is Mona Mae eyes me suspiciously. "S'that all you're getting?"

Is she a member of the book club I didn't notice? Vanessa has called everyone to let them in on her secret, that she thinks I'm crazy. I'm sure of it. "I'm just getting this. Do you have a problem? Is it illegal in this godforsaken place to buy a mix? I didn't do anything wrong!"

Mona Mae shrugs. "Three-fifty." She holds out her hand. "I've never made 'em from a box." She looks away as I count out the money.

For so long after Rosabel's death, people avoided my gaze. I felt ashamed, like I had somehow contributed to her ending. When I left them all, just after Father's death, they seemed relieved to see me go. No one outside of my family showed up to see me off. Maybe that's what Sandy Salts thinks of me as well.

By the time I walk in the door, I feel like a crazy soup Dee might have concocted. Full of fruits and vegetables from her garden, with a dash of chocolate and cinnamon. There isn't one part of me that's comfortable in my skin. I left home just six months ago so sure of who I was and how I would leave those ugly memories behind. Now I'm not so certain the memories haven't been controlling me all along.

I throw myself on the grape-and-tan sofa, hoping to fall into another lengthy slumber where I can sort everything out. Instead, I hear a little cough. At first, I think – hope – that it's just Gentry, stretching his claws on something he shouldn't. But then I hear it again. I sit up and notice Dee's tiny body, hunched over on the stairs.

"Dee? What's going on? Why are you here this time of day? Are you sick?"

"No. Well, I had a migraine. But I took my ginger and magnesium concoction and I'm doing better. Just sittin' here, trying to take it all in."

My heart sinks. "What do you mean by that?"

"Vanessa stopped by to bring my book club book while I was home for lunch. Told me about your shenanigans. Thought she'd be nice and let me know about it before you hit me with that brick." She crosses her arms. "Then my old friend Bev from the beauty shop stops by to pick up her book. I'll be darned if you didn't tell her the same nonsense. Don't know what you think you're doin,' girl. Seems you've made quite a spectacle of yourself."

"Oh... I... was going to tell you..."

"So, you think your zoo man stole my Gentry? Is this a game to you?"

I'm startled. "No! Why would you think... I want to

figure out if he took your brother! I was going to tell you tonight. I'm trying to help you, Dee! So you can bury him, like you said."

Dee pulls her arms tighter across her small chest. "Did I ask you to help? Did I, missy? I didn't need you to tear the scab off this old wound. Now everybody in town will think I'm harborin' some kind of nut."

I shake my head. "I didn't mean to hurt you. I want to fix that hole in... in you."

"I've got a nice big scar over mine. It's yours that needs some work." She wipes her nose on the corner of her shirt. "Maybe you should look in your own backyard if you want to fix things gone wrong." Tears pour down her face.

It's only a minute before they pour down mine for the second time today. "No! That's not it at all! Dee, I love you! I wanted to help!" I'm trying to grab her arm but she pushes me away.

"Tend to your own business!" she snaps.

I'm trying to fix things for Dee. Like I couldn't for Rosabel. Why can't she understand?

"I have lots to work on, I know. That's why I moved here. And I'm doing better..."

"I still have that application you filled out to be my boarder. It had two phone numbers listed. I thought hard about it. Decided I should make a call, in your best interest."

"What?" I try to see her face through the avalanche of emotion that is careening off my face. "What are you talking about?"

"I called your brother. The one you're always goin' on about. I was worried 'bout where your mind has been and thought your family should know. He was workin' on some whirly-do, somethin' I didn't understand. He says, 'Why don't you talk to my wife.' Sorry, but he's a married man now. I think you're wrong about her. She seemed awful nice. And concerned about you. Called you 'darling', for one."

I feel like I'm going to throw up.

"She said they're goin' to come down next weekend and check on you. Maybe take you home for a bit. 'Til things settle in your head. She promised me it wouldn't affect your big inheritance."

There is no way any of this is actually happening.

"Keilah? You in there? Say something." She puts her hands on my shoulders. "This is for the best. I'm worried about you."

I push her arms off mine and run for my bedroom. I'm shaking harder than I could ever remember doing before. I'm scared of what my body might do next. I remember that Rosabel used to say if you took deep breaths, you could get through almost anything.

Reach for the stars, Robin. You can find the answer to anything if you give yourself the chance.

I thought Dee was sweet and kind, the replacement for Rosabel I had been waiting for. Someone who truly cared about me. I don't understand how she could betray me like this.

Just breathe, Robin. The answers will come.

I force my mind away from Dee, to the innocent memories of Rosabel. The times we sat on her porch, laughing and making up silly voices. Our make-believe universe in the barn, with Kenner perched on her lap while she told endless stories of our brave citizens fighting off the Evil Ones.

Planning prom together, knowing it was only the end of one adventure and we would soon begin another.

I think about the day she was killed. Saving those children. Another entirely selfless act. The end of the day, when Kenner held me tightly, I wondered how I would go on.

"They were both doing their best."

What had he meant?

My arguments with Mother in the months after her death were always the same. She couldn't understand why everyone else in the family was moving on but I wasn't.

How can you say that, Mother? I get up every morning. I go to work. I've made my peace with her death. I even made my peace with the fact that her father killed her. Isn't that what I'm supposed to do?

I rush to the bathroom and throw up. The memories flood in now like the first irrigation water of the summer. Strong and out of control. As if it had happened yesterday. I can't escape them. I lie my head on the floor, wishing desperately for sleep. Instead, I fantasize about my life. There is my Rosabel, laughing at something silly I said. She and Phillip and I are sitting together in a flat spot, on a green-and-black checkered blanket in a field full of golden wheat. It's sunset and we can smell the end-of-the-day sun and Mother's barbecue grill.

"Keilah? Keilah, answer me! Are you ok? Did you get into my mushrooms? Should've told you about those sooner. Should I warm up the car and get you to the hospital?"

I sit up and rub my eyes. It has enveloped me now. I can't shut it out anymore.

"Dee?"

Her face comes into focus. "It's awful…"

"Shhh..." She presses my head to her blouse. "Let it all out. Let it pass."

I push her away. "No, you don't understand." I look up at her wire-rimmed glasses, stained with dried tears. Her little face is so sweet, so fragile.

Keilah, quit this nonsense. You know darned well it wasn't Rosabel's father who ran her over. It was yours.

Chapter Thirty-Six

SANDY SALTS
2012

"I DON'T UNDERSTAND. Did he hurt you? There are places we can go. Get you some help…"

Memory is a funny thing; sometimes it hits you all at once, and sometimes it comes in bits and pieces. In my case, it came at first in tiny droplets. Now it's coming as a giant downpour. Those who've been holding it from me can no longer contain the flood.

I gulp before I say it out loud. "He killed Rosabel. My father." The words hang in the air like a heavy cloud of smoke.

Dee sits back on her ankles. "What? Oh, Keilah, that can't be!"

I shake my head. "He was on a run for parts that morning. Probably not paying attention to much of anything. And Rosabel – being Rosabel – only thought of the children. She probably wasn't paying attention when she ran after that kid. He hit her. Killed her."

"Oh, my… How did you figure it out?"

"Little pieces came flooding in all at once. Pieces I've pushed away for too long." I grab my knees and try to squeeze every last emotion out of my body.

"Everyone around me spoke in whispers after she died.

There was no family discussion. No one disagreed when I blamed Rosabel's father, but they didn't agree. They just stared. And the fact that he killed himself, it fit the story I had made up for so many years and no one told me differently.

"Mother and I had these awful arguments after Rosabel died. Mostly they are still a blur. I just remember telling her to be quiet and leave me alone. Maybe she didn't say it in a way I could understand. Kenner was... all wrapped up in his life. And Father... I thought he still hated me so much for what I did in high school that he couldn't look at me. They never just came right out and told me, not ever."

"But are you sure, Keilah?" Dee starts picking her teeth.

My phone buzzes, but I can only handle one event at a time. I take a deep breath. "Our pickup disappeared for a few weeks after Rosabel's death. It came back with a shiny new coat of paint."

Dee strokes my hair. "You poor thing."

"Father was never the same. He never smiled again. I don't think he spoke more than two sentences to anyone. Kenner would say things like, 'I drove by and saw Father at the cemetery again.' I never thought about what he meant. I was drowning in darkness."

"Oh, Keilah."

As the memories continue to flood back, I think about the folded paper that has been in my wallet for the last five years. The missing piece that had never really been missing. "Hold on for a minute, Dee," I say, jumping out of bed. I run down to the grape-and-tan couch, where my purse is lying on its side. I grab my wallet and run back up to my bedroom, pulling out two crumpled pieces of paper. I shove

Gentry/Colin's obituary back in and unfold the other. "Here," I say, breathing heavily. "Read this."

"Why? How will this help you? I..."

"Please," I beg.

Dee unfolds the paper and scans it. She pushes her glasses down farther on her nose and sucks in a large breath. Then she reads it out loud:

> "*Rosabel McCallister, age 19, died yesterday of injuries sustained in a pickup-pedestrian accident on County Road 51. The driver of the pickup, who asked that his name not be released, was not cited and no charges will be filed. No other injuries were reported.*
>
> *A beloved and well-known member of the community, Ms. McCallister lived her life in service to others. She volunteered at the Pepperville Preschool and spent many afternoons pushing delighted young ones on swings at the after-school program. She was the only child of Ted and Penny McCallister.*
>
> *A memorial fund set up by the Brownwell family will go to cover funeral expenses. If you would like to contribute, contact Kyan Brownwell: bigboss@ brownwellfarms.com*"

There is familiar, scratchy handwriting at the bottom of the page. It is that of a customer who came in daily to the coffee shop in Pepperville and signed his charge slip with a scribble and a smiley face: one of Rosabel's legions of fans.

"Keep reading, Dee," I command. "You have to read it out loud."

She clears her throat. "'*I was there shortly after, Keilah. I know your daddy sure feels sorry for what happened. Don't blame him as he'll be re-living this for the rest of his life. It was a terrible tragedy. We loved her so much. None more than you. I'll keep you all in my prayers.*"

Tears fill my eyes once more. "I came all this way, all these months, to read that. Something that had been in my wallet all along."

Dee presses me to her chest once more. I can smell the ginger carrot muffins she baked early this morning. That seems like a lifetime ago. She holds me tightly for several minutes until I'm not sure I can take it anymore.

We go downstairs and I watch while she eats some three-bean soup and I sip some ginger tea. I'm exhausted from the day's events, so we sit in silence for most of the meal. Finally, Dee looks at me with concern and puts her hand on mine.

"That's so much to deal with, Keilah. How in the world will you? Your brother's gonna be here to get you. Can you work this all out?"

I've almost forgotten that Kenner and Sonnet will be coming soon. She would be relishing the idea of torturing me for every one of the twelve hours it would take to drive home. "We'll help you recover, love." Ugh.

"I'm not sure yet, Dee."

She pats my leg and hops up to her feet. "I'm here if you need me."

I smile at her. The one person who knows the truth – all of it. "I know. Thanks, Dee."

"I'm sorry I got lathered up about all of this. Shouldn't have yelled. The reason... the reason all of this business with

Gentry is so hard for me... is that... Daddy used to talk when he was drinkin'." She begins picking her teeth.

"What?"

"That it was a nice couple from California. Gentry went off with a nice, rich couple in California who couldn't have kids of their own. So, it wasn't your fancy man at all."

For the second or third time today, it's getting too hard to keep track. I feel like I've been kicked in the gut.

"What? How can that be? I don' think..." I want to tell her about the obituaries. About Dmitri and Gentry, and how Rosabel has connected us together through Dee. I'm sure of it.

"That's what Daddy said. And that's the end of it," Dee replies firmly. "No more talk of Gentry." She kisses my forehead and heads to her bedroom.

There is no more fight in me today. I can't pull her out of her fantasy world any more than she could've pulled me out of mine. I'll save Gentry's story for another time, when she is ready.

I go back and forth all night about it all: the truth of Rosabel's death, and how my family, so lacking in basic communication skills, couldn't even discuss something that affected me so deeply. I don't know if going home to confront them will change any of this. But shouldn't I try?

I can't allow Sonnet to come and poison my new life. If I'll be forced to go home, I need to do it on my own terms. And then there is the matter of my inheritance. Will my going back affect that? The farm is still important to me.

After I get into bed, I remember the text I'd gotten earlier, when I was pouring my heart out to Dee. I reach over to my nightstand and see that it's from Kenner:

Heading your way next weekend. We'll get things straightened out for you. It'll be good to have things back to normal.

Chapter Thirty-Seven

JOURNAL – PEPPERVILLE
2012 – EIGHT MONTHS LATER

The Salty Sun, Established 1902
Vanessa Withers, Reporter
Casper Quickenmier, 87

Jolly old Casper, player of accordions and expert in gourd carving, went to be with his maker yesterday morning. Casper was out on a morning walk, visiting neighbors when he slipped on a soggy box of donuts someone left on the sidewalk. Fortunately, his end came quickly.

Casper grew up in nearby Shakersville with three golden-haired older sisters who always made sure he was looked after. His parents died young and left the oldest sister, Versalia, to raise all of the siblings. She instilled in them a love of the accordion and all four went on to travel the country playing pop songs while Versalia sang along. The Quickenmier Quartet had a write-up in the New York Times, which named them among the top 50 "Up and Coming Traveling Siblings in the Contiguous United States."

After a brief time in college, Casper settled in Sandy Salts with his wife, Chandra, and his two girls Zabrina and Zabra. They opened the Salty Stew and

Sundries. His grocery store – offering homemade soup daily – was a staple in our community for nearly 40 years until ill health forced him to close the doors last fall.

Nothing made him happier than watching his grandchildren frolic at his feet while he carved family members' faces into his beloved gourds. Casper always said, "If your family and your work can create the perfect 4/4 rhythm, your life is worth something."

Come join in a celebration filled with accordions, meatballs, and laughter on Saturday at the dance hall at 6 pm. The grocery store will supply donuts, now packaged in fluorescent boxes.

"Fifty miles left? Seems like it's taken us a few months. A girl my age don't have too many of those left." Dee leans forward from the backseat of Phillip's pickup, the smell of garlic-pickled beans strong on her breath.

"I really appreciate you coming with," I say, though at this minute I'm not sure that I do. When she volunteered to come with Phillip and me to visit Kenner, I hadn't taken her seriously. She felt she owed me, though, and I couldn't deny I needed the extra support.

"You want to head to the hospital first thing?" Phillip asks.

"Yeah. I need to see him for myself."

Two nights ago, the call came from Mother. "Your brother's in the hospital. Slit his wrists in the barn. Don't know anything more."

For the first time in my life, I actually asked to speak

with Melanie.

"Your brother was found in the corner of the barn. Where you played as children, evidently. Luckily one of the new farm hands was confused about where to find a wrench and discovered him. No note or anything." She sighed loudly. "There are all sorts of rumors. And Sonnet doesn't want the family there. She thinks that since he was in the barn, it was something WE did to him. She's even got a guard posted at his door 24/7 to keep us away."

After talking things over, Phillip and I decided I needed to go see him, whether Sonnet agreed or not. Phillip didn't want me going alone. Even after all the growing I've done this year, he knows that seeing my family could send me back to that dark place.

"These are them green rolling hills you always talk about. Just like a painting. How much farther, Phillip?"

"Almost there, Dee. Keilah would know better me." He smiles at me and then grabs for my hand. "You ok, babe?"

I nod. "Better when we're on the other side of the road."

"I'm just so sorry for causin' what I did. You don't think that's what set this in motion?" Dee has apologized repeatedly for "stickin' her nose where it don't belong" and calling Kenner. The past eight months have included daily "I'm sorry, this is just for today" baking.

"No, Dee. You asking him to come get me didn't cause this. He was never going to come. Sonnet has a firm grip on him. The reason he didn't show was all about her."

We waited, Dee and I, in an uncomfortable silence. I was processing what I had always known but just discovered. I think she was too. When I called to see when to expect him, he told me he didn't have time to talk. I didn't press him, even as months went by without communication. I was relieved he wouldn't disrupt my new life.

When we reach the edge of town, I guide Phillip to the hospital. Nothing looks different, except maybe a new coat of paint here or there.

"You want us to go with you?"

"Not right now, thanks, Dee. Maybe you can stretch your legs a bit."

I take the elevator up to the fifth floor, where we always joked they "keep the crazies."

When I ask the nurses about Kenner, one of them, a flute player in my high school band, motions for me to step into the break room. "You know you're not supposed to be here. Sonnet's hired a big goon to sit outside the door. That guy needs a personality and a shower."

I peek around the corner and see a man about the size of Kyan leaning back in a folding chair, reading a copy of *Survivalist Monthly*.

"You know, I never had the chance to thank you. Freshman year, you and Rosabel were the only people to speak to me. I had that horrible acne and everyone acted like I was diseased. If it wasn't for lunches with you two, I might have ended up like your brother."

A chill runs down my spine. I've been back in Pepperville less than an hour and Rosabel's good deeds have already resurfaced. "Thank you, I..."

"The goon goes to dinner in about ten minutes. He always goes to the deli across the street, and they can be real slow if I call ahead and ask." She winks.

"Oh, thank you so much. Do you know..."

"What happened? He hasn't said. But there have been

rumors for months that he has been seen with someone."

I can't imagine Kenner cheating on Sonnet. It's actually a little exciting to think that he might break free. "Do you know who?"

She looks down at the ground. "I don't know how you feel about this. But I've heard it's Charles O'Cann."

"Rosabel's prom date? Are you sure?"

"It's a small town. You know how rumors are. Oh wait, he's leaving! Give him a minute and I'll run and call the deli!"

When the appropriate amount of time passes, I enter Kenner's room. He is staring straight ahead, looking at nothing.

"Kenner? Sparrow? It's me, bud." His face is pale and pulled tight and his hair is prematurely greying at the temples. His arms are bandaged from his wrist to his elbow. He looks ten years older than me.

He turns his head to face me just for a moment. I see a spark of recognition. Then he squeezes his eyes shut and rolls to face the window.

"It's ok. You don't have to talk." I lie down next to him, pulling his body in close to mine. Just as he did the day Rosabel died. I smell the comforting and familiar scent of his hair.

"I was lost for so long. I didn't understand what happened to Rosabel. Maybe you tried to tell me and I wouldn't listen. It must've been hard for you too. You loved her so much. But now I know all about Father. I don't hate him for it. I don't know what I feel.

"And Kenner, you know what? Someone loves me. Someone besides Rosabel. You and me – we're worth loving.

That's what she wanted us to remember."

I rub his bony shoulder with my free hand. "I heard that you may have found someone to love as well." His neck tightens and he pulls away just a little.

"If that's true, I'm glad. You deserve that in your life. Don't let Sonnet or anyone else tell you different. I don't know what happened, but I want you to know that I love you. Even though things have been rough between us, I'm always a part of you. Don't forget that, Sparrow."

"Hey, lady, you need to leave. This is a private room. No visitors!" I look up to see the guard has returned, carrying a large Styrofoam container. My friend, the nurse, is standing by his side, mouthing the words, "I'm sorry."

As the elevator descends, my anger grows. I need to confront them all. Make them apologize for keeping me lost all those years. Now Kenner is caught in the same trap. I used to blame everything on Sonnet, but she is the symptom. Mother and Kyan are the real problem.

Phillip is leaning against his truck and I fight that sizzle that still permeates my body when he is near. Dee is doing some kind of stretch on the sidewalk. Her rear is sticking in the air and she's got one foot pushed forward. People are staring at her as they walk by.

"How'd it go? Did you see him?" Dee asks.

"Yes. He's broken. Even more than I was. Phillip, can you open this?" I pound my fist against the pickup door.

He comes over and rubs my back. "Tell me about it. What happened?"

"Let's go. I'll tell you on the way." I stare at Dee, who is now chanting something I can't understand. "We need to leave now, Dee!"

After we're all on the road heading out of town, I release everything. "He's not even Kenner. There's nothing. And there is one more thing. He might be gay. At least that's the small-town rumor, which might mean nothing at all."

"Whooo, Keilah. That's a pickle from a whole different barrel. You feelin' uncomfortable about that?"

"No, Dee. If he's finally found the right someone, I'm glad. It's just hard to think of him so torn up about that and everything else that he ended up here."

It is dark when we reach our property. Phillip pushes the code for the wrought-iron gate (thanks4thefarm) that crosses our road. BROWNWELL FARMS adorns the top, something Kyan had insisted was necessary when he married Melanie. As we approach the farmhouse, I can see that Mother has turned all the outer lights on, illuminating the two-story wrap-around porch. The large wooden front door is also lit, highlighting the stained-glass portrait of the rolling hills in the center. I never cease to be amazed by the beauty of our home.

"Well, Keilah, it's just as gorgeous as you said. Feel like I'm visitin' the home of a hooty-toot from Hollywood."

Mother opens the door to greet us. My insides tighten up. She looks exactly the same. I even recognize the green-flowered dress she is wearing.

We trudge to the porch, exhausted from a long day on the road.

"You're late. Thought I'd have to throw supper out."

"We stopped at the hospital first." I think about hugging Mother, but she's not one for affection.

"Mother, this is my friend, Dee."

"Nice to meet you, Ms. Brownwell. Lovely place."

I can see her eyeing Dee with disapproval. She stops when she gets to Dee's hair. "And this is Phillip," I say quickly.

Mother offers her hand to Phillip as Dee and I step inside.

"How are you, young man? So nice you could visit."

Phillip makes small talk with Mother while I show Dee around. I can smell a familiar dinner in the oven.

"Mother made her pot roast. I'm sorry, I told her you were a vegetarian," I whisper.

"Don't you worry about it, Keilah. I'll find something to chew on."

We take our things upstairs, Dee and me in my old room and Phillip in Kenner's. I see the blackout curtains Rosabel sewed for me while we were in high school. I think about Mother's voice calling me to a bland breakfast of something fried with a side of watery coffee. Seeing the endless rolling hills filled with green, leafy crops every day. Some of the things that defined me as Keilah Middle-Name-Unimportant Brownwell since birth.

"Hard to tell a young lady ever lived here," Dee comments. The room is empty, other than a bed and a small nightstand. It has been sanitized of any memories of my time with Rosabel.

We head downstairs for dinner, and I see that the Macassar-Ebony table is set for seven. Kyan's three daughters and Melanie arrive and the conversation is about nothing but the girls' glowing accomplishments for the next two hours. Dee is forced to eat Mother's hard rolls and celery sticks because Mother even cooked the vegetables in meat broth.

Every few minutes, Dee drops her fork on her plate. "Sorry 'bout that. Celery's hard to cut."

Not one mention of Kenner, or what happened. It's like he doesn't even exist. We don't talk about Rosabel or Father either. Kenner has joined the ranks of the invisible. I want to confront Mother and Kyan, but there is no time. They are all going to bed and my head and heart still hurt.

I don't sleep at all. I can't stop thinking about Kenner. How difficult life must've been for him after Rosabel died. He was an outsider too. He had to work harder than I could've imagined to fit in.

Chapter Thirty-Eight

PEPPERVILLE
2012

"THAT WOMAN'S "wound up tighter 'n an eight-day clock," Dee says as she pulls on her fuchsia socks.

"I know, Dee."

"That's why it isn't goin' to make any difference whether you confront her or not." She straightens her shirt and then grabs my chin. "Ya hearin' me, Keilah? No need to make a scene."

I shrug.

Phillip is almost done with breakfast. Mother can't get enough of him. Buttering him up like a thick slice of Rosabel's homemade bread. "More syrup, Phillip? Can I get you a cup of coffee to go?"

"No, but thank you. I usually only have one in the morning."

I can hear the familiar pounding of Kyan's feet as he comes through the back door.

Now is my chance.

"Dee, would you mind helping Phillip load up the car? I need to speak to my family."

Dee frowns.

"So, I've been meaning to ask you, Phillip, what is it you see in a scraggly farm girl?" Kyan has the same sneer on his face he's worn every day of his life.

Phillip seems shocked. He clears his throat, not prepared for this question. "Well, she's beautiful and smart and..."

Kyan's phone rings and he gets up from the table, pointing a finger at Phillip. "Gotta take this."

I motion for them both to leave and Dee shakes her head forcefully but complies.

"Mother... we need to talk."

"Oh? What about?"

I usher her into the living room, to the couch where she told me the gruesome details of Rosabel's death without mentioning Father.

"I've been wondering why you never told me that Father killed Rosabel."

Mother's hands go to her neck. "He didn't kill anyone! It was an accident! What a horrible thing to say about your own father!"

Kyan hears Mother and storms into the living room. "What's going on here? You causin' trouble? I knew it would happen."

"I was asking Mother why she never told me about Father killing Rosabel."

Kyan crosses his arms. "You were told. We didn't think we needed to put it on the theatre marquee. You were just too flaky to understand. Don't go upsetting Mother over nonsense."

A united front. As always.

"And Kenner. You haven't mentioned a word. Do you know what's going on with him?"

"Now don't you go bringin' him into this, girl. This is all about problems with the marriage. None of our business.

Lovers' spat is all."

I let out a big breath. "Well, they are gossiping at the hospital that he is gay. Are you going to push that under the rug too?"

Kyan laughs. "Here we thought you'd gotten yourself together. Few months ago, your friend called up, wantin' us to come and get you out of her hair. Crazy Katherine. Always with the drama."

I am starting to shake, but I take a few deep breaths, the kind Dee says remove the "googly bits" from the system. "I don't understand why you've both always hated me so much. And Kenner. We just wanted to be loved."

Mother starts to cry, or at least sounds like she is crying. There are no actual tears on her cheeks.

"You're a selfish, mean girl. I never did understand what happened to you, Keilah. You don't appreciate all you've been given. Always such a disappointment," she says in a low voice.

"You didn't give us love! That's all we wanted!" I shout.

She makes a *pssssh* sound.

"That's enough! You've upset Mother after all she did, welcoming you and your friends. It's time for you to leave. You've got no respect for family!" Kyan shouts.

I stare at them both for a minute. Kyan is rubbing Mother's shoulders and she is gazing back at him lovingly. They are who they've always been. Phillip comes inside from loading the truck. He glances at Mother's face and then mine.

"Keilah, we'd better get moving. I've got to work in the morning." Phillip's mouth is set and he is speaking directly to the fireplace. "Thank you for your hospitality. Dee says thanks as well." He takes my arm firmly and we are out the door before another word is uttered.

We ride in silence until we reach the cemetery. What would have hurt me years before has left me numb. Everything here leaves me numb.

I want Phillip and Dee to meet Rosabel. Daisies, roses, and stuffed animals frame her headstone. She is still just as loved and remembered as she was six years ago.

"How-t-do, Miss Rosabel," Dee says, curtseying. "Honored to be in your presence."

I ask them both to wait in the pickup while I visit Father's grave. He is buried next to my grandfather, Harlen, who unknowingly set us up to become the family we are.

"I think I understand now, Father. You didn't send me away for punishment. You sent me away to find myself. You knew I was lost. Maybe you even felt guilty about taking away my Rosabel..." I'm starting to get choked up, reliving it once again. "You took away my best friend. I'm still working on that one."

A few miles down the road, Dee gets restless. She makes groaning noises and moves around in her seat.

"Do you need to get out and do some stretches? It's going to be a long trip home." I didn't bring headphones. This may be a trying trip.

"Well, I didn't get too much to eat. I'd like to stop for some real coffee and pie when we get a chance. No offense, Keilah, but that coffee tasted like a burnt Barbie doll."

I look at Phillip. We are at least two hours from anywhere to eat. He shrugs.

"But more 'n that, Keilah, I want to know what happened. How'd things go with your family?"

"I... We're not going to work it out. Not right now, maybe never. They can't even talk to me about Rosabel's death. And I don't know what will happen with Kenner."

"Such a shame. You did a fine job of patching things up with Vanessa."

"And with Nova. That was the tough one," Phillip adds. "I was really proud of you for standing your ground."

I smile, remembering the day after discovering Father's secret. I decided there should be no more hidden stories. I waited until I could hear Nova's new boyfriend honking in the parking lot. "By the way, I'm the one with Phillip. He wants to be with a person he doesn't have to share."

She stared at the door and then at me. "You want my leftover? You can have him."

"You tell 'er good, Keilah," Tucker yelled from the back.

"Just know that he'll come back. They always do. You're nothing compared to me." She smiled her trademark smile.

I picked up a tray of yesterday's cinnamon rolls and resisted the urge to dump Tucker's hard work all over the front of her tight, pink t-shirt. "'Scuse me, Nova," I said, pushing past her. I turned around when I got to the door. "Today's boyfriend is waiting. You'd better hurry before he's gone too." She stormed out of the store. I expected things to be bad the next day, but she acted as though we'd never had the conversation.

That night, I sent Phillip a message: *So, you said to text you when I got things all straightened out.* There was a knock at my door. Phillip was standing there, with his phone in his hand. I reached for mine. *No more Nova. Now I can really see the stars with you.*

"Well, you did your best. That's all you can do," Dee says, patting my shoulder. "You've got your eyes open now, seein' things for what they are. Life's too short for those worries. We have to make the best of the ingredients in our own pantry."

I nod.

"My stomach is sure a growlin'. Let's find us a gas station soon."

I open my purse, searching for any kind of snack that might keep Dee occupied.

"Say, you two oughtta think more about that. How life is just so quick. For my Gentry, it was only a few good years."

"I thought Rosabel would be here forever. I never guessed her life would end before it really began."

I find a candy bar and hand it to Dee. We haven't been able to discuss Gentry, or Colin. She is firm that he went to California.

Dee begins to chew loudly. "Yeah, the more I think about it, the more I know what needs to happen. Remember the other day at the gas station, when we was havin' that conversation, Phillip?"

"Um... not sure I know what you..."

"Yeah, you remember. You told me these past eight months have been the best of your life. That you couldn't imagine living without Keilah. And then you..."

I feel my cheeks becoming hot. I'm a little upset that they continue to have conversations behind my back.

"Okay, okay, I get it Dee. You're right about that," Phillip says. "Life is short. I kinda wanted to do this somewhere else." Phillip pulls the pickup over to the side of the road. Right in front of the sign that says, NEXT GAS STATION, 50 MILES.

He unbuckles and pulls me a little closer, taking my hands in his. "Keilah, I've been thinking about this for a while. Dee's got a point about making today count in case it's our last. Would you want to... Would you do me the honor of..."

My heart is racing.

Dee thrusts the candy wrapper between our faces. She has wound it tightly into a circle. "Phillip wants your hand in marriage, Keilah. He just can't seem to spit it out." She hands the plastic ring to Phillip. "Put it on her finger, just 'til we can find a decent one."

Phillip slides the plastic on my shaky finger. It isn't very round or pretty. It is perfect.

"Oh my gosh, Phillip. Yes! Yes!" I never thought I was good enough for happiness like this.

Dee pushes our heads together. "Now comes the kiss. Seems like you two need my help for everything."

The next ten hours float by. I can hear Dee rambling on about the cake she will make, how she's been wanting to make something tall and fancy for years but she didn't have a good excuse until now. Her words are background noise. My head is full of memories, good and bad. I stare at my candy wrapper ring in amazement. How did I ever get this far? I'm even more than I imagined I could be without Rosabel – a whole person. Keilah DeRose Brownwell.

The day before Rosabel's funeral flashes in my mind. I was standing in her bedroom looking through her Folder of Life, that special folder. Trying to figure out what to say. And then that paper fell out. Her list. She had made an alternate list for Miss Seagull to read, in case she didn't like the first one my Rosabel had come up with. My fingers shook as I read it: Number One: Find Patty and Henry, my real parents. Number Two: Forgive them.

It is hard to sleep. I have so much to digest. Some things to tuck away for good and others just beginning to unfold. It is an entirely new life that I never dreamt was possible without Rosabel as my guiding force.

The next morning, I wake up for work and find a note on the counter:

Dear Keilah,

Left you some chocolate spelt muffins. Never asked if you were allergic to any of these concoctions, but too late to worry about rashes now, as you'll be moving out soon. We should go through my box of family things. You can see what I kept of Gentry's. Quite a fine little fellow.

The book club will want to throw you a bridal shower. They love the chance to have a good party. They've learned all sorts of things they can share. Keep your eyes on the windshield and out of the rearview. That's what I always think, anyway.

Love,
Dee

Epilogue

The Salty Sun, Established 1902
Vanessa Withers, Reporter
Gentry Modelty

Deeloriandra Fisher invites you to join in a celebration of life for her brother, Gentry. Gentry was taken from his family in Friendly State Park shortly before his 5ᵗʰ birthday. He was a joyful, musically-gifted soul who made everyone around him smile.

There will be a short service with a reception following at Ms. Fisher's home. She asks that you bring any musical instrument you may have for a jam session. Refreshments will be provided by Ms. Fisher and Jack's Beanery.

Please dress casually and wear only natural bug repellent.

THE END

STUDY GUIDE

1. What would have happened if Kenner faced the same stipulation for collecting his portion of the will?
2. Do you think Keilah's perception of Rosabel was accurate? Why or why not?
3. Was Keilah's interest in Gentry genuine, or was she trying to distract herself from her own problems?
4. Would the citizens of Sandy Salts have been as accepting of another child's disappearance if he/she came from a "good" family?
5. Why does Keilah's mother dislike her so much?
6. Who was Sonnet protecting by having a guard posted at Kenner's door?
7. Is there more gossip than reality is daily conversation?

CPSIA information can be obtained
at www.ICGtesting.com
Printed in the USA
BVHW031315031220
594826BV00008B/44

9 781733 663908